Advance Praise for The Language of Water

"The diverse ensemble of charact[ers in this] debut novel includes royalty and subs[istence farmers,] elderly, fierce warriors, and dedicated p[hysicians—all com]pelling, complex, and struggling with [events] that can shatter souls. But the core protagonist in the novel, the only one truly powerful, is the natural environment.

"The action takes place in 2100, when climate change has created extremes in the global distribution of, and access to, water. The divide between Haves and Have Nots is an ever-widening chasm. Regional conflicts sparked by dwindling natural resources are rampant. Agriculturalists have developed a plant, the pea cactus, that grows in harsh environments and can be processed into a variety of goods, but worsening floods and periods of drought make this, at best, a last-gasp measure.

"It is a world severely out of balance, but not quite out of hope. Clark-Stern captures the inflection point toward which we are barreling at break-neck speed, the moment when humans—having contorted ourselves to our limits in a desperate effort to maintain life as it was before climate change—are forced to decide if we want to die clinging to old ways or give up illusions of power and embrace something new.

"*The Language of Water* is a balm for nerves frayed by the fear of impending environmental disaster and a bracing vision of how balance might be restored to our off-kilter world."

—Kate Boyes, author of *Trapped in the R.A.W.*-

"Elizabeth Clark-Stern has created a marvelous adventure that takes us into a mysterious future where the climate is out of control. Her characters vibrate with creativity, passion, and imagination as they bring an evolving world to life."

—Beverly Olevin, Kirkus Award-winner for *The Good Side of Bad*

"I found this novel's complex characters and the richness of their relationships—in love and in war—tremendously compelling. Sara, Kethuda, Ruqia, and the rest of the cast are skillfully drawn. A story about the future devastation wrought by climate change has the potential to be a grim read, but instead Elizabeth Clark-Stern has written a gripping feminist tale exploring love and power, violence and forgiveness, despair and hope. *The Language of Water* is a page-turner and a paean to resistance."

—Gwynne Garfinkle, author of *Can't Find My Way Home*

The Language of Water

The Language of Water

by
Elizabeth Clark-Stern

Aqueduct Press

Aqueduct Press
PO Box 95787
Seattle, Washington 98145-2787
www.aqueductpress.com

Library of Congress Control Number: 2022950579

ISBN: 978-1-61976-234-3
First Edition, First Printing, May 2023

Cover Illustration: "Sappho" – copyright © 2008
Karlie Markendorf, oil on canvas, karliemarkendorf.com

Book and cover design by Kathryn Wilham
Printed in the USA by McNaughton & Gunn

Dedicated to my beloved author, Dylan Nicole Hansen,
who tells me her stories, and helps me tell mine.

In memory of Masha Amini, whose Kurdish name is Zhina. She died at the hands of Iranian police for daring to modestly adjust her hijab to show more of her proud beauty as a woman of independence and value. May she rest in peace and continue to inspire women all over the world.

PART ONE
WIND

1 – Sara

HER given name was Fatima, a perfectly respectable Kurdish name, but she called herself Sara, the code name of her revolutionary heroine, Sakine Cansiz.

On this quiet morning, Sara hurried barefoot across the dusty floor, her heart quickening as she opened the cracked windowpane. A glimpse of her face appeared in the glass: broad Kurdish nose, thick black braid coiled onto her shoulder, eyes that Papoo used to call "the darkest jewels in the night sky."

She leaned out the window, searching the village streets for movement. The soldiers of the Kurdish Women's Protection Unit, the famous YPJ, would arrive at any moment for recruitment day, January 1, 2100.

Sara shouted out the window, "YPJ. I am here. On this day I am eighteen!"

No sound but the wind whipping dust along the deserted stone streets.

Sara first saw this band of sister-soldiers when she was a little girl, pulling herself up to this very window to watch them rush by. Young women, proud, laughing, their heads bare, their bodies strong in vintage camo fatigues, their boots solid as small mountains. She used to march around the house, pretending to be the mighty Sara who led the YPJ against ISIS almost a hundred years ago. Mamoo and Papoo applauded, though Sara knew, even as a child, that her parents did not want a life of violence for their only child. But how else were women to find justice?

Sara was afraid. The YPJ of 2100 fought gangs of ISIS brides who sold young Kurdish virgins to wealthy men across

3

the Middle East. And there were rumors of other covert missions, even water poaching, punishable by death.

Sara swallowed, her throat dry as sand, as she took her tin cup off its peg and placed it beneath the spout of a small, covered bucket. She punched a code and watched grainy water fill the cup with the first eight ounces of her ration for the day, collected last night at what people called the "Kiss-Off Station." A simple procedure: when Sara pressed her lips to a metal button on a metal pipe, the sensor in the button read her weight, age, and state of hydration, dispensing the minimum quantity required to sustain her existence for 24 hours. It also read her DNA, shutting off if she attempted to double dip.

Sara sipped, grimacing as the gritty liquid moistened her throat. There were rumors. Old men in the streets said, "Be grateful. Drink slowly." What did they think was coming, mud? No matter. Soon she would no longer have to haul the stupid bucket from the public pump every evening. *When I am YPJ, my arms will be burdened only with an e-arrow rifle and a water canteen.*

Outside, the wind whipped through the brown haze, revealing houses of mud and stone in the hillside across the way. Laundry on clotheslines snapped with each gust of dust. The clothing of the Kurds used to be brilliantly colored: geometric patterns in the dark red of a child's cheeks, the yellow of mountain wildflowers, the blue of the morning sky. Now, every garment was putrid green, like Sara's own scratchy frock, fashioned from the pea cactus, a high protein succulent made of genetically engineered eatable cotton, cactus, and dried chickpeas. It required very little water, and could grow anywhere in the world, supplying food, clothing, and myriad necessities to the warming world. In Sara's village there was no water for cleaning, so people hung their pea cactus garments out for the dust to scrub.

Sara's country was Rojava, once a northern region of Syria, now its own nation; so beautiful in her youth, high mountains covered with rich green grass for goat-grazing and abundant snow whose melt-off swelled the Euphrates River. Now, the mountains were barren of snow, the bright green grasslands replaced with gray-green paddles of pea cactus as far as the eye could see. It was not so much the loss of the beauty that weighed so heavily on Sara. It was that Rojava suffered from the perma-drought, the final stage in the drying up of a city, a nation, a continent.

This left her homeland at the mercy of the country that controlled the headwaters of the Euphrates, the Kurd's time-honored enemy: Turkiye.

All of that is about to change. The YPJ will fight for our water rights. And I will be with them. She waved out the window, confident the YPJ were there, momentarily hidden by a cloak of dust. "I am here. Where do I sign up?"

No reply.

What if they won't take me? I'm short. I've never shot an e-arrow rifle. My feet are soft as dainty pillows on a sultan's couch. I have no boots and no money to buy them.

Her thoughts went wild, her fingers drumming the window ledge. She glanced around the room at the stiff couches, the cheap American movie posters. Nothing left of the Kurdish wall hanging her mother had sewn from fabrics of turquoise, orange, and gold. No smell of Mamoo's fig pie, No coughing from the smoke of Papoo's pipe.

cha cha cha cha cha

Sara saw a beloved winged visitor coming toward her out of the dust.

cha cha cha cha cha

She slid her cup onto the ledge. A tiny speckled bird landed, his long tail thrashing.

"Rexie, my darling." She lifted her right baby finger, pointing it at his tiny lizard-like tongue, bobbing her finger up and down, capturing an image of the full reach of Rexie's tongue.

"Got it. My teacher doesn't believe you're devolving into a dinosaur. Now I have proof." She moved her baby finger to the center of her forehead, sending the image through the In-Phone embedded just under her skin, the spot ancients referred to as the "third eye."

"When Mr. Askay gets this picture, he will say, 'I admit that tongue looks more reptile than bird, but Sara, birds *are* dinosaurs, so how can they devolve?' I will say, 'This is no bird tongue, it is adapted for a dry world. Punctuated equilibrium—evolution leaping forward.'"

She contemplated the photo of Rexie in the picture gallery just inside her frontal lobe. She was amused at the thought that phones used to exist outside the human body. They were said to be flat, funny, buzzing things. People kept dropping them into toilets or leaving them on barstools, so scientists, ever eager to prioritize convenience, discovered how to implant stable microscopic sensors into the human nervous system, centered in the brain, but with radiating sensors placed throughout the body. This genius innovation was crowned the In-Phone. All citizens of the world received them, in the first international technology treaty in history, a sign of true global benevolence, they said. How all of this was financed, and who controlled access to anyone's personal In-Phone was left to the imagination of cynics and the overwhelmed. Sara's belief was that the In-Phone was financed in the waning hours of the United Nations by elder billionaires from various countries who wanted to leave a truly democratic legacy for the world. They insisted on privacy laws as a condition of their philanthropy, but just as in the olden days of external phones, it was prudent to be cautious when sending information through a veil of intrusion.

Originally it was thought that the In-Phone would be an energy-saving device. But this claim, like so many others promised by scientists and government officials, proved false. A quota had to be set on the number of energy units used in any one In-Phone exchange. Certain transactions, such as snapping and sending a photo, depleted the weekly quota. The most expensive transaction of all, the holographic meeting of two or more parties, could cost up to a month in quota-usage.

Some believed the In-Phone had mystical properties, a portal to the chamber of our dreams and the cosmic Source of all energy. Sara had great curiosity about this and had enjoyed long discussions with her teacher about how to access images on the In-Phone from the dawn of time.

A shrill voice cried out from the other room.

Sara pushed Rexie off the cup. "Go. She will catch you and throw you into a stew." Rexie vanished into the dust. She gulped the remaining water.

Her stepmother, Fidan, a large woman in a vintage red gown, entered with a motion that brushed aside anyone else in the room. "Is it wise to gurgle down one-fifth of your ration so early in the day?"

"It is my choice."

Sara's stepsister, Nazan, shuffled in after her mother, carefully taking up as little space as possible.

Fidan ignored her compliant child and moved closer to Sara. "You think you are so special, my little Fato? Just because it is your birthday, you think the Turks will open their headwaters to us 'down-streamers' and give you all the water you want?"

Silence filled the room. For the moment, the three women were united in their hatred of the Turks.

"I was thirsty. And my name is not Fato, or Fatima. It is Sara."

Fidan laughed in open mockery. Nazan followed with a shrill giggle, squeezing something under her arm. Sara leaned closer: folded blue fabric. A birthday gift? Surely not. She had received nothing from them since her father's death.

"You think by calling yourself Sara you will become a hero?" Fidan said. "You are Fato, who scrubs floors."

"Nazan can scrub the floors from now on. I am 18. I am joining the YPJ."

"Of course, you are," Fidan said in a sudden change of mood. "But first, tonight, is the festival." Her eyes slid to her meek daughter. "Show her."

Nazan brought forth a vintage gown of Kurdish design: deep blue green, triangles of white, an orange border, with a lemon-yellow hijab.

Sara touched the fabric, soft as Rexie's wings. "Where did you get it, a museum?"

"Your mother wore it when she presided at the Equal Voice Council," Fidan said. "She spun it herself, in light wool. I promised your father I would get you a good husband. You must debut in decent attire."

"I don't want a husband. My teacher, Mr. Askay, says that the independence of women—"

"Your teacher, he eyes you like a ripe pear."

"I remember pears," Nazan said, gazing out the window at a withered tree that had once borne fruit.

"At least try it on." The edge in Fidan's voice was clear: disobey and you get the lash. Sara had been whipped with much less provocation. She peeled off her flimsy pea cactus dress and stood naked, studying the face of her stepmother: what profit for Fidan was hidden in this "gift?"

Nazan pulled the resplendent gown over Sara's body, placing silky white slippers on her stepsister's feet.

"I have never felt anything so soft against my skin," Sara said, and, for a moment, she imagined herself a bride, valued by a compassionate man who would care for her. She had not known love since her parents died, and she longed for true, abiding love, but rarely admitted it, even to herself. She had a deeper longing. Her feet seemed happy in these soft slippers, but they had a greater desire to slide into sturdy boots. And love? Surely it would come another way. Not in this masquerade.

Fidan glanced anxiously at the door. "You are very beautiful, little Fato. I am so sorry, but we will die, if we do not get our own well."

Sara stared, amazed, at the first tears she had ever seen in her stepmother's eyes. "Your own *well…?*"

"They promised they would not beat you, if you submit like a good whore."

A singing missile flew past Sara's ear, an e-arrow, made of electric charge, visible only when it hit the target, appearing as an arrow-shaped apparition burning with deadly precision.

The missile misfired, setting ablaze a movie poster of a bare-chested American cowboy.

Fidan crawled to the wall, pulling Nazan with her.

Sara hurried to the window. ISIS brides were heading toward the house, their eyes barely visible behind full-faced black hijabs.

Behind them came the women of the YPJ, their faces bare, their boots smacking the ground. Sara cried out in desperate joy as she saw a tall YPJ woman leap like a mountain goat, knocking down two ISIS babes in one blow. *She must be Ruqia, The Flying Warrior, as brave and fierce as my namesake, Sakine.*

"Ruqia!" Sara called, waving.

The Flying Warrior turned at the sound of her name, a face of angles and hard lines. A warrior's face Sara admired at once.

"Help me, Ruqia, I am sold for a well."

Their eyes met across the town square.

Sara's joy was short-lived. The sound of feet thumped up the stairs, and the door opened with a crash. ISIS women shoved a black hood over Sara's head. She screamed a muffled cry to Ruqia as they carried her away.

2 - Kethuda

SHE picked up her mother's ruby necklace, a prized heirloom from the Ottoman Empire. *What about the down-streamers?* Her belly grew hot, her legs suddenly weak. "I can't think about them now. I have to get through the next few minutes," Kethuda said out loud.

An older woman with a spine like a question mark appeared. "Yes, Madam President?"

Kethuda tossed her head, feeling the slap of her perfectly knotted black hair on her back. "I'm not the President yet." The room was barely a closet, used for storing supplies for Turkiye's proud Kebon Dam. "Does a President need a conscience, Mihiri?"

The older woman bowed, her spine arching to the floor. "Yes, Madam, I believe it is beneficial."

"How much do I owe, and to whom?" Kethuda asked.

"How much what, Madam?"

"Water."

Mihiri was silent. Kethuda knew of the Kurdish blood in her servant's body. Though the woman never spoke of it, on certain days, Kethuda glimpsed a turquoise and orange scarf, poking out from the neck of Mihiri's dull pea cactus dress. The geometric design harkened back to the time when the northern part of Kurdish territory stretched into Turkiye. Uprisings were frequent, many Kurds and Turks slaughtered. Finally admitting defeat, the Kurds in Turkiye remained largely underground, while open rebellion rose in Rojava, Iraq, Iran. Now the question of achieving a united independent Kurdistan

11

was a distant dream. All they wanted was water: the "down-streamers," a yawning mouth, begging to be quenched.

Mihiri fastened the ruby necklace around Kethuda's throat.

"It's lighter than I thought," Kethuda said." Mother wore it often. The rubies made her lips seem a dark, pomegranate red."

"Yes, Madam President. You are beautiful." Mihiri opened a crack in the shuttered window. They could see the massive expanse of the Kebon Dam, water splashing over the spillway in abundance.

"Allah is good," Kethuda said, looking to the mountains dusted with snow. An old Turkish legend told of the Earth disappearing into the sky during winter, renewing the mating of the god and goddess that bore the children of humankind. No one spoke of this any longer. There was still snow in the mountains above the pea cactus fields, but how much longer would it be there?

"Now then, Madam. Have a look at yourself," Mihiri said, guiding her mistress to a full-length mirror, hanging like an afterthought in this room packed with vintage cardboard boxes and old computers. Kethuda scrutinized her image: still youthful at forty, the strong bones of her cheeks and the line of her jaw etching the perfect profile for her office: feminine, but with masculine strength, her long golden gown the color of the sun. Perhaps this was an error. Recalling an image of what was scorching, dehydrating. The sun seemed to follow everyone these days, even in their dreams.

"Mihiri, bring another gown, white for clouds, the snow, with a tinge of pale blue, for water." Kethuda knew she must deliver an image to her people that illustrated what could happen when the ravages of climate change intersected with female power. From this inaugural day forward, she would no longer be Kethuda. She would be a fountainhead of security, even a hint of the divine. She would not claim to be a goddess, yet she must look like one: A Goddess of Water.

Mihiri said, "We only brought a few items, your keepsake trunk—"

"Find something," Kethuda said, realizing her voice sounded too high-pitched—too, God forbid, *needy*. She slipped off the golden dress and stood naked before the open window, snapping the shutters shut with her jeweled hand. *No, no, this is not right.* She peeled off the rings and bracelets and unclasped the ruby necklace. The Goddess of Water must be at one with her people, without vain trappings, one message: I am terrified of *thirst*, just as you are.

Mihiri hurried in with a gown Kethuda had not seen for years. "Couldn't you find something else?" she said in a voice that betrayed deep sadness.

The older woman bowed low. "There was nothing else. You said it must be white, like a cloud—"

"Stand up, woman. You have done your best. It will serve."

Mihiri stood as tall as her curved spine would allow, slipping the white dress over her mistress's naked body.

"My mother's wedding gown," Kethuda said, imagining her mother's enveloping embrace. Ayse named her daughter Kethuda after a powerful queen of the Ottoman Empire. Her father had never liked the name, claiming that it sounded like a twentieth century bicycle horn, *Kay-thoooo-dah*. Her mother ignored him, loving everything about her only child.

Tears came, unbidden, as Kethuda saw herself in her mother's wedding gown. "No, not a day for feeling," she said, wiping her face with her strong hands and pulling on her pea cactus boots covered with alum so they shone like silver bullets.

She peeked through the shutters at the workers on the platform installing floodlights to enhance the live feed of her image on the World Board, a global feed that would broadcast the Inauguration on the In-Phone of every person on the planet.

Turkish people—now *her* people—were arriving in large numbers: young and old, rich and poor, many women and nongendered, not as many men, some coming with the blind hope that *this time* the person on the Inaugural podium could guarantee they would never know thirst, others coming to heckle the newly elected President, a *woman.*

She touched her forehead, bringing up images of world leaders peering at the Inaugural platform on their In-Phones. The predictable crowd appeared: male members of The World Water Rationing and Refugee Team, referred to on the street as RAT, an alliance of the United States, Europe, Scandinavia, Canada, Japan, the new United Korea, and Turkiye. Russia and China remained isolated, maintaining their own In-Phone system and water refugee policy.

Relations between the former Ottoman Empire and the West had always been tense, especially between Turkiye and the United States. It was worse in this new alliance, responsible for regulating water rations at "Kiss-Off "stations across the globe. The quantity of water was always under review based on a country's policy of being "Closed" or "Open," to water refugees. RAT took over water ration management from local authorities on the questionable wisdom that it would lessen the prevalence of the greatest crime in the late twenty-first century: water poaching.

The male RAT leaders seemed impatient with Kethuda. ("When will this woman get the show on the road?"), bemused, ("The true power in Turkiye has nothing to do with this dolly"), or wary, ("She is either being manipulated, or manipulating the world for nefarious ends"). This onslaught of babbling was pure conjecture on Kethuda's part, but she knew these men and the fear that propelled them into public office. Some of them may have feared that she would do an end-run around RAT and team up with the Closed alliance of Russia and China to create a new authoritarian empire that would push all water refugees into the remaining countries. This was a card she would have to keep in mind, as a threat, if not a reality…or the other way around.

She switched away from the men, digging her fingernail into her forehead at an angle, opening a private channel where she could find the faces of women. When water scarcity became a permanent global pandemic, terrified nations found the illusion of security in male-dominated regimes. The ascent of women in the early twenty-first century had rapidly declined. The one exception was the world-wide Right to Abortion, as political opportunists and ideologues alike crumbled in the face of *thirst*. Hailed as the beginning of International cooperation to fight over-population, it was paired with the Global One Child Act. This spawned grief rituals in every country, as women and men on both sides of the political divide mourned the loss of siblings in families, and the beginning of life in the womb.

Kethuda's private In-Phone pathway brought up the face of Shogofa in Afghanistan, where women had defied decades of Taliban rule by establishing a network of home schools for girls. These women wore burkas and moved in secret, establishing grass roots justice at Kiss-Off stations, now led by a groundswell of women and men who monitored water rations for tampering.

Kethuda sent a silent message to Shogofa, "I am with you. The women of Turkiye are with you."

Shogofa did not lower her burka—was any In-Phone channel really secure?—but she blew a kiss, signaling her support for Kethuda's ascent to power.

"They are waiting, Madam," Mihiri said.

"Yes, yes." Kethuda scanned the hopeful faces of the world's women, stopping when she found the round white face and dark blue eyes of Nina Navalny, descended from the early twenty-first century dissident, Alexie Navalny. Nina was young, too young to be leading an underground revolution, but since the economic and spiritual collapse of Russia, young women and men rallied with the cry, "Democracy at Last" for the country of Pussy Riot, Anna Akhmatova, and Tolstoy.

Kethuda could feel the scrutiny in Nina's eyes. "She looks to me to bring female power to our shattered world."

"Who, Madam?"

"Women. They look to me, wondering if I will keep Turkiye Open. Will I continue to send water from Kebon to the down-streamers, or will I curdle, like over-cooked pudding."

Mihiri attempted to suppress a giggle.

"Laugh," Kethuda said. "I will not beat you!"

"Yes, Madam," Mihiri said. "I think you are not a wiggly dessert. You are a woman of flesh and blood."

"That remains to be seen," Kethuda said, wiggling her hips. They laughed, their bodies momentarily relaxing.

Kethuda released the pressure on her "third eye" and turned back to the male leaders leering down at the podium from the safety of their In-Phones. The bulbous, white-whiskered face of the American President, Sam Boatwright, came into view, flashing her a "thumbs up." Kethuda longed for the days when the predominantly Latinx United States was ruled by a woman Hispanic President. In those days, as an Open country, it was home to millions of water refugees from South and Central America. But the country had been thrown into panic as the sidewalks of Florida, New York, and all coastal states disappeared under the swelling sea. The white minority imposed strict limitations on the immigration of Latin American water refugees. Mr. Boatwright, a Mississippi politician who had moved to Ohio when his state went under water, was catapulted into the Presidency by a slim white majority. He declared America Closed, sending troupes to the Southern border armed with hi-powered, cowboy-style e-arrow rifles. As thousands of water refugees amassed on the Mexican side of the border, they built "Temples of Return," out of dry sagebrush and pea cactus tumbleweeds. These beautiful, ghostly structures were replicated in perma-drought countries across the world. Sacred structures that gave meaning and the presence of divine love to where "the dry go to die."

Kethuda hated Boatwright, and yet, she knew Closing his country had saved American lives. Since her election, Mr. Boatwright had turned a sympathetic eye to Turkiye, calling her "President Babe."

Boatwright's cozying up was a radical shift from America's long-standing critique of Turkiye's human rights policies. Even the term "human rights," had fallen out of use in favor of "water rights," defined as which humans in which countries were entitled to how much water, for how long.

"I will tell them you are almost ready," Mihiri, said, hurrying off.

Kethuda's sweating body churned with terror and excitement. She had dreamed of this day as far back as she could remember, watching her mother bow, always bow, to the will of men, especially her father, President Hamza the Great, whose power was as natural to him as her mother's subservience was to her.

A hand touched her shoulder. "Mother?"

She sighed. "No, Papa. It's me."

"Of course," he said, resting his forehead against his daughter's back. "I thought, for a moment—the gown—"

"Do I look like her, on your wedding day?"

He cupped his large hands on her shoulders, turning her to face him. She was always surprised when she saw him this close, his face cracked with age; but the aura of his power shone through as if he were still a young man, with a forehead descended from the sultans of the Ottoman Empire, metal-gray eyes, full lips parted, to devour, or kiss. "She would be so proud of you."

Kethuda caught the slight tightness in the corners of his eyes. She leaned back. "Would she? I think she would give me that look that always shot right through me when I laughed too loud, or jumped too high, or beat boys in a foot race. 'Don't blow your own horn, Kethuda.'"

His hands were heavy on her shoulders. He said, "She would be amazed, frightened for you, as I am." His nostrils widened, taking in the scent of amber oil on her neck. "But I'm certain she would look at you today and say, 'You are the woman I could never be. And I love you for it.'"

Kethuda closed her eyes to dam the tears. "Did you remember to bring it?" He held out a silken cloth, azure blue, the color that river water used to be before the climate turned it brown. Her mother's hijab, worn with the pride of a devoted Sufi. Kethuda touched it, fluid as a magic stream from some forgotten dream. But who believed in magic these days? "Papa, our water is beige at best. I can't promise to restore this color to our water."

"What can you promise? Let's hear it."

She heard a knife's point in his voice. They had spent hours rehearsing her speech. To go through it one more time, she would become even more his monkey.

He moved closer, his breath hot as desert wind on her neck. She swirled suddenly, squawking and hopping like a baboon. "Monkey see, monkey do!"

He laughed, hollow and aggressive. His grip was tight on her wrist.

She hated the quiver in her voice, the fear he could evoke with one stroke, "You would have me show up on the podium with a black eye? The world already suspects I am your creature."

His eyes narrowed. She could smell it on him now: the *fear*. She had smelled it in him since she was a child. She had talked about it with her mother. They both knew who he really was: the shivering bush rabbit pretending to be a hawk. Ayse never called him on it. She was too coiled in her own fear to step into the power of her own self. *I will do otherwise. I will play along as his monkey, conquering my own fear until I become a true woman of power.*

Slowly, begrudgingly, Hamza released her, as if he could read her thoughts and wanted to distance himself.

She draped her mother's hijab around her shoulders, a billowing blue shawl, turning away from her father, running down the metal stairs, her silver boots clanging like steel drums.

She marched onto the platform, blinking in the brilliance of the floodlights, her ears burning with the roar of the crowd. She stepped to the podium, touching her sternum to activate the microphone temporarily implanted to carry her voice to the world, a voice that must echo with authority and feeling, "I welcome you, those around the globe, and people of Turkiye. I am proud to address you for the first time as your President."

She paused for the ovation, paid for, in part, by her father. It was impressive, necessary. She inhaled, raising her voice, "On this Inaugural Day, I want to share with you a sacred icon from our National Museum—" She retrieved a clay statue from inside the podium, lifting it above her head. "Discovered in an ancient village in Anatolia, where the Turkish Empire was born, I give you the Seated Woman of Catalhoyuk."

Female voices of devotion rose from the crowd. This was not orchestrated. The Seated Woman was sacred to all women of Turkiye.

"She is our Earth Goddess," Kethuda said, caressing the base of the statue. "Behold Her pendulous lactating breasts, her hands on a throne flanked by leopards, each bare foot resting on a skull. Life and death in one magnificent image." She held the statue to her breast, her eyes closed in prayer, "Goddess of our Blessed Earth, I ask for your wisdom, your protection, your love." She placed the statue on the podium, one hand on the goddess's head, the other reaching out to the crowd. "In the twentieth century, President Ataturk promoted a secular Turkiye. It was needed at the time, and we honor him for his leadership. Today, we are in a different time, with different needs."

She glanced sideways at her father.

His eyes were stone. Behind him, the crashing waters of the dam poured over the spillway. The wind carried mist onto her face. "Today I will no longer be known as Kethuda, daughter of Ayse and Hamza the Great. I have a new name: *Ataturka.*"

The crowd gasped. Some murmured approval. Some whispered with weary suspicion.

She placed Seated Woman on the podium, bowing to the statue as she lifted her mother's hijab to the crowd. "I have never married. Never known love. I have devoted my life to serving the common good for you, the people of Turkiye."

She wrapped her mother's hijab around her own head. "Today I embrace the divine wisdom of Mother Earth and Allah. We need them both as we watch our snow-capped mountains recede, our countryside become desert. I promise you, I will be the divine steward of our water. You, my people, will never know thirst!"

The crowd exploded with relief and adoration, shouting down the low growl of skepticism.

Kethuda smiled at the crowd, the muscles in her arms burning as she held aloft the Seated Woman of Catalhoyuk. *Papa thinks I am his. He does not know the quiet rebellion burning in my heart that could destroy him—that could destroy myself.*

3 – Sara

SHE was curled into a ball in the back of the van. No windows. Her hands tied, the mask pulled off so she could breathe the stench of sweat and urine. Sara recalled the moment when she saw Ruqia and they found each other's eyes. *Did the ISIS slavers murder The Flying Warrior? What if I caused the death of a great hero of the YPJ?*

She steeled herself against this, breathing gently, telling herself her job was to get through the next moment, and the next.

How can I survive when every dream has been taken away? On the surface it seemed pointless to continue to live without hope, and yet, Sara had no thought of suicide, even after her captors had disabled her In-Phone and left her alone in the dark.

"What keeps me from despair?" she asked an unseen listener, her spine bouncing with the rough motion of the van. She thought of her teacher, Mr. Askay, with his soft gray eyes and his scruffy black beard always a little askew, as if while standing at the mirror to trim it, his thoughts had drifted to the life cycle of the solar system, and the beard went out of orbit. If he were here beside her, he would say, "What is your plan, Sara? You must escape. Remember the report you wrote on twentieth-century Kurdish women? They always found a way."

"I have no plan," she said, seeing his face in her mind: that proud slender nose that looked longer when viewed from the left than the right. In class when he fired out a question, everyone fell silent. She was always the first to shoot up her hand and offer an answer. She must do that now, in the darkness of her mobile prison.

"My first plan is to remember my namesake, Sakine Cansiz," she said out loud. "In 1979, she and other women were sent to the horrible Diyarbakir prison in Turkiye. The guards raped them and beat them with clubs, planks, electric cables. The women stuck together. If one was weak, another woman volunteered to be tortured in her place. In this way, they survived. Not one became an informant."

She paused, waiting for Mr. Askay to say something, knowing he was only in her mind, but wanting to hear his voice, see the spark of curiosity in his eyes.

He would tell me I must be as strong as my namesake.

But strength eluded her. In its place pulsed a great fear that she would never see Mr. Askay again. She wept until she could no longer see his face, her mind retreating, her body pure sensation, roiling with the movement of the van.

Though she could not see outside, the desert felt strange, as if it were an ocean made of sand. The last time she had left her village was many years ago, when Mamoo and Papoo took her onto the first run of the Sun Shuttle. What an adventure it was! People from all over the Middle East joined journalists and scientists from all over the world to make history in the maiden run of a sand-roving mega-bus, powered by synthetic photosynthesis. As they crossed the Euphrates on the Sun Shuttle Bridge, Sara shouted for joy to hear the mighty rushing of the river below.

These memories, what she called her "golden treasures," allowed Sara to drift into a deep sleep. She dreamed of the desert, the stars, the wind gently covering the figures of Mamoo and Papoo until they were sand sculptures lit by the stars.

She woke with a jolt as the van slammed to a halt. The wind had picked up. Cracks of light came through the bottom of the blacked-out windows. And, what was that strange sound? Sara pressed her ear to the locked door: a sound she had not heard since she crossed the Sun Shuttle Bridge years ago. The Euphrates. No longer a rushing torrent, it had the sound of timid water, dribbling its way downstream.

Next came female voices, one shrill. The door opened and hands pulled Sara out and smacked a black hood over her head. Rough palms pushed her forward until she landed on her knees in the hot sand. She could hear the gurgling of the Euphrates, close, very close.

"I will take off your hood so you can drink," a woman said with authority, perhaps the Commander. "If you look back at me, I will kill you."

"I will not look at you."

The hood came off. Sara gasped, her eyes blinking in the cloudless dawn light, her mother's lemon-yellow hijab whipping around her face in the warm breeze.

In front of her lay the muddy stream that was once the mighty Euphrates. A great sadness settled in her heart. "The Turks," she said. "They horde our headwaters for their spas and golden swimming pools." A far darker grief came upon her, for it was a Turk's e-arrow that had taken the life of her mother.

The ISIS Commander spat onto the sand. "The Turks have a new bitch. Calls herself Ataturka, the virgin queen, married only to her people."

They both laughed bitterly.

"Lying whore," Sara said. "This Ataturka is 'married' to the wealthy bastards who run Turkiye. The men who ordered the slaughter of my village, of my mother...."

Sara wanted to see the face of the woman Commander who hated the Turks as much as she did. She could sneak a glance. They didn't dare kill her. She was the merchandise. "This gives you pleasure, selling girls to wealthy fat cats? Have you sold me to a Turk?"

The Commander scoffed. "You will be happy where you are going."

"A happy whore?"

"Yes. A family who would sell their daughter does not want her. Where you are going, you will be wanted."

Sara shivered at the graphic thought of what it would be like to be "wanted." "And you, Commander, do you want this life?"

"You waste time. The Turks prowl the desert like snakes. They will rape us and kill us, not because we sell women, but because we sell water."

"You think you are better poachers than the YPJ?"

The Commander sighed like a dying ox. "The world called us terrorists. We fought for our God. We were vanquished by the West, our men murdered, the few left in hiding crushed with shame and mental shock. I am not proud to sell women. I love my husband, an ISIS warrior crippled by war. We survive like any other animal. Allah must want it so, or he would have brought rain and snow long ago."

Sara could feel the depth of the Commander's pain. She sighed in mirror despair. "Please, untie my hands so I can drink."

"One hand only."

Sara stretched out her right hand, barely able to move it after it having been bound so tightly for so long. She scooped up the cloudy water, thinking of Rexie, her little T-rex wren. If he were here, she would offer him the first sip. She drank and spat it out. More silt than water.

The Commander laughed.

Sara scooped again, forcing herself to swallow.

Ooodle, wok, oooodle, ooooo

What sound was this? A machine? A weapon?

It repeated, doubling, tripling, louder, louder: *Oooodle, wok, oooooodle…oooo, wok*

The Commander stepped forward. Sara saw her face: Proud nose, full lips dark eyes enlarged in panic. They stood together, watching a dark cloud moving toward them like a great blanket. The other ISIS women joined them.

"The Turks?" the Commander said. "The sound of a Sun Tank?"

Sara listened to the call, *OOOdlllee! Wok. Wok* "No—" she said. "This is the sound of *birds*. Big ones. My teacher said it was a myth—"

The herd appeared out of the dust devil, huge, egg-shaped bodies, crested heads atop long snaking necks, their pillowed feet galloping into the river, greedily slurping the water, pecking each other.

"Dinostrich!" Sara said, pulling free of the Commander, plunging headlong into the flock. "You are *real*."

The largest bird snapped at her with his sharp beak.

"Eat me or kill me," she shouted, dodging his next blow, "but take me with you."

E-arrows sang over her head.

The Commander shouted, "Don't shoot the Kurd. Then we have nothing."

The dinostrich scurried away. Sara, in their midst, joyously joined their cry: "Ooooddle, ooodle, wok wok wok."

4 - Kethuda

SHE was safe and cool in the pea cactus-leather seat of her Ataturka-mobile, a small, self-driving, white vehicle, with a clear e-arrow-proof top. It had the ability to rocket across dry plains and pea cactus farms. Unlike the Sun Shuttle, the Ataturka-mobile could take Kethuda from her Presidential quarters in Ankara five-hundred miles away in only half an hour. Her destination was the body of water that told the real story of abundance or scarcity: the reservoir south of Kebon Dam.

Kethuda quelled her growing anxiety by tapping her finger to her forehead to view reviews of her Inaugural speech. Some writers were giddy with optimism: *Woman President Ushers in New Era of Feminine Power Married only to the Common Good.* She winced at this one, written for the International In-Phone Press by her own spin-doctors. Reading it afresh, her stomach turned: how could any mortal woman live up to that?

Other critics countered, "The Common Good? Whose Good? The only 'good' is giving disproportionate water to wealthy Turks who brought this woman to power and her father before her. What of the poor Turks? What of the middle class? What of the Kurds, dying in the desert? What of all the water refugees petitioning to enter Turkiye from South America, India, Africa?"

Kethuda's belly grew warm with guilt. Was there anyone in history who came to power without the corrupting influence of the privileged class? She could think of no one, telling herself she wanted power to help all of her people. She was an Open country, sending water from Kebon to the down-streamers, and letting in a few Africans a year to fill service jobs. Why should she feel bad that she couldn't help *all* people?

"There is no substance to this 'Ataturka,'" wrote a journalist from Great Britain. "Merely a woman constructing an image borrowed from our Virgin Queen, Elizabeth I, who executed her rivals while blithely commissioning Shakespeare's plays. All *show*."

The phrase "She has no substance" played over and over in Kethuda's mind, for this was the secret terror hidden in the chambers of her heart: I am *nothing*.

She pictured the face of her mother, Ayse, her dark brown eyes filled with love. *What would Mama say to me now?* She would say, "Kethuda, dearest, if you could stand up to your fear, just once, the deepest secrets of the universe would open to you." These words were from a Sufi poet, re-written ever so slightly. Ayse did that, re-write the masters, to suit her own star.

The vision of her mother gave Kethuda the courage to finish reading the reviews, the most generous from Elena Maria Juarez, writing from her high-rise cubicle at *The New Yorker*, no doubt watching sea water rise outside her window. Ms. Juarez was famous for her articles on how the fear surrounding climate change had caused global politics to regress to the patriarchy of the Middle Ages. Nowhere was this truer than in the United States, where the policies of male leaders had marginalized Latinx Americans, while shutting out millions of Latin American climate refugees. Ms. Juarez wrote, "In our era of planetary misogyny, a female President bursts onto the scene. All women present themselves to the world in the hope that their character reflects esteem, utility, and a positive regard for others. Re-naming herself to reflect one of the most powerful of Turkiye's historical leaders, Ataturka—wearing her mother's wedding gown—claimed to honor both Allah and the ancient Earth Goddess of Catalhoyuk. Was she not presenting her best self to the world?"

I want this to be true. I want to be a woman of esteem. I want to be good. For whom? Not only for my corner of the world. For Shogofa in Afghanistan, for Nina in Russia, for women everywhere who sent private messages of love and support at my Inauguration.

She moved her fingertip sideways, pressing the implant portal on her forehead with her nail. A cache of images flashed from the World Board: lines of school children at a Kiss-Off station in Viet Nam, holding out their cups for water, Indians digging in the desert for underground water they would never find; in America, wealthy Floridians living in luxurious penthouses perched above the rising sea, while other Floridians crowded together in makeshift houses in the branches of palm trees. Her body shuddered, her finger dropping to her lap.

The Ataturka-mobile stopped at the reservoir. "Mother," she said to the air, "come with me this day. There is much to be managed, many choices to be made. Many people with great need." She listened, hoping for a voice from within.

Nothing. And yet Kethuda felt her mother's love, always.

Water droplets from the reservoir drifted onto the clear dome of her car. A black speckled bird swooped down, smacking into the glass. Kethuda shrieked in fright, startling the bird. It looked at her with wild eyes, its long tongue sucking up drops of water: a creature dying of thirst.

She got out of her Ataturka-mobile, scooping the bird off the dome, holding it for a moment, feeling the fluttering of its heart. She opened her hands, and it flew off toward the reservoir. She followed it, watching it dive into the water, sipping and gulping. Her stomach tightened: she had never seen the water level so low. She took a deep breath, and strode with a semblance of confidence toward the rim.

The men of the Executive Council were waiting on a platform, speaking in hushed tones, their faces turned away from Kethuda, toward her father. She had grown up with these men, some uncles, some acting like uncles. When she was little, they wore suits with black coats, even in summer. Now, no one wore suits. Their olive green pea cactus shirts seemed particularly bland in contrast to the blue water.

"Did you know the reservoir was this low?" Her voice was an accusation, delivered with authority. The men slowly turned their faces to her, their bodies remaining aligned with her father.

"Good morning, Ataturka," Hamza said with a smile of possessiveness, or fatherly love, always hard to tell which.

"Good morning Papa. Good morning, Council."

They nodded in greeting, no shift in their bodies, no bow.

Her eyes scanned each of them. "I get daily reports in text, but *seeing* it so low— Aren't you alarmed?"

Hamza shrugged, his face lifted to the rising sun. "I see the data, my dear. We all do. You are new to this, Ataturka. The water supply fluctuates. It will rise again."

"You would do *nothing*?"

The oldest "uncle" tucked his drab green shirt into his pants and walked toward her. "You are a powerful goddess now, Madam President. Maybe you can make snow."

Laughter rippled among the men.

Kethuda looked at the water, inhaling slowly, watching more birds, some like the speckled one that had crashed into her car, one white seagull that must have lost its way. She said with a leader's voice, "This system of dams has been re-built many times with water drawn from sources all over the country. Sit down with me. Let's construct channels of abundance."

The men looked away. Hamza stared at her.

"I don't understand," she said. "Do you want our people to die?"

"This system was re-tooled only a few years ago," Hamza said. "Managed well, we have enough for the foreseeable future."

"For whom?" she asked.

The question hung in silence.

Only Hamza would look at her. She did not look away from him.

"You've inspected the reservoir," he said lightly. "Go home. Paint your nails."

"I will not go home. I see your game, Papa. You mean to parch them out, all the poor wretches downstream. When there is almost no population left in Rojava, Syria, Iraq, Iran, you think you can *order me* to send troops to scoop up those countries one by one. The New Ottoman Empire."

The men acted as if they have never heard of such a thing, expressions of shock, denial, nervous laughter. Bad actors, all of them.

"I like that name," Hamza said. "*The New Ottoman Empire*. When the time comes, *Ataturka*, you will do whatever I say." He stepped closer to her. "Make your high and mighty speeches to the world; we both know you want power. To rule, to dominate, to conquer."

Her voice was larger than life: "You will never understand, Papa. I want the power of goodness, not your geriatric own-the-world crap. I won't do it, Papa. I am the President. I am Ataturka, the divine Queen. *I* am the New Ottoman Empire, and I will route the water as I damn well please!"

Hamza seized his daughter's throat. Her breath stopped. His eyelashes brushed her cheekbone as he squeezed her throat. Her legs gave way, and she fell into darkness.

5 - Ruqia

THE Flying Warrior hated to lose. From the moment she saw the young Kurd in the window, only a girl really, crying, "Help me, Ruqia," she vowed to save her. But there were too many ISIS sex traders, too few YPJ. Ruqia had to retreat, even as she watched the ISIS brides carry the girl from the house, toss her into their sand-colored van and sputter away, coughing up oil fumes in what must have been the last fossil fuel buggy in the Middle East. The YPJ had no vehicle, only the Sun Shuttle to get them across the desert. From there it was all on foot. And what of the girl? She would be stripped of her beautiful Kurdish gown, anointed with perfume, and left to lounge, naked, on silken sheets, waiting for her sultan.

I failed. The thought throbbed in Ruqia's mind as she looked out across the Rojavan desert. The wind had died down during the night, allowing Ruqia and her band of sisters to breathe the night air without coughing up balls of dust. They split up at first light, each dyad tasked with their core mission: find the Turkish water pipelines buried in desert caves. The proud and brave YPJ, reduced to water poaching, punishable by death.

Dawn without wind was so rare, Ruqia thought for a moment she had fallen into an alternate universe, where the sand was water and she was able to walk on it. No separation between the orange-gray of the sky and the gray of the sand.

Ruqia could see the girl's village, a speck on the horizon, like a crumb on the brim of a plate. How long had it been since the girl had been carted off? One day? Two? The sand-colored van might still be somewhere out in the desert.

The blood-orange sky paled as the sun broke the horizon, robbing Ruqia of the fantasy that she stood on a vast interior lake. Unexpected tears came to her dry eyes. She wiped them away, her hands rough as sandpaper. There was a time when her hands were soft. In Mosul, after the Kurds defeated ISIS, the whole world had seemed safe and soft. Then came the perma-drought, the slow receding of the Tigris and Euphrates. She could not sit at home, waiting for the day when her family's faucets dried up. She took off her hijab and left it in the hands of her weeping mother.

"The women of the YPJ don't wear anything on their heads," Ruqia had said. "They can't look different from men on the battle field."

Her mama had taken her daughter's hands and studied them. "A woman's hands," she had said, "meant for the joy of husband and children. For making pea cactus *Kifte Gosht*. Only you know how to make it taste like meat."

"I can't stay home and cook, Mama."

"But you play the *oud* at our dances. No one plays like you." Ruqia loved to play the *oud*, often called "the Kurdish balalaika," or, simply, a lute. The *oud* had strings mounted on a deep basin of treated wood, giving it a sound like a cello inside a mountain cave. She loved her instrument, but on that day, she was stern, "Mama, just because I'm a woman, it doesn't make it right for me to stay home and strum."

"But you will not be fighting," said Papa. "Only looking for water."

Ruqia said nothing. Best for them not to know that the remaining forces of ISIS were hell-bent on controlling the water from Iraq to Iran to Syria to Rojava. Fighting and killing were the order of the day.

Papa's eyes studied her face. "My daughter does not kill," he said. "We are Kurds. In our branch of the family, we are true to the most ancient teaching of Islam, 'No killing.'"

She held his eyes. "Yes, Papa."

"Promise me," he said.

She nodded, not averting her eyes. "Show me the nest of the Pharaoh Eagle Owl before I go."

Papa smiled. They kissed Mama and climbed a favorite rocky slope. Inside a shallow cave they found large brown eggs in a nest of pilfered pea cactus. Soon the mother Pharaoh Eagle Owl swooped down upon them. They laughed and waved at her.

"We will not hurt your babies," Papa called. Ruqia grabbed him, and they descended the rocky cliff. She was able to get a good view of the magnificent bird, its ears curved upward with such elegance that it was said that the Pharaohs of ancient Egypt modeled their headdresses after it.

Not long after she left home, her mama and papa died with many others in an ISIS bombing targeting the Kurdish section of Mosul. After that, everything soft in Ruqia turned hard. She learned to shoot the e-arrow rifle better than she ever played the *oud*. The YPJ entered Baghdad. Ruqia killed so many brawny ISIS men, she lost count. At night she grieved for her parents, wandering the alleyways of brothels, drinking flasks of 90-proof pea-whiskey, seeking solace in the soft bodies of women.

That all seemed a long time ago, yet it had only been three years.

"Our mission is water pipes, not your Kurdish virgin." The voice belonged to Gran, senior markswoman of the e-arrow rifle. Despite her advanced age, her falcon eyes and steady hands took down her prey, by her account, every single time.

"Damn you," Ruqia said. "I was only admiring the sunrise, so rare without wind. Look at it: orange, blue, like the pattern on my mama's quilt."

"Sure you were," Gran said, wiping her face with the tail of her mother's patchwork hijab, the only keepsake from the family lost in the bombing of Aleppo. Gran—who had another, now forgotten name—had been barely ten years old when she watched her mother peel the hijab off her own head and press it into her daughter's hand. A smile, and her mother was gone. After decades of repair, the hijab brushed Gran's cheek like frayed feathers. She never took it off, and the YPJ let her wear it, knowing she needed to wear it or she would become a lousy shot.

"I can't get the sand out of the cracks in my face," Gran said, rubbing her cheek.

Ruqia smiled. "By the beard of Allah, I'll find you a Turk water pipe. We'll crack it open and bathe your pretty face."

"You don't believe in Allah."

"I used to. Then I saw the world. There is no God."

"Allah is with us *because* of the violence of the world," Gran said, placing her hand on her comrade's shoulder. Ruqia's body relaxed. So good to be touched. But this was only Gran, not a lover. Ruqia had not felt that kind of touch since the brothels in Baghdad. It embarrassed her to admit that she was not only thirsty for water. *Could I die of thirst for sensual touch?*

She banished this indulgent longing, moving forward in her sturdy pea cactus boots, blinking from the brightening sun, and yet, ever-vigilant, she spotted a print in the sand of a bare human foot, a small one, and just ahead, a shoe print only slightly larger than its bare mate.

"A boy?" Gran said. "ISIS uses kids as water scouts. They have a better record than we do, skimming off the Turks."

"I think it might be a girl; the shoe print has a pointed toe. Not a shoe for the desert. This poacher must have been discovered by the Turks."

"No Turkish boots in the sand," Gran said, searching the ground with her smart eyes.

"Right. Odd. It's like this child came out of nowhere. If the Turks shot him, or her, the blood has been sucked into the sand."

They followed the footprints to a low mound of Earth, its open mouth beckoning them down into darkness.

"I smell a water pipe in that cave," Gran said.

Ruqia leaned closer to the sand, discovering a fresh set of non-human prints that had entered the cave from another angle. "A bird?"

Gran knelt beside her, staring at the large three-toed print. "Can it be?"

"Dinostrich?" Ruqia said, measuring the print with her hand. "A big one. Thirsty bastard. He chased our boy, or girl, into the cave, killed it, ate it, then pecked into the water pipe?"

"Where's the water?" Gran asked.

"Maybe an inner pool far down in the cave?"

Gran pulled out a small e-arrow hand gun and stepped toward the cave. Ruqia's hand was firm on her friend's arm. "We are out of range for In-Phone light. I don't want you falling."

"I'm an old woman in need of protection?"

"Yes, you are." Ruqia pulled out her long knife, its silver handle carved with a geometric Kurdish design. She didn't mention to Gran that shooting off an e-arrow handgun could cause a cave-in, but her friend was not wrong to propose a weapon. *Can I kill an ISIS warrior or a giant bird with a knife?* Her hand trembled. If she could find water, it was worth the risk. No fear allowed.

She walked slowly into the mouth of the cave, the darkness so complete, she had to feel her way along the rock wall, her boots treading inch by inch in case of a sudden drop off.

She paused, listening for the sound of life or the gurgle of water. Her feet halted. A sound. Faint. Incomprehensible. She dropped to her knees, inching forward, one hand on her knife, the other on the rough Earth of the cave floor.

The sound grew louder.

Breathing. In....out....

Something in the cave was alive. A bird? A boy? A girl? Ruqia's hand crept along in the darkness, stopping as her fingertips felt something familiar: fabric, light wool, like her mother's best Kurdish dress, smelling of mud and blood. Her fingertips continued to move across the fabric, aware that she was trespassing on a stranger's body, but she couldn't help being drawn to know the figure in the dark by touch alone.

The light wool fabric gave way to a silken cloth like the hijab Mama made for Ruqia on her thirteenth birthday.

The breathing stopped, a moan, a movement.

Ruqia's fingers roamed the silk until they touched human skin, moist with sweat.

Someone's fingertips touched her own. A gasp, then the stranger's fingers moved to Ruqia's face. Time seemed to pause as the hands of both humans touched the face of the other. A knowing passed between them, a knowing beyond the world of sight and talk and judgment, fingertips learning the anxious forehead of one, the trembling chin of another, the arch of an eyebrow, dry, cracked lips.

Ruqia was reluctant to speak, to break the spell, to end an exploration that satisfied a deep a longing.

Gran shouted from above, "Are you okay in there?"

"I found something—" Ruqia called back, touching the soft hand beside her.

The voice of a young girl said, "Who are you?"

"I am Ruqia, of the Women's Protection Unit."

"You? The Flying Warrior?"

"At your service."

The girl's voice quivered, "I saw you, from the window I cried for your help."

"You are *she*?"

"Yes. I am Sara. I escaped from ISIS with birds that my teacher calls dinostriches. One followed me in here, poor mama; she died at my feet. I am so thirsty—"

Ruqia pulled her canteen from her belt, placed it on Sara's lips. The girl gulped and gasped. "Thank you."

"Of course. I am sorry you have suffered," Ruqia said.

"I want to join you, become a soldier. I have no combat training, but I'm a good learner. Best in my class—"

Sweat pooled on Ruqia's brow. *This girl is a child. She has no idea what awaits her.* "Drink, Sara. We can talk later—"

The girl sipped, swallowed, and moaned with relief. "Please. I am sold for my sexual organs. I have nowhere to go. I have wanted to be YPJ since I was a little girl." Sara tensed her bicep, putting Ruqia's hand on it. "See? I am strong."

Ruqia touched the sleeve of the girl's Kurdish gown. "A gown for a bride, not a warrior."

Sara's voice trembled. "The ISIS women will find me if you leave me here. I lost a shoe. They are good at footprints. Please, General Ruqia, I have a good mind, a strong body, a loyal heart. I have so much to give to YPJ."

Ruqia moved her hand from Sara's arm and found the girl's face, wet with tears. Something shifted within the iron fortress of the Flying Warrior. She held Sara's face. If common sense ever had a foothold inside this cave, it was gone now. Ruqia said, "Your training will be brutal. Many don't make it through."

"I am tougher than you know." Sara's voice fluttered like the wings of a nightingale.

"We will you take on a trial basis."

Sara's breath filled the cave like a windstorm. "Innana has answered my prayers!"

"Who?"

"Warrior goddess of ancient Sumer."

"Whatever," Ruqia said. "Stay here, I need to inspect the cave."

"How can you do that without light?"

Ruqia moved her hands along the floor. "I don't need to see water. I can smell it." Her fingers touched liquid, and her heart skipped a beat. But, no, the scent was blood, not water. No pipeline, only the dead carcass of a bird devolving into a dinosaur.

6 – Kethuda

THE bruises from her father's attack still hurt. The skin would heal, but not her rage. *He could have killed me.* How remorseful he was, giving her mouth-to-mouth resuscitation, so that when she woke his lips were on hers. She cried out, and he pulled away, weeping with shame at his violent attack. Or was it show-shame?

She avoided him in the ensuing days, one thought dominating all others: *I must find a new form of power that is all mine. A model that can spread across the world.* Was this grandiose? As overblown as her father's inflated clamp on power? Important questions, but, in her mind, she heard her mother's quiet voice urging her to see that the only way to stay alive was to become a true leader to the people of Turkiye: to re-imagine a form of power the world had not seen in four thousand years.

Kethuda disguised the bruises on her throat with a thick pea cactus hijab and boarded her Ataturka-mobile, setting its course for Anatolia, in central Turkiye, home of the ancient city of Catalhoyuk.

She had not been here in years and found it remarkably well-preserved for a four thousand year-old village: the foundations of houses close together, no streets, only slender alleys for carrying food and supplies.

Kethuda swept her hand along the crumbling wall of the central courtyard, imagining the sculptor, or sculptress, creating the statue of the Seated Woman, a pregnant Earth Goddess flanked by leopards. Predator power and mother love in one image.

Since she had held the Seated Woman aloft at her In-auguration, the statue had become a rallying cry for women around the world. T-shirts of the woman with pendulous breasts showed up in Europe, South America, India, Afghanistan, Saudi Arabia, even the Closed countries Russia, China, America. Nina Navalny was arrested for wearing one, her face beaming in proud defiance.

Kethuda's thoughts tumbled out: we can't go back to this primitive way of living, and yet, isn't our climate catastrophe forcing us back to a collaborative society, not unlike ancient Catalhoyuk? A community of true equality, all people valued. Archaeologists had found no evidence of gender roles for women or men. All worked side by side to ensure a sufficiency of food and water for everyone. No evidence of domination. No slaves. No rulers.

And what of today? Couldn't there be a new form of power, a unity of *humanity*, seeking not to dominate but to collaborate?

I sound like a babbling idealist. And yet, they did it here, in Catalhoyuk. How do I take the seeds of this society and bring it to our planet, now?

Kethuda nodded to the attending archaeologist, a middle-aged man in a broad pea cactus hat. He bowed, smiling at her as a man admiring a beautiful woman. She nodded back, ignoring the nervous flutter in her stomach from male attention. This made her sad. Since the extinction of butterflies, the grieving world had been infested with "thornies": spindly purple insects with thorn-like appendages. A person could no longer have "butterflies" in a nervous stomach, but no one could manage to say "thornies." Snow-capped mountains were not the only casualty of climate change: metaphors had suffered as well.

Kethuda turned away from the archaeologist, hungry for more history to back up her theories. Her fingernail found the sensor in the center of her forehead, and images from the history of all past political models: capitalist, socialist, communist, democratic, totalitarian flowed into her mind, a story of dominance and oppression, with occasional oases of short-lived compassionate societies woven like golden threads in a vast red carpet. Notable was the South Indian monarch who had suddenly became horrified that he was torturing his people and instituted state-sponsored Buddhism and the Chinese Emperor who had ushered in a golden age of art and peace; other examples popped up in the history of Europe, Africa... But even in the great democracies of the West, the golden threads of justice ultimately gave way to domination, privilege, and corruption.

Is evil encoded in human nature, as everyone says, or is there an evolutionary door we have not opened?

The wind rustled her heavy pea cactus hijab. She looked down at her white dress: the robes of Ataturka. Am I lying to myself? What is this pretense of longing for a golden age of equality? Didn't I suck up to the rich and engage in corruption in my rise to the Presidency?

She reached for a pile of bones, cradling a fragile skull in her palms. What did this person know about being a human? What did they know about equality, and intimacy that I don't know, that I may never know?

An all-too familiar voice greeted the archaeologist.

Hamza.

Her body seemed suddenly as fragile as the skull in her hand. She put the skull back and absurdly searched for a weapon. These people had had no weapons. Their only enemy was the natural climate shift of monsoon and drought.

Her father's voice was a marvel of jaunty denial, "Ataturka. Your beauty brings a ferocious glow to this dreary place. My tutors used to drag me here when I was a boy."

Her toes stretched beyond the tips of her sandals, finding warm dirt. This brought a bit of comfort, as if the Earth Goddess Herself sent courage up through Kethuda's feet. "You lie, sir."

He was oddly amused. "Always catching me, my darling. But isn't that what daughters are for? My tutors never let me go anywhere. I hated them for it. I desperately wanted to be a regular kid, go on field trips with a gang of misbehaving ruffians." His voice lowered, "I didn't come to this place until years later, with your mother. She always brought us here, before finally agreeing to go out to the sumptuous meadow, beyond these filthy ruins. We took off our shoes and waded in the stream, so cold from the melting snow. Remember?"

"The sun was brighter then."

"Your mother wore long skirts, ever devout."

"Was it devotion, or pleasure? She used to say, 'I love to feel the wind blowing my gown around my legs.'"

He chuckled, his eyes evasive.

"I remember Mama brought me here as a child," Kethuda said. "A special journey, mother to daughter, to show me where they unearthed the statue of 'Seated Woman.'"

"I was here as well."

She could only look at his right foot, tapping nervously in a shoe as shiny as a new Sun Sports Car. "You were here too? Really?" She knew he was lying, but this suited her purpose. "Mama told me all about Catalhoyuk: no defined gender roles, the children raised by the whole community, and, most interestingly, some of the families in these houses could have become quite dominant, but didn't. There was some sort of 'cap' that prevented it."

His foot stopped tapping. She gripped the dirt with her toes.

"A 'cap' on the rise to power?" he asked. "Are you afraid someone will dig it out of these bones and topple your empire?"

"I'm curious, that's all."

He snorted, "Such a little hypocrite."

She looked down, her body burning: he had hit a vein of truth.

"I don't remember anything about that," he said. "Ayse told me lots of stuff in those days. Always reciting that Sufi damned poet, Roofie or Rudi, whatever his name was. I liked his sonnets, actually. Some of it quite passionate." He sat on a stone.

Kethuda stole a glance at his hands, palms on his knees, as if holding down his fury. "Mostly I loved to watch Ayse danced the Sufi whirl of devotion. She never looked like a damned dervish. Often, she danced free style, just for me." He looked off into the distance.

Pity flowed into a familiar part of Kethuda's heart, the part that knew the depth of his love for Ayse, the depth of his grief at her loss.

Hamza looked at his daughter.

She wanted to look down, but that was the way of a coward. She faced him, President to President.

"You are my sun, my moon, my star," he said with a voice that did not lie.

She smiled gently: their code of forgiveness.

This is the prison I live in, not his violence, but his love.

7 - Sara

JOY filled Sara's heart as she pulled on Ruqia's spare boots. "I am YPJ," she shouted, flinging her arms to the sky.

Ruqia stared, amazed.

The old woman scowled.

Sara danced, the hem of her mother's dress brushing the toes of the spare boots as the wind lifted the sand, and the women coughed and spat out their meager saliva.

"So sorry," Sara said—but the mishap did not dampen her joy. In this moment, nothing else mattered—not the threat of pursuit by her ISIS captors, or the deepening disapproval on the face of the old woman called Gran. "If I die today, I will have known the freedom of *choice*."

Ruqia nodded, "Those boots are too big for you."

Sara regarded the woman she first met by touch in the cave. Light and sight revealed a tall, thin woman with long calloused fingers, a buzz of brown hair cropped off with a blade, large intelligent eyes beneath a brow too creased for one so young.

Ruqia's eyes carefully measured Sara. *She is seeing me in the light, just as I am seeing her. She is judging me: is this girl a clown or a savior?*

"I don't mind that the boots are too big," Sara said. "I love them. They are the answer to my dreams!" She kicked the air, careful not to let sand fly up into their faces.

"What's all this mirth?" Gran asked. "Do you know what we're doing here, girl?"

Sara suppressed her joy. "You are water poachers. Looking for pipes that carry the water the Turks sell to the Saudis, the Israelis, and Innana knows who else. Punishable by death."

"Innana?" Gran said, crossing her arms over her chest. "I have no patience for retro-pagans. We are engaged in life-and-death, missy."

Sara planted her feet in the sand. "I am not afraid. I will do everything I can to help you find the water pipes. When you find them, how will you get the water back to Rojava?"

Gran smirked to Ruqia, "See? Too many questions. She'll bring trouble."

Sara looked closer at the old woman. "You look familiar, Gran, if I can call you that. My mother was a member of the Free Women's Movement of Kurdistan. Her name was Gita Roxan. The Turks murdered her and all the other Free Women making council that day."

"Gita Roxan was your mother?" Gran said, her voice lighter, her face slowly uncoiling from its harsh judgmental lines. "I met her once, at a meeting in Kobane. Taller than you. Same Asian-type Kurdish eyes."

Sara exhaled slowly, picturing a younger Gran shaking hands with her Mamoo. "You sat in council with her? I was a child. My Papoo watched me while Mamoo was in the meetings, so I never knew what she did. Even now, I don't know."

Gran's face softened, her lips proud. "We sat in a circle. No one higher than the other. We rotated the leadership of the meeting. Your mother was a great one for educating. She said, 'The word leader means 'to guide,' not 'to tell everybody what to do.' Gita was very fine. She listened, wrote down the ideas of others, then turned to another person she knew had a different opinion, and asked them to speak."

"Yes, Mamoo listened well," Sara said.

Gran nodded, "Gita was a pioneer in Equal Voice Council. We are judge, jury, and lawmaker. We are equal. We work hard. Often after hours or days of debate, we come to *yes*."

"Council is still happening?" Sara asked.

"More important than ever, with this Ataturka woman on the throne." Gran moved close to Sara, "You can call yourself 'Sara' after the revolutionary hero, but that's a fairy tale. What have you done to make yourself fit to be a soldier?"

Sara swallowed, "I will prove myself."

Ruqia touched her forehead, her eyes widening slightly. "Shuttle in ten minutes. Gran, I get your concerns, but, this is my call. Sara, please kneel."

Sara gasped, kneeling in her mother's dress, her toes tickling the inside of the roomy boots. She knew the joy of this moment would never go away, no matter what happened.

Ruqia placed a hand on Sara's head, "Are you trustworthy, Sara Roxan?"

"I am. I will honor the values and goals of the YPJ and the Free Women's Movement of Kurdistan as long as I live."

"You are held to this. To hold our secrets, endure torture or death, to keep our intelligence from our enemies."

"I will die," Sara said, closing her eyes, imagining fatal torture. "I will suffer torture unto death rather than disclose secrets of the YPJ." *Can I really promise this? Scrubbing floors has been my greatest discomfort....*

"Enough," Gran said. "Get up, girl. We must hurry."

Ruqia tossed spare fatigues at Sara and helped her fold her mother's dress and lemon-yellow hijab, placing them gently into her YPJ backpack along with Sara's one tell-tale white slipper. Sara kept her face serious for Gran, though her arms felt like wings as she rolled up the legs and arms of the borrowed fatigues.

"We only get four cups a day in the field," Ruqia said, digging for something in her pack. "But we get four salties each.

Sometimes we sneak an extra here and there. They taste like shit, but the salt in the pea cactus helps retain fluid."

"I think they make it worse," Gran said, digging the drab green crackers out of her pocket and slapping them into Sara's hand.

The Sun Shuttle appeared in the distance, its translucent panels whirling in spirals from its worm-shaped core. Dust devils flew into the photosynthetic appendages, momentarily slowing the Shuttle's lighting speed.

Ruqia strapped a pack onto Sara's back, flashing a smile that mirrored Sara's joy. "Thanks," Sara said, tugging on Ruqia's sleeve. For a moment they were back in the cave, connected only by touch.

As the Shuttle came toward them, a baby dinostrich appeared at the mouth of the cave. "It must have been hiding in there with its mama," Sara said, clutching the fluffy little creature to her breast.

"Come on!" Gran said, heading for the Shuttle.

"Can't we take him with us?" Sara said.

Ruqia laughed, wild and free, as the dust whirled around them. "The only reason we didn't eat his mother is because we didn't have time." She took the baby out of Sara's arms and dropped him onto the sand.

Sara stared at Ruqia defiantly, unbuttoned her shirt, scooped up the baby, and secured him on her bare breast. "I will care for him. He's my responsibility."

Ruqia howled, "You are such a little mama." She grabbed Sara's free hand and ran with her to the Shuttle. "That's what I'll call you, 'Little Mama.'"

"What can I call you?" Sara said, stumbling to follow in the large boots. "The Flying Warrior is too long."

Ruqia glanced back, winking. Sara smiled, dust brushing her teeth. The wink was a badge of honor. *We are comrades.* She climbed the ramp into the Shuttle, and it took off. Sara, pulled down her long black hair and, leaning out the window, let her hair whip in the wind.

The baby dinostrich *peeped* from inside Sara's shirt.

Gran nestled in her seat, her skeptical eyes roaming over Sara, looking for a chink.

From the Shuttle, Sara watched the towns and villages of Rojava pass by, each town structured around a central Kiss-Off Station where children came and went with their small buckets, men hauled water buckets on carts and women carried bottles on their heads.

"Allah weeps to see His people reduced to this," Gran said.

"Maybe we can find a solution," Ruqia said. Gran nudged her. Ruqia glanced at Sara and turned away.

Sara sensed that her comrades held a closely guarded secret. She would have to prove herself before they trusted her with it.

They traveled across the expanse of the desert and into the foothills. The wind seemed to blow the Shuttle up the mountain, past pea cactus farms tended by families, their children running along with the Shuttle for a heartbeat, before being left behind.

Beyond the farms, the country was uninhabited. In earlier years, it had been covered with snow. Now it was simply barren Earth. They traveled far into mountain wilderness, until the three of them were the only people left on the Shuttle.

"Where are we going?" Sara asked, stroking the head of the baby bird.

"You will see, Little Mama."

The Sun Shuttle ground to a halt with a low moan, like an animal dying or being born. Ruqia and Sara rolled out a massive water tank that had been stored in the back compartment of the Shuttle. Ruqia pushed a lever, and the tank produced wheels. Gran wiped gooey pea cactus oil on the joints of the machine, and it waddled down the ramp onto rocky soil.

Ruqia guided Sara to stand back as the Shuttle rotated its panels, like the translucent wings of a dragon and took off back down the mountain.

Ruqia uncapped the enormous water tank and drank from its large mouth, gulping with relief and pleasure. "It's unregulated around here," she said. "Don't tell Ataturka."

"Leave some for the rest," Gran said, taking over, drinking, passing it to Sara. They rolled the tank down a narrow hill, through a gully, to an opening between two trees covered with hanging vines. Gran and Ruqia looked both ways and rolled the water tank through the vine doorway, pulling Sara in behind them.

"What is this?" Sara said, staring in wonder as soldiers of the YPJ, mostly women, but quite a few men, danced in a circle, leaping, stamping, clapping to the strum of an *oud*.

"Physical Conditioning," Ruqia said, nudging Sara to help roll the water tank to the center of the square. The soldiers broke their dance and dashed for cups and lined up to drink.

They toasted Sara. She bowed and smiled and opened her shirt to reveal her little dinostrich. Oh, the fascination that followed: "A mascot!"

"One more mouth to feed," said Gran.

"I had a bird at home," Sara said. "He was a wild wren. I called him Rexie because, like this one, he's devolving into a dinosaur to mitigate dehydration."

She cupped water in her hand, and the baby drank every drop "Please let me keep him. When he's an adult, we can cook him for feast-day."

A great laughter erupted. No soldier believed Sara could cook a beast so close to her heart. Sara held tightly to the bird, unsure if the YPJ would let her in or cast her off, like any other wild creature on the outskirts of an uncivilized world.

8 – Kethuda

KEBON Dam was beautiful at night, water pouring over the spillway, calming her mind. Kethuda wondered if it were possible for a prisoner to be separate from her jailer, especially if the chains were not made of iron but of a more indestructible substance, like the will to power. Metal could be melted down; the desire for power, so deeply seeded, resisted destruction. *To discover my own power, I must know who I am. I must face my own nothingness, find substance where there has been only the reflection of the will of my father.*

She shivered, pulling her cloak around her shoulders, her feet close together in her silver boots.

How different it had been on Inauguration Day, when the lights of the World Board had been brighter than the sun. Now, in darkness, the sliver of the crescent moon was the only light sprinkled on the surface of the spillway.

As a child she had always been excited to wake in the night. She could walk freely through the rooms of the Presidential Palace, past the sleeping guards, the pack of Great Danes wagging their tails, to the Hall of Portraits of the Sultans of the Ottoman Empire.

In recent years the stuffy paintings of Turkish monarchs had given way to some of the greatest art in the Western world. Kethuda felt a special kinship with one called *A Favorite*, by French artist Jean-Auguste-Dominique Ingres: a sensual nude lounging on silken sheets with her beckoning bare feet and the curve of rosy hips, but mostly her face, a subtle rage behind her dreamy eyes as she waits to pleasure her master.

A Favorite, once the pride of a French museum, had been procured by the Saudis and given to Hamza at the closing of their water purchase contract. How many precious works of art had served as climate barter now that water, the overabundance or lack of it, had reshaped the world?

This painting was particularly fitting. It was no secret that Hamza had his own version of a harem. As far back as Kethuda could remember, women came and went beneath the averted eyes of her mother. When Kethuda was ten, she asked, "Why do you put up with it, Mama?" Ayse had sighed, moving away from her daughter into a slow Sufi swirl. Kethuda was enraged by what she saw as her mother's cowardice and swore never to be like her. *That was long ago. Now, aren't I more of a coward than my mother? In every practical way I am powerless against Hamza, just like the harem girl in the painting.*

Kethuda watched a cloud cross the moon. The downstreamers claimed they have not seen clouds in years. In Rojava, they said the stars were so bright on a dustless night, they outshone the moon. It seemed absurd. Clouds came from all over the continent, brought in by the wind, and yet, the arid countries observed that the wind above their land lusted after dust, exiling clouds to moist climates.

The trio arrived: official state hydrologist, official state climatologist, official state engineer. They muttered respectful greetings, shuffling their feet, glancing over their shoulders.

"My father must not know of this meeting," Kethuda said, summoning authority in her voice. "At his age, he is becoming weary of policy-making. He told his ministers that the depletion of our snow pack is a natural cycle. I need to know the conclusion of each of your disciplines."

Their mute response was broken by the call of a mourning dove, shorter than it used to be, conserving energy.

Kethuda smiled wryly. "Seems the dove knows what you are unwilling to tell me."

"If our model proves true," said the climatologist, "we will not see an uptake in snow pack. Not in our lifetime."

Silence, even from the dove.

"We are still in relatively good shape," the hydrologist said. "Better than most. With continued rationing, we should have enough for our people and to fulfill contracts with Israel and the Saudis, at least for the next year."

"After that?"

"We may have to renegotiate our contracts. Keep more for ourselves."

"More for Turks who can afford it," Kethuda said.

The hydrologist wiped his bald head, "Those who can pay will get more, but we shouldn't have too big a problem in the water ghettos of our less fortunate citizens. The public pumps in Ankara and Istanbul—"

"Kiss-Offs? They are *insufficient*, even now," she said.

"They aren't dried up."

"They will be... Are you telling me that by next year, we must reduce the volume of water we pipe to the Israelis and the Saudis, risking a war?"

The engineer's voice was slow, studied, "War would not be in our customer's best interest, nor ours."

Kethuda glanced up at the slender moon, a cloud curving around it. "I think you underestimate what a country will do when faced with de-hydration," she said, thinking of the people who had no clouds. "And what of the down-streamers?"

"We can't go there," said the hydrologist. "If your father were here—

"He's not. I have already syphoned off water for our customers that was once used to fill the Tigris and Euphrates. Those people downstream are surviving on what amounts to pond scum. If I close the Last Gate..."

"They will find other resources," the engineer said.

She laughed, high and sharp. "They already call me Water Witch."

"Good. That means you are doing your job," the hydrologist said. "Preserving water for our people and selling it at a fair market price to our allies."

The cloud dissipated. Kethuda stared up at the naked sliver of the moon. "I want all your data sent to my desk by the end of the week. I will take it under advisement. Go now, gentlemen. I appreciate your scientific rigor and your discretion."

They disappeared into the darkness. Her stomach churned: the bastards would tell Hamza first thing in the morning. *There is no one I can trust.*

Her mind searched for women leaders she could reach out to: Shogofa of Afghanistan, Nina Navalny in Russia, Elena Maria Juarez at *The New Yorker*, no doubt ready to turn her desk into a boat and set sail across a submerging New York City. Nestled in local support, they would tell "Ataturka" to continue to send water down stream, to be a great woman of open heart, open country.

It was not so easy. These women aspired to power, but had none. Were they not hampered by their own goodness, nursing the illusion that they could prevail through grass roots rebellion? Kethuda envied them on one count: Shogofa, Nine, Elena Maria, they all had a circle of loving women around them.

I have no circle of women, only these men with their lips on the phallus of power. And what illusion am I nursing? That I can discover a way of leading the world without sucking up to power, and yet, I know, deep within me, that without power, a noble heart is useless.

9 – Sara

THE days that followed blurred into a dream. Sara got her own uniform and proper-fitting boots, and learned the movements of the Physical Conditioning dance. She was tasked with hauling water into Camp from donation sites all over Rojava. She did this with the help of some of the men. "I thought YPJ were all women," she said to Ruqia.

"We were," Ruqia said. "But things got more complicated. So many enemies, including the perma-drought. It made sense to combine our Kurdish combat units into a genderless whole. It only works because of the chastity contract."

"The men honor it?" Sara asked, glancing at a young male soldier serving their breakfast of pea cactus mush.

"They're devout Muslims, and the contract is sanctified by Allah," Ruqia said, pushing away the mush and sneaking off to indulge in her secret stash of black-market Turkish coffee.

The Camp resembled a Kurdish settlement with laundry ropes connecting pea cactus tents instead of stone houses. While the census varied, depending on how many soldiers were off on missions, at least a hundred were stationed in Camp and the surrounding burnt forest. The black spires of the dead trees provided good cover for the Camp, but they gave Sara nightmares. She dreamed they were ISIS brides coming for her with poison-tipped javelins.

Each night at dusk, the soldiers formed small circles for Common Hour.

"Like the Council your Mamoo led," Gran said to Sara. "The leader's role is to keep order when things get heated and make sure everyone in a conflict has her or his say." Sara hugged her knees, sitting on the ground between Gran and Ruqia.

Gran opened the meeting with silent time. "You can pray to Allah, or whomever, or just be here with your thoughts and each other." After a few minutes, she asked, "Does anyone want to bring up a matter for the good of the order?"

A young woman quartered in Sara's tent raised her hand. "Sara—or whatever her real name is—she's Ruqia's favorite. I don't like her. I want her to go back to where she came from."

Ruqia raised her hand. "You think I'm neglecting you?"

"Yes," the girl said, twirling her long black hair. "You liked us all before what's-her-name came."

"My name is Sara. I was born Fatima, my stepmother called me 'Fato.'"

"The Kurdish Cinderella," the complainer said with a smirk.

Laugher erupted. Gran raised a hand. The laughter waned as quickly as it began.

Ruqia raised her hand.

"No," Sara said. "Don't defend me." She turned to face all the women, her mouth dry. "I was very much a Cinderella. My Mamoo was killed by the Turks. My Papoo married a nasty stepmother and died grieving my mama. This stepmother sold me to ISIS sex-slavers. Our Flying Warrior took me under her wing out of compassion. If she gives me more time, it is because I am stupid and weak, knowing nothing of soldiering or the world. You are seasoned warriors, the women I have worshipped since I was a little girl. If I cry out at night, it's because I dream that the burnt forest is ISIS, or sometimes I think it is the Turks come to kill us all."

An anxious rumble followed. "We all fear the Turks," said one young man, glancing shyly at Sara.

Gran raised her hand for silence. Sara noticed a subtle shift in the eyes of the other women. They no longer seemed to see her as a snotty little girl taking their General away from them, but a frightened girl, wanting only to be seen and known for who she is.

The young woman who first complained raised her hand. "Sara has made an important point. She fears the forest turning into ISIS or the Turks. Both have spies everywhere. Sara names what we all feel: how long before the Ataturka bitch orders her army to slaughter us?"

Sara's face flushed with relief. *She called me Sara, not Fato. They do not hate me. They listened to me.* Her heart warmed to think of her Mamoo, raising her hand as Gran did, leading Council. *Maybe one day I can be such a leader.*

This promoted much discussion about Ataturka and the water depletion in the Euphrates, and how large the Turkish army was, and how few the numbers in the YPJ.

At the close of the meeting, all participants recited the pledge, "Happy are they who call themselves Kurds." They vowed to bring their joys and grievances to Common Hour, confirming that YPJ was a community of soldiers and human beings, the latter always first.

As the meeting broke up, Ruqia told Sara, "Little Mama, you spoke with great courage and vulnerability."

Sara stared in awe at Ruqia: the most admired woman in Camp. When she performed the Physical Conditioning dance, the others moved away to watch her fly into the air and land just in time to shoot an e-arrow at a spinning ball. This only made Sara more anxious to face Ruqia in private tutorials on the art of shooting the e-arrow rifle.

"You're the champion of warriors," Sara said to Ruqia at their next shooting session. "You are so patient with me. May I call you 'R'?"

"Only if you let me call you Little Mama in front of everybody."

"What are the moments you have loved the most in your life?" Sara asked, and then burned with shame: *where did that come from?*

Ruqia swallowed, glancing away. "It was a long time ago."

"I'm sorry. I don't know why I said that."

"You're afraid of shooting," Ruqia said. "You'll do anything to distract us from the real work. I don't blame you. These rifles are complicated. Two settings, *sleep,* like when people used to put animals to sleep with a tranquilizer dart, and of course, *kill,* which seeks lethality. If you forget to select one of these, it defaults to *kill.*"

"Give me time to learn how to shoot it before I mess with the settings," Sara said, pointing the heat-seeking arrow at a squirming chameleon strapped to a target, flashing its color from red to gold. "Isn't it endangered?" she asked.

"No more than you or me. They crawl all over the forest."

Sara dropped the weapon. "Take it off, please. I want to practice with a blank target."

"This is a war camp, not a petting zoo."

"I can't hit something that wiggles so much."

Ruqia howled, "You think the enemy will stand still for you?"

Sara lowered her head in shame. "I keep thinking of the red and gold butterfly that used to land in my Mamoo's fig tree when I was a girl. I can't get it out of my head."

Ruqia scoffed and wrapped her arms roughly around Sara, closing her long fingers over Sara's small ones that held the e-arrow weapon.

"Look at the target, Sara. What do you see?"

"A living thing that doesn't want to die."

"Horse-shit! Look again. What do you see?"

Sara squirmed. Ruqia's arms held her in a fierce grip. It hurt. *I can't tell her that! I must be a warrior.*

Sara scraped the roof of her mouth with her dry tongue. "I see the enemy."

"More like it! How do you feel about the enemy?"

Sara felt Ruqia's calloused fingers touching her like divine sandpaper on a porcelain vase. "I hate the enemy."

"Yes. Whose face do you see in the body of the squirming snake?"

"Ataturka."

"Yeah. Ataturka. She who would kill us all."

Sara trembled.

Ruqia held her tighter, saying in her ear, "Shooting is not only about hate. It is the finest art form on the planet. You see something move—something you hate—something that wants to kill you. Your eye sends a signal to your arms, your fingers, your whole body, so that every cell in you, every part of you, it all comes together in that one moment. You aim. Your target moves. You follow it with all that you are, body and soul, whatever the hell that is. A signal comes up from your gut, and you know it is now or never. You shoot—" Ruqia pressed Sara's finger on the sensor. A missile ejected, silently sizzling into the writhing flesh of the chameleon. It flashed orange and purple and golden-green and went limp.

Sara gasped, panting for breath. She felt Ruqia's body relax.

"You were holding your breath, Little Mama."

Sara nodded, inhaling.

"Good. You were engaged. Some people check out. They are not warrior material. I could feel it in your body, Sara Roxan, the capability to love it."

"Love it?"

"Your weapon, not just a gun, an extension of your body, your whole self. Even now, killing this stupid snake we will secretly enjoy for lunch, I feel the joy of the art, as if I had created a beautiful sculpture. In the moment of the kill, I am complete."

Sara's breath slowed down. No feelings came. Only a desire to please the General, to be a good warrior, to learn to love to kill.

10 - Kethuda

SHE stood on the balcony of her Presidential apartment, gazing into the torch-lit darkness of Ankara. Far off, a singer grieved for his lost love, merchants sold candles and pea cactus liquor. A woman called out, "Gourmet *salties*: keep hydrated in style." Musical bells echoed from *ferry-cycles* sweeping back and forth in the street below. Kethuda loved these late twenty-first century inventions: a bicycle transformed into a small urban ferris wheel, each person peddling to the sound of soft bells. As a girl Kethuda had loved everything about the ferry-cycle except its putrid green color. Her father had commissioned extravagant paint in brilliant shades of the rainbow. The popularity of the musical transports skyrocketed.

Kethuda leaned against the balcony rail of what people called the "Ataturka Apartment." After a month in the Presidential Palace, she had realized that its grandeur did not match her image as a servant of Allah and the Earth Goddess. She chose this relatively modest apartment to downplay her privilege and play up her unity with the common people. Hamza was horrified that she had taken up residence in the "slums" of Ankara. Kethuda relished his disapproval. She loved this apartment, loved listening to the sounds of Ankara: the laughter of children, the murmurs of lovers, the smell of pea cactus rum.

This night, she poured real rum into her coffee cup, toasting all those happy imbibers out there in the dark.

My people survive. The texture of their lives has changed, but their spirit endures. "I must find the voice of my own self," she said out loud, "and offer that to my people."

"What a very fine thought," Mihiri said, carrying in a new shimmering white gown and blue hijab embellished with speckled black feathers. Kethuda was dimly sad that a bird had died to make this decoration. Perhaps it came from the black speckled bird that had sucked water from the dome of her car at the reservoir? It was probably going to die anyway, and she had to admit the effect was stunning. Luminous feathers encircling her face like a crown.

She admired her reflection in the full-length mirror. The expansive room behind her added to the effect: sea-green pea cactus couches in the style of ancient Roman, pale purple walls peppered with fine art, vintage mahogany tables adorned with pea cactus lavender-scented shells, and through the open door, the bedroom with her mother's antique marble vanity. Lavender was imported at great cost from northern countries who grew it on platforms above flood level. Mixing it with pea-cactus created a scent far more luxurious than the sour acrid smell of pure pea-cactus.

Ayse's jewels were carefully tucked out of sight. Not appropriate for the People's President. But Kethuda had spared no expense on the King-sized canopy bed, its sheer white curtains swaying softly in the warm night breeze.

As she turned sideways in the mirror, it was impossible not to notice that she was a superior specimen of femininity, head tilted slightly upward, conveying authority without arrogance, confidence without a lust for power. Impossible not to feel self-adoration—deserved, or not—yet a voice within her chimed in from under the façade. *Ka-thoooo-dah, who the hell are you beneath this concocted masquerade?*

She dismissed all thought, hurrying away to slide into her Ataturka-mobile. In moments, she was crossing the threshold of the Grand Ballroom of the Presidential Palace.

She smiled, not at the men bowing and kissing her hand, but in answer to the urging of her inner voice, *rise up, claim power, whoever the hell you are. I will send a press release to Elena Maria Juarez at The New Yorker tomorrow. I will thought-message Shogofa in Afghanistan, Nina Navalny in Russia, women all over the world on my private In-Phone setting to report my political victory tonight over these suck-up men.*

They were all here, the ministers who had witnessed Hamza strangling her at the dam, the trio of scientists she had met under the crescent moon, and the customers of Turkiye's precious water supply: the Prime Minister of Israel, the King of Saudi Arabia. All of these men stood together, whispering like old school chums.

Everyone seemed excited to talk about the two-state solution for the Israel and Palestine. Climate change had proved the final impetus. All the effort that used to go toward killing each other was now needed to resettle the entire region away from the swelling Mediterranean. Palestinians and Israelis worked together to build as many desalinization plants along the coast as possible. Some remained barely cordial to each other. Some became friends. Some even intermarried.

Hamza hovered beneath the ballroom's crystal chandelier, reaching for the skirt of a young serving woman. She gasped and spilled champagne on his shirt, feigning shock as she backed away. Kethuda smiled at her from across the room, and the girl nodded with gratitude for the approval in the new President's eyes.

The Israeli Prime minister made straight for Kethuda, bowing, kissing her hand, asking if he could place her finger on his forehead. She agreed, ignoring the tightness in her belly: Israel was among the driest countries on the planet.

"Madam President, I want you to see the public water station at the Wailing Wall," he said.

"Such a monumental achievement," she said with studied sincerity. "Transplanting Jerusalem stone by stone as you flee from the rising sea; so it is with our beloved Istanbul."

"Yes, Madam President, our desalinization plants are running at full capacity, and yet we need your continued support."

"You have stopped dumping your brine residue into the ocean?" she said.

He bowed. "Yes, Madam. As per the request, no, the *demand*, of the World Water Rationing and Refugee Team. We will not destroy our coastal marine sanctuaries by poisoning them with our brine waste products."

"Thank you," she said, wondering what land-swelling creatures were being poisoned by the brine, including the swelling communities of water refugees.

The Israeli minister politely pressed Kethuda's finger against his sweating brow, opening his In-Phone portal for sharing. "See for yourself, Madam President: Israelis, Palestinians, Muslims, Christians, standing in line to fill their empty buckets. Without your water, our people would die of thirst."

She moved the tip of her finger gently onto her own forehead until the images from the Prime Minister's In-Phone came into view. A daunting sight: women and children in sleeveless pea cactus shirts, standing in line in the hot sun; elderly people dragging their buckets of water home; one boy holding the head of his dying baby goat to let it sip from his hand.

"I am grateful we can send some of our water to you," Kethuda said, removing her finger. *If this is happening in Israel, what is happening here? I get written reports, but I have been too afraid to go among my own people lined up at Kiss-Off Stations all over Ankara.*

She collected herself, returning her gaze to the Prime Minister. "And let me congratulate you on the two-state solution. Israelis and Palestinians living in peace, at last."

He put a hand to his heart. "Many of us did not want it. But it is what the water wants."

She smiled. "That phrase is tossed around a lot these days. I think everyone has a different idea about what the water wants."

"I must ask you what Israel wants: to join The World Water Rationing and Refugee Team."

"Are you displeased with our ration decisions?" she asked.

"You have seen the images," he said. "We need more water."

"It is not up to me alone You must draft a petition addressed to all leaders of RAT."

The Israeli minister's eyes grew large. Saying "RAT" was worse that uttering the most base sexual slang. She concealed her amusement as he bowed and wandered off.

The Saudi King was next, kissing Kethuda's hand and placing her finger on his forehead without asking permission. "I must show you," he said in the voice of a man addressing his lover. In public, he supported female Saudis' right to drive, run for office, and own property. In private, he was a customer of sex traffickers and had recently displayed a terrible tantrum when his beautiful Kurdish virgin escaped in the desert of Rojava.

"See how many of my people are served by your water," he said, his eyes combing the strong lines of Kethuda's nose, her chin, her body concealed beneath the diaphanous folds of her white gown. "Many of my people will go thirsty without your support."

"You have it," she said, withdrawing her finger.

Hamza was watching from across the room with pride and ownership. This sumptuous State Dinner was not only to flatter her, it was to reward the loyalty of the patrons who had swept her into power. In honor of the occasion exotic food had been shipped in, including the meat of the mythical dinostrich from the desert of Rojava. Apparently this beast wasn't a myth and was said to taste like alligator left too long in the sun. No one seemed to care. It was the privilege of the rich to dine on devolving dinosaur while the servants ate warmed-over pea cactus soup.

She stared back at Hamza, her inner voice pleading, *where are you, Kethuda? You do have substance. Find it. Don't slip away.*

A fanfare from the State Orchestra brought silence to the room. Hamza lifted his glass. "Tonight, we celebrate the love and protection given to the Turkish people, and to our partner nations, by the most beautiful President in the world, our own Ataturka." Chants rose to the vaulted ceiling, where a Medieval painting of a bloody battle seemed to come alive in her name. She stared up, watching the men slaughter each other, blood appearing to drop from the ceiling.

"Take your seats," Hamza said, gesturing to the long banquet table set with plates of silver and gold. "Tonight, we dine on the raw meat luxury: dinostrich tartare."

The Saudi King and the Israeli Prime Minister offered to guide Kethuda to the head of the table. She politely declined. The room spun before her eyes, as if she stood on a mighty ship in a wind storm. She touched the vintage white linen table cloth. The room was not spinning. She was.

Is there any way for me to be my own woman in this puppet show?

A young Turkish man in classic red fez perched on a vintage velvet stool, aiming his *oud* at the empty dance floor. He bowed to Kethuda, to the table of men, and began to strum. A pulsing, rhythmic, sensual song.

A woman entered: statuesque, African facial tattoos, golden pantaloons belted to her hips, full bare breasts the color of a warm summer night. The men whistled and cheered as she moved to the center of the room, her thick black braids sashaying across her back, like serpents swaying to their own drum.

Kethuda's body grew calm, her focus leaving the men behind as she watched the woman move with brazen female pride. Who was she? A water refugee from Africa, surviving by feeding the appetites of men? And yet, she was no victim.

She commanded the floor, her body pulsing with bold grace, her eyes bemused.

The music entered Kethuda's body, and with it, a wild joy. She strode past the Saudi King and the Israeli Prime Minister.

Hamza grabbed her arm.

"What are you going to do, Papa? Strangle me in front of all these people?" She broke away, joining the African woman on the dance floor.

Shock spread through the room. The *oud* player faltered, forgetting his tune.

Kethuda looked proudly into the eyes of the African woman. "I will follow you."

"I wouldn't take off your clothes, if I were you," the woman said, her accent round with African tones.

Kethuda laughed, holding out her hand. "I am Kethuda."

The woman smiled, shaking the President's hand. "I am called Gai."

"Play!" Kethuda called to the musician, who took off his fez, shook out his curly black hair, and resumed the erotic strumming of his *oud*. Gai bent her knees, moving her hips as she rose, arms in a graceful spiral, head back, lips apart. Kethuda mirrored her, feeling the pure joy of her body in motion.

Gai picked up the pace, stamping the floor in a syncopated beat. Kethuda followed, locking eyes with Gai as they moved together, hips going one way, breasts the other.

Kethuda could see Hamza impatiently gesturing for the men to sit down at the table and eat. They stumbled in the process, all eyes glued to the dance floor with disbelief and desire.

The smell of wild game entered the room as the young servant women carried in trays of raw, pulverized dinostrich. They paused, amazed at the sight of their President dancing with a half-naked Black woman in primal female glory.

"I'm sweating like a wild boar," Kethuda said as she twirled close to Gai. Are you sure I shouldn't strip?"

"I smell rum on your breath, Madam President. Don't do anything you will regret in the morning."

"You talk like a sister, not a subordinate."

"You would have me grovel?"

"Not unless it's part of the dance."

Gai's smile outshone the brilliant candlelight of the chandeliers. "Let's go the other way," she said, sinking her fists into the shimmering golden cloth on her hips, strutting forward.

Kethuda copied her, chin high, hips rocking in the sheer joy of being brazenly a *woman*.

Hamza's face grew red.

"Let him fume 'til his blood boils," Kethuda said under her panting breath.

"He could murder you, Madam," Gai said, changing the dance to a twirl, cupping each naked breast with her elegant fingers, lifting them high, like the great treasures of humanity they were. Kethuda found her breasts beneath the sweaty folds of her white gown, lifting them, shaking them, as if she had become the moving statue of the Seated Woman of Catalhoyuk Herself.

The men howled and clapped, whistled and cheered.

Hamza sat down at the head of the table, stabbing his dinostrich.

Kethuda stared back in defiance. He could not touch her. Not tonight. Not since her body had discovered what her mind had not: unleash the power of the female body, and the world is yours.

11 – Ruqia

RUQIA's heart lost a beat as her boots hit the ground. The sand-colored ISIS van chugged toward them in the desert. *It was a terrible mistake to bring Sara into the field; the bitches picked up her small footprints, even in new boots.*

Sara ran just ahead, pacing Gran, glancing back at Ruqia with such trust, such devotion.

"Hold on," Ruqia called, her voice dropping from its usual confident register as she felt a throbbing pressure at the base of her throat, a pain both diffuse and sharp, bringing with it a flood of images: her tiny bare feet running out of her house to dance in the monsoon, laughing with Mama and Papa; flocks of wild geese covering the sun, their proud *honks* echoing across the fertile plains; her grandparents' sheep grazing on the gently sloping hillsides, snow covering the shrubs and forests in magical white.

I can't think of this now. She looked across the wind-swept desert, the only sign of life a limping gazelle, migrating from Africa in search of a habitable climate. As possible death approached, Ruqia couldn't help remembering the Earth as it used to be.

The motor of the van sputtered.

"They can't catch us—" Sara said, eyes wild, as she turned to Gran. "I'm so sorry. They're here because of me."

Gran clicked her teeth. "And they want you alive."

"I know," Sara said. "They will kill you to get to me."

"We won't let them," Gran said. "Shoot to wound. It is easier than aiming for the chest."

"We can do that?" Sara asked.

"I do it always," Gran said. "Allah prefers."

"To Hell with Allah," Ruqia said to Sara. "Shoot to kill."

A chorus of female voices in the van shouted, "Death to YPJ."

A murderous energy rose from the balls of Ruqia's feet. She leapt into the air, landing beside Sara. "Put your setting on *kill.*"

Sara touched the sensor. "I'm sorry. You should have left me behind."

"Whatever you do, stop apologizing."

Ruqia pushed Sara and Gran into a swirling ball of dust, their only cover in desert warfare.

The ISIS women piled out of the van: four of them in black, their full mask hijabs whipping in the wind.

"I know the one in front," Sara said, spitting dust. "The short one. The Commander. My lost slipper is poking out of her pocket." Sara shot her e-arrow rifle into the wind before Ruqia could stop her. The missile landed in the sand at the ISIS Commander's feet. All hooded heads turned to the dust ball.

Ruqia pulled Sara back as ISIS circled them.

"Don't save me," Sara said.

"Then stop screwing up." Ruqia leapt sideways and shot a hooded woman in the leg. The wind dispersed the smell of burning flesh, muffling the victim's screams.

The other three ISIS warriors fired, but Ruqia leapt so high, every missile landed in a fizzle at her feet. She caught the look of awe in Sara's eyes. *This is why we have destroyed the Earth; we are possessed by our need for hero-worship in an innocent's eyes.* The thought was ill-timed. It made her lose focus.

Sara seemed to sense this and fired at another hooded woman, missing her mark. Gran coughed. "I can't see to shoot, but they can't see us either."

Sara grabbed Ruqia's sleeve. "Let me surrender before they kill us all."

"Shut up."

A missile grazed Sara's left arm. Blood poured from it, dripping coils of red onto the sand. Ruqia grabbed the wound. Gran tore off her flimsy hijab and wrapped Sara's arm.

The three of them looked up. Something was happening. The wind was dying down.

Their dust devil spiraled into the ground. They were exposed. So were the ISIS women. They stared at one another across the empty space.

In the stunned silence, Gran popped off two shots, wounding two women as Sara shot frantically with her good arm.

The ISIS Commander grabbed her chest and fell to the Earth.

"Well done," Ruqia said.

Sara gasped, "I only meant to wound her. Oh, my God, what have I done?" She ran to the Commander, pulling off her black hood, looking at her face, a face that mirrored all the women in the desert that day: proud nose, full lips, eyes startled, yet still.

Sara leaned close, "You are the Commander. You took me to drink at the bank of the Euphrates. We said how much we hated Ataturka. You told your soldiers not to kill me."

Ruqia joined them, staring in wonder at the strange intimacy of Sara and the Commander.

I, the Flying Warrior, have killed many women and men. I felt nothing; killing was simply a fact of war. I have never felt this great mourning for a dying enemy. Sara feels everything so deeply—great joy, great sorrow. What magic does she bring to my frozen heart? Why do I want it? Why do I fear it?

The heavy eyes of the Commander found Sara's face. "You are the merchandise—"

"I am so sorry. I aimed for your shoulder—"

"Allah will not forgive you."

"I will not ask Him," Sara said, taking out her flask and dribbling water into the Commander's mouth.

All the women watched in silence as the Commander swallowed.

Death came, as quiet as the ceasing of the wind.

12 - Kethuda

SHE slowly raised her eyelids as bright morning light penetrated the white lace curtains. She had been dreaming that she was moving into a new place, a large empty room with full-length windows, tall white walls, and a ceiling very different from the one covered with the bloody battle scene in the Presidential Palace. This ceiling was blank, as if ready to be painted upon. The real estate agent was eager to make the sale. Kethuda studied the space, not sure she would take it.

A new space? A new home… But do I really want it?… She lifted her head, feeling its ache, the memory of the previous evening tumbling out. *By the breast of Seated Woman, I danced with an African in front of all those men!* After the dance, she had refused the plate of dinostrich, declaring in a drunken swagger, "A new species, and we kill it for pleasure?" She ordered plain pea cactus soup, and invited the African woman to put on her shawl and join her at the head of the table. All the male guests were intrigued and amused, except her father.

A knock on the bedroom door brought her out of reverie. "Yes?"

"It is Gai, Madam."

"Gai?"

"We met last night, on the dance floor."

"Of course, enter."

Gai opened the door. It took a moment for Kethuda to recognize her in modest white shirt and black trousers, the tendrils of her black braids rolled into a knot on top of her head. Her face was more mature than it had seemed the night before in the rosy glow of the ballroom: a face that had seen the trials of the world, a scar across her eye, deep ridges on her brow causing the vertical lines of her tattoo to appear to move like waves on water.

"You're the dancer. What are you doing here, dressed like a servant?"

"You hired me last night, Madam."

"I did?"

"Yes, Madam. In addition to the rum, you had some wine with our soup. Quite a lot. It is not surprising you can't recall. You said to me, 'Teach me to dance, and become my personal assistant. But you must wear clothes.'"

Kethuda chuckled, holding her head, "Where is Mihiri?"

Gai placed a tray on the bed table with Turkish coffee and a dull green pea-bun. "She was here when I escorted you home. You hugged her and told her she could retire."

"Oh, my God, what a wretched thing to do."

"Oh, no, Madam. Your Mihiri wept in relief, touching her curved back. You said, 'It hurts?' She sobbed and said, 'Yes, Madam.' Then you did a marvelous thing, You took out handfuls of your mother's jewels and gave them to Mihiri."

Kethuda looked into Gai's large eyes, luminous as black stones polished in a mountain stream. "It doesn't sound like something Kethuda would do. Must have been Ataturka, the merciful."

"Yes, Madam."

Kethuda sipped her coffee, rubbing her aching head. "I remember, vaguely… Did I sign a note for Mihiri, so no one would think she stole the jewels?"

"Yes, Ma'am," Gai said, wrinkling the middle of her nose.

"What?" Kethuda said.

"Are you sure you won't grieve the loss of your mother's jewels?"

"Mother didn't wear them unless Papa insisted. She preferred light, inexpensive gems. The ones I gave Mihiri were from the Ottoman Empire. I won't miss them. I must present an image of religious devotion to my people, not a bedecked sultana."

"You are a fox on a mission, Madam."

Kethuda chuckled, amazed at the woman's boldness. Was she a person of authority in her country of origin? Kethuda remembered an image on World Board of the bodies of dehydrated giraffes on the African plain as far as the eye could see. Did her new assistant come from such suffering?

"As she left, Mihiri told me to take good care of you. She held the jewels close and said, 'My Mistress is kind. But wealth will not help me if there is no water to buy.'"

Kethuda smiled, "I was very wise to hire you—what is your name again?"

"Gai, half the word for God, not that I am one." She placed a stack of documents on the vintage mahogany desk. "From your scientists. Apparently, something about last night made an impression on them." Her eyes rested on the statue under glass. "Madam, is it She?"

"Yes. The Seated Woman of Catalhoyuk, our Turkish Earth Goddess."

"Does she give you power?"

Kethuda sat up taller in her bed, a kernel of fear poking its way into her belly. *Who is this woman that she asks such questions?*

Gai looked at her. "What you did last night, dancing with me, a toy in the service of men, was a demonstration of unity with all women. You must be guided by a powerful Goddess. Or you must have had a mother in league with your God."

"My mother? She was very loving, but far too humble. She had no power."

The tattoo on Gai's forehead wrinkled. "Humble? My *yeyo* taught me that the word humble comes from Greek: humus. Your mother was a Goddess of the Earth."

"Whatever she was, she had no power," Kethuda said, holding her throbbing head.

"I think you do not understand, Madam President. You make two animals of power and love. It is not so. My *yeyo*, Maasai for mother, she was called Tabana Meru, a woman who was the equal of the mountain, Meru. She was powerful as a mountain for my brother and me because her love was so great. I think you danced with me last night out of your love for yourself as a woman. Your mother taught you that gift."

The fear in Kethuda's belly dissolved, and in its place, wonder, and the hint of something she had longed for all her life: self-respect. "Dancing with you was a crazy thing to do. An impulse."

Gai smiled, resting her hand gently on the glass dome of the Seated Woman. "An impulse from somewhere deep within."

Kethuda felt a wave of nausea, as if she had stepped too close to the edge of a precipice and the next step would send her over the edge. She chewed her pea-bun, talking with her mouth full, "Maybe you can help me solve a mystery. The civilization that worshipped our Earth Goddess was free of gender-bias. Truly egalitarian. Some houses had the capacity to dominate, but they couldn't. Something 'capped' their will to power."

Gai tilted her head, looking at Kethuda through the bottom of her eyes. "Are you always so philosophical this early in the morning, Madam?"

Kethuda laughed. "Do you have an answer to this 'cap'? Something from the Maasai?"

Gai's smile faded. She looked out through the sheer white curtains, as if seeing far beyond. "I grew up with our family in low houses of mud and dung, arranged in a circle with our precious cattle in the center. My papa had four wives, each with her own house. The RAT committee watched us closely after passage of the International One-Child Policy. My brother and I are twins. When this accident occurred, the second wife could not bear children, but she helped raise us both, as did all the other wives. You had only one mother, Madam?"

Kethuda smiled. "Only one, though my father had many mistresses. I never knew them. They lived in separate apartments all over the city. Very different from what you describe."

"How lonely for you and your mother," Gai said. "The question of the 'cap' would not have come up for the Maasai. All worked together in our circle of houses. Adults looked after the children, who were considered very precious. We were given great freedom. All we had to do was play for the first seven years of our lives. Those years, for me, are filled with the memory of rolling in the red Earth, chasing my brother and my cousins. When I was eight, we learned to milk the cows, and we went to school."

"Did you feel love from your father?"

"Yes. He was always going to Nairobi, where he worked as a lawyer. He taught me what he knew. 'You will make a brilliant attorney for our people,' he told me."

Gai stopped, turning her face away from the window. Kethuda could not take her eyes from that face, the tattoo roiling with memory. "RAT did not make a priority of our Maasai people. All my father's efforts to petition for more water were ignored. The RAT said Africa was a 'lost cause.' We watched people fashion empty termite mounds into Temples of Return, where the dry go to die."

Kethuda shivered. Hamza had been part of the decision-making to abandon Africa. Ayse had been very upset about it, arguing for the possibility that a new technology could come along one day to bring water to the African continent. Hamza had laughed. "One day? We have no time to wait for your fairy tale and no way to bring water to a dying country." Kethuda and her mom began to hear stories of Temples of Return, some works of art, copied recently by down-stream countries, some even sighted in Turkiye.

Gai's eyes trembled like black diamonds on a broken necklace, "Our Tabana Meru, our *yeyo*, worked with the last of her strength to get passage for my brother and me to come to Turkiye. We wept and begged. We did not want to leave *yeyo*. She insisted. Our father insisted. We knew she would build a Temple of Return after we left, the most beautiful in the whole of the world. Someone took a picture of it: vintage plaid blankets of the Maasai coiled like red waves on the banks of the dry Mara River."

Gai looked up slowly, her face still, as if lit from within. "*Yeyo* went away in body. Her spirit lives inside the mountain of me." She placed her hand on her heart. "I feel her every day. Do you feel your mother in your body, Madam? I am sure she is there."

Kethuda stared, unable to feel anything. "I never thought about it. Not like that. What does that have to do with finding the 'cap' on dominance?"

"The question is irrelevant when there is love in a community. Anyone who gets uppity gets laughed at, with loving kindness, brought into the heart of the community to be healed."

"Healed?"

"Yes, Madam. The will to power is a disease."

Kethuda could barely breathe. "Do you think this happened in Catalhoyuk?"

"Why not?" said Gai, turning to her mistress, in a voice as light and firm as a school teacher's. "Has your body touched the ground this morning, Madam?"

Kethuda sat up, swinging her legs to the side of the bed, her bare feet slapping the floor. "By the uterus of the Seated Woman, I've never been so sore in all my life."

"I think you have never danced like you did last night, Madam. Shall I draw a powder bath for you?"

Kethuda groaned, "That won't help my aching muscles."

"No, Madam, but the tiny microbes of the bath powder will devour your dead cells and, frankly, give you a more pleasant scent."

Kethuda giggled at the delicacy of her new assistant's words. "You're saying I stink?"

"Yes, Madam. And I have inspected the mechanism on your Sucking Toilet. If you had it upgraded, you might not need all of these lavender scent shells."

"If you make the flush stronger, my whole body will get sucked down, not just my poop!" They both giggled at the thought of the President bring sucked down by waterless bathroom technology.

Kethuda studied Gai and saw a woman who was obviously well educated, and appeared to know a great deal about the temperament of men and the vulnerability of women.

Gai met Kethuda's scrutiny with her head held high. "Your father has been asking to see you."

Kethuda felt the old tug deep in her belly. *Meet his need... meet his need...do it at once, Snap to. Snap to.* She tightened her lips in revulsion, not for her father, but for herself.

"You must tend to your body before you take on the requirements of your office," Gai said. "I have brought my e-arrow firearm, in case your father loses self-control."

Tears of relief filled Kethuda's eyes. "No one has ever protected me from him. Not my mother, no one. Thank you."

"You will find your voice with him, Madam, and I will be here."

Kethuda wiped back tears, her head throbbing, her body aching.

Gai took her mistress's hands, leading her in gentle stretching. They moved together across the pale purple pea cactus floor, Kethuda moaning with each stretch.

"An answer to your 'cap' may be in the body," Gai said. "People in Catalhoyuk moved their bodies each day to survive, yes?"

"I think you are a goddess," Kethuda said, lifting her arms as if carrying sheaths of grain. "The people of Catalhoyuk—women and men alike—carried the babies, the grain, ground it, grew it, their bodies as curved in old age as Mihiri's."

Gai lifted the ends of the sheer white curtains of the balcony window, moving inside of them like a goddess of fabric. She pulled Kethuda in with her. The people in the streets below could see two feminine figures moving in the morning light. They cheered, as if at the sight of the Earth Goddess in motion.

"You are the People's President," Gai said.

Kethuda stepped onto the balcony in her nightgown, waving to her people, wondering if it were actually possible to become the person they all needed and loved.

13 – Sara

I have taken a life. Sara leaned out the window of the Sun Shuttle, holding the Commander's body in her arms. Ruqia did not understand. Why hold your dead enemy? The wounded ISIS prisoners wanted to hold their Commander. It was causing disruption on the Shuttle, but Sara would not let go.

She carried the body through the mountain trails into the Burnt Forest surrounding YPJ Camp. No one understood why the Commander had not been buried in the desert. Sara offered no explanation, digging a grave in the forest, allowing the wounded ISIS prisoners to grieve as she allowed them to perform the Muslim burial rite.

In the days ahead, Sara watched, amazed, as Ruqia unveiled a new side of herself, not the flashy warrior, but a person who intimately knew the trauma of death. Ruqia never rebuked Sara for expressing grief, regret, and remorse. She brought her water and rubbed her shoulders. Sara wept and coiled into a ball. Ruqia did not say shallow words, but silently wrapped her arms around Little Mama as they laid quietly, back to belly, until Sara's tears washed them both to sleep.

The other soldiers in Camp spread rumors. Dangerous ones. Women were not allowed to have carnal relations. When confronted by a cadre of adoring young recruits, Ruqia snapped, "Sometimes I hold Sara like a mother holds a child. It is treatment for post-traumatic stress."

One night, Sara woke to the sound of whispers outside the tent.

"Incoming map of new sand cave formations," Ruqia was saying.

Sara peered through the opening: Ruqia and Gran huddled around a small fire, sharing data on Ruqia's In-Phone.

Gran clicked her teeth. "Not too far from where we found Sara."

"Dose the fire. Let's go."

"Sara will be mad with you," Gran said.

Sara crawled out of the tent. "I'm coming with you."

Ruqia's eyes reflected the orange-gold of the firelight. "No. I think you have too much empathy to be a soldier, Little Mama."

"I've been target practicing every day. My aim is getting better. Right, Gran?"

Gran tied up the filaments of her patchwork hijab. "Better. Not great."

"So, don't give me a rifle. Let me help navigate. I'm good with maps. Good with dust. I'm strong. I can carry a mountain of *salties*."

Ruqia's face was moist with sweat, her long fingers wrapped across the handle of her e-arrow rifle. Sara wondered if 'R' would have been a famous oud player if the world hadn't warmed.

Ruqia said, "We don't know what we'll find out there—Turks, ISIS, water refugees ready to kill us for a canteen."

"I took a vow to give my life and death to YPJ," Sara said.

"You two can stay here and fuss. I'm off to find a water pipe," Gran said, stamping out the fire and heading into the darkness.

Ruqia and Sara followed, no words passing between them.

Ruqia knows I can't sleep without her body next to me. Maybe she needs me as much as I need her?

They hiked through swirling dust, sipping their rations, sleeping in open desert beneath a tan pea-tarp. Hours became days as they slipped into villages to get Kiss-Off rations. When the wind settled at night, Ruqia and Sara would crawl away from the snoring Gran and curl together, breasts to back beneath shooting stars.

On the third day, Sara woke to a familiar sound. *Oooowok! Wok, oooook wok.* Dinostriches.

She shook Ruqia. "They're excited. I know the call—"

Ruqia must have been having a lovely dream, for she creased her nose and rolled over. Sara crawled into the pea-tarp and nudged Gran.

"ISIS?" Gran peered at Sara with milky morning eyes.

"I don't know," Sara said, rubbing Gran's crinkly face. "I need you to listen."

"So? Quibbling dinosaurs."

"It *means* something. I heard calls like this when I was running with them and we found a pea cactus farm."

"What they chirp when they encounter a food source—"

"—or *water*."

"What?" Ruqia said, crawling in beside them.

They packed up quickly, passing the morning water flask and pea-cactus breakfast squares.

The desert was a veil of dust, the sun a quiet blur of light.

Sara forged ahead. "What if ISIS—or the Turks—planted a recording of *Wok! Wok*! to lure us into a trap?" she said, her heart fluttering. But something was different. Her boots sank in lower than they had before. She knelt and placed her palms on the sand. "*Moist*…it feels……*moist*."

Gran slapped her hand on the ground. "Praise Allah."

Ruqia pressed her hands into the Earth. "We will thank Him later. This could still be a decoy." She pulled out her knife, walking slowly along the pathway of moist sand.

A yawning opening in the Earth appeared through the curtain of dust.

The sound grew louder. *OOOgggle, woook, wok*

"By the ponytail of Innana," Sara said, "do the lights on our In-Phones work out here?"

"Maybe," Gran said, "but we might need every bit of our energy quota for something else."

Ruqia said, "We have three heads, three In-Phones. Sara, try your light."

Sara pressed the tip of her ring finger. A pleasant light shone out to guide their way.

"Sara, do you mind going in first," Ruqia said. "You're good with birds. They give me the creeps."

Sara pointed her finger-light and entered the cave. At the bottom of a long shaft, a flock of dinostriches pecked at something buried in the sand. No sign of ISIS or Turks. Sara called for Gran and Ruqia to follow.

"Look at their beaks," Ruqia said. "Much stronger than a bird's, more like, what did you call them, Sara?"

"Crested dinosaurs. We can move closer. They won't eat us—I don't think so, anyway." She crawled in beside the dinostriches like she was joining old friends at the dinner table. But this was no banquet. Something much more precious: "They're *drinking!*"

Ruqia and Gran lunged to her side. There, unmistakably, were the sturdy beaks of the feathery dinosaurs pecking a hole in a pipe buried in the floor of the cave. Sara moved in closer. "Hey Oogle, oggles, there's enough for all of us." One of the dinostrich lumbered aside. Sara scooped water into her palms, carrying it to Gran. "You're our elder. Take the first sip."

Gran drank from Sara's hands. "Tastes like the tears of Allah—"

Ruqia slurped greedily. "Best Turkish water I've ever tasted."

They drank until they were giddy and filled their canteens to the brim.

Ruqia took pea cactus squares from her pack. The dinostrich lifted their magnificent heads toward the food as she dribbled bits in the sand, leading the beasts out of the cave.

Gran ceremoniously lifted a square metal box from a secret chamber in her back pack. "Sara Roxan, you found the pipe. You can be the first to open the box."

"The secret?" Sara said. "We should do this together."

"No," Ruqia said. "Your curiosity got us here. The unveiling is yours."

"Pandora's Box?" Sara asked with a measure of anxiety.

"The opposite," Ruqia said. "Trust us."

Gran punched in a sequence of numbers on the box; the lid popped loose. Sara reached inside, lifting out what looked like a giant flat egg with tiny black feet.

"This is the miracle technology?' Sara asked, aghast.

Gran chuckled, placing the device over the hole in the pipe, latching the tiny black feet in place. "Today we witness the maiden voyage of the Water Thread of Rojava, crafted by an International team of women and men, the Scientists for Humanity. They worked in secret for many years. No one knows where their laboratory is. We are honored to launch the prototype. It may work. Or it may send us all to Allah ahead of our time. Pray with me, please."

Sara and Ruqia exchanged a glance, bowing their heads. Gran whispered a prayer. Sara wanted to grab Ruqia's hand but channeled her desire into reciting Sumerian Princess Enheduanna's Hymn to Innana, the first words signed by an author in human history.

Gran placed her left hand on her forehead, pulling out an illegal quantity of energy from her In-Phone while placing her right hand in the center of the device.

Nothing happened.

From outside the cave, *Oogle, oogle mwook, mmm,* the dinostriches licking their food.

Time passed. One minute. Two minutes. The women barely breathed. Three minutes…

A low, sucking sound grew louder as a surge of invisible energy roared up out of the egg-shaped device, blasting out the mouth of the cave.

The women stepped back. The stream of water—transposed to air—flowed past them, HO2 as air, a pure, homing, energy.

Ruqia sobbed, reaching for Gran.

"What the hell—" Sara said, daring to stick her hand into the thrust of energy: a blast of air, much stronger than the one she felt from the fan in Mamoo's kitchen, and this air had the slightest tinge of...*moisture.*

"Don't ask me to detail the science," Ruqia said, her sobs of joy turning to laughter. "Tonight, if all goes well, the Thread— this gush of transformed energy—will dock with its sister device in Rojava and turn back into water."

"It's sister? Another big flat egg with little black feet?' Sara asked. "Can it transport sea water?"

"Yes," Gran said. "There is a subtle chemical that bonds with sodium and turns it into fresh water at the other end."

"This technology can save the whole world," Sara said. "My teacher, Mr. Askay, always said that if some genius technology could come along and solve the water crisis, we could survive." She pulled on Ruqia's shoulder, savoring the salty scent of her sweat.

Gran pulled something out of her pack, a device that looked like a cross between a compass and a tiny slot machine. "We call it The Fooler. While the Thread is sucking water out of this pipe, it is calculated to send data back to the Turks. They will have no idea the water level in their precious pipe is being poached."

Ruqia clipped it to the Water Thread's black feet. "YPJ will be dancing in Camp tonight."

Gran wiggled her fanny, grabbing Ruqia's hand as they danced the Kurdish *Cuckoo Trot.*

"The Turks won't know where the poach is coming from, but they will notice the water level dropping," Sara said.

Ruqia and Gran sang so loudly, they didn't hear the warning.

Sara couldn't join their mirth. A powerful new force had been unleashed in the world. Her teacher, Mr. Askay, had said to the class, "We must look carefully at all new technology, past the ego of discovery to the unintended consequences lurking in the dark."

14 - Ruqia

IT had been a week since the Water Thread had begun pouring into Rojava. Ruqia was like a virgin bride on her honeymoon: the world in a glow of love and wonder.

But there was still work to be done. This night she crawled on her belly toward the mouth of the cave, touching *standby* on her e-arrow rifle. Turks were patrolling the desert, kids in fancy pea cactus uniforms. If they had been proper soldiers, they would have made an effort to find the cave housing pipe 12 and done a routine check. Instead they told salacious stories about the girls, tossing their pea-cigarettes into the sand.

Ruqia was worried. The next patrol might not be so incompetent.

A sunset of coral and orange burned through the dust as if heralding the dawn of a new world. Did this unusual display have anything to do with the debut of the Water Thread? If Gran were here, she would say it was a mystical signal from Allah. Ruqia didn't believe such nonsense. It was merely a beautiful sunset, unrelated to the thrust of moist molecules thundering silently over her head. She missed Gran, but admitted in her secret heart that she was glad Gran chose to go for supplies and reinforcements. It gave Ruqia time alone with Sara. They had discovered a language, not of words, but of glances, giggles, hugs, back rubs and foot massages, memories of the past, and now that the Thread carried water home to Rojava, a fragile hope for a future.

A fledgling dinostrich waddled toward Ruqia in the shifting deep red of twilight. Where had it come from? The herd had moved on. It would be humane—and delectable—to eat it, but she would never hear the end of it from Sara.

"Ooogle, ooogle, wok, wok!" Sara called from inside the cave.

Before Ruqia could stop it, the baby squeezed under the invisible thrust of the Water Thread and darted into the cave.

"Wok, wok, wok," Sara called. She was up to something.

In the sky, bands of reddish-gray dissolved into darkness.

One star appeared. It seemed to be looking down at the Water Thread, as if wondering if it could bring water to its solar system light years away.

"R! Come here!"

Ruqia slid down into the cave to find Sara holding up a pea cactus square bent into a tight cylinder. Sara's face was radiant. "You think I'm pining for my bird back in Camp?"

"Now that you mention it—"

Sara cradled the baby dinostrich in her arms. "Look what I got this one to do: make a hole in the pipe next to the egg thing—"

"The Water Thread."

"—A hole big enough for a straw."

"A straw?"

"So we can *drink*," Sara said. "You first, General R."

Ruqia pushed the straw into the tiny hole in the pipe, and sucked. Ahhh, the water was so clean, so good. She sucked and swallowed, swallowed and sucked.

Sara laughed. "Allah, or Inanna, or Jesus or the Turks may strike us dead, but tonight, we have fresh water!"

"Your stepmother must have been some piece of work," Ruqia said, handing the straw to Sara. "You're always afraid some powerful a-hole will come thundering down on you."

Sara looked down at the bird.

Ruqia moved closer. "You're brilliant. I tried to punch a hole with my knife, but all I got was a bent knife. You figured out how to manipulate that bird. Your Innana is not going to punish you. She's proud of you."

Sara blushed, turning her eyes away from Ruqia, dripping water in her hand for the baby dinosaur.

Ooodlle, Oooosss, it sang, slurping greedily. Sara caressed its soft feathers, lulling it to sleep.

Ruqia and Sara drank until they were drunk on water. Sara ran out of the cave to pee. Ruqia followed. They had survived on meager rations for so long, what glory to drink *unlimited.*

Sated at last, they lay down at the mouth of the cave, the stars quivering down at them through the silent stream of the Water Thread.

"We should make up new constellations," Ruqia said. "I've heard that when desert winds scrape away new layers of Earth, new stars appear."

"Sounds like a myth. I'd rather just bask in it, like I did when we had clouds. I remember seeing a cloud that looked like a herd of sheep, then, the next moment, it became the tail of a fish."

Ruqia studied Sara's face in the starlight, that proud Kurdish nose pointed toward the heavens as if taking in each star.

"I'm thinking I will stop praying to Inanna," Sara said.

"Going back to Allah? Really?"

"No. I thought the ancient warrior Goddess would understand me. Now I think she's just another superhero somebody cooked up to make us feel better." She lifted her fingers to touch the energy stream of the Water Thread, laughing as its force slapped her hand away. "Now I believe God is right here."

"In the Thread?

"In water, in all of its forms." She turned to Ruqia, her dark, almond-shaped eyes darker in the starlight. "Water has all the properties of a god, or goddess. But unlike some of the pagan gods, water doesn't resist or pout if It doesn't get Its way. It flows to us. It carves the Earth, makes mountains, digs rivers. Some places in the world, it still makes clouds, and where the air is cold, it makes that miracle called snow." Sara's palms cradled the air of the Thread's perimeter, as if holding a sacrament for prayer.

"What about when water floods the other half of the world, drowning people, and just for spite, leaves us to die dry?" Ruqia said.

Sara moved her hands to her rest on her chest. "I wish my teacher were here, Mr. Askay. I never asked him that question. I was mesmerized by his pictures of snowflakes, wanting the world to be beautiful. Now, I think water, like us, is not all good. It can be really mean. It can hurt us, do acts of evil, like I did when I killed the Commander."

They were silent, looking at the stars.

Sara turned to Ruqia, her black pearl eyes shivering.

"Do you need me to hold you?" Ruqia asked.

"I don't need you to hold me like a mother or sister. I need you to hold me as a lover."

Ruqia stared back, her heart racing.

Sara exploded with laughter. "R, you should see your face."

Ruqia flushed. "God, Sara, what took you so long?" Their bodies lunged together, their kisses wild with joy.

"One of us should be on guard," Ruqia said. "But I want you so much, I don't care if I die—but I want you to be safe."

"I am safe, as long as I die in your arms."

15 - Kethuda

SHE squirmed to find a comfortable resting place for her bottom. The desk chair was made of compostable pea cactus, lumpy, with an occasional thorn that poked her presidential flesh.

She swung her legs sideways and bolted out of the chair, turning her back on the stack of scientific reports that had been gathering dust for days. She cursed under her breath and ran to the open window.

The dry wind whipped the sheer white curtains like the wings of an unknown goddess. "I know how you feel," Kethuda said to the billowing fabric. "Thoughts flailing for moorage in a rocky sea." She tugged on the curtain, curling it around her lightly clad body. "Spin me into a cocoon. Make me a bee, a bug, a caterpillar—anything but President of Turkiye."

Gai sat motionless across the room, like a panther lounging in her lair. She touched her forehead with quick beats, *tap tap tap*. This used to be called "texting" when phones were external. Now, thoughts could be communicated directly through the In-Phone with a gentle rhythmic tap. Whomever Gai was thought-calling, the conversation was engrossing. She looked up, pressing her finger firmly on her forehead, ending the call. "Yes, Madam?"

"I disturbed you. I'm sorry."

"I was just thought-calling my twin brother."

Kethuda felt a dull pain. "What is it like to have a twin brother?"

"He's my buddy," Gai said, her smile putting the sunlight to shame. "Our Maasai God is neither male nor female, inclusive of all sexual identities: Engai. My brother is named for the first half, 'Eng.'"

"What is he like, your twin?"

"A silly man, always scolding when I flirt with danger. I tell him he can't be big brother, always protecting me. 'You think you are Maasai warrior of old,' I say to him sternly, 'rescuing the woman. You need to get with it. This is the twenty-second century.'"

A dark pool of envy curdled in Kethuda's heart. "I think he loves you very much."

"Love? Of course. They have an expression in the West, 'hang the moon.' Do you know it?"

"I think it means you love someone so much, they hang the moon in the sky for you each night."

"Yes, Madam. Since our birth, he hung the moon every single night. Even when we smacked each other, *Yeyo* said we always made up and ran off to play."

Kethuda imagined the beautiful children, fussing and running out into the savannah. "You told me of your village. Where was it exactly?"

Gai looked out the window at the high-rises of Ankara, the strokes of the black tattoo on her forehead poised to block strong feeling. "Our circle of houses was just outside the Maasai Mara, our great National Park. The lion, zebra, wildebeest, the secretary bird, the elusive leopard; they were our friends. My brother and I, we played with baby zebras in the Mara River."

"How terrible that your African animals were shipped to Montana."

Gai's silhouette was motionless against the sunlit window, "Yes, Madam. The Maasai Mara is burnt by the sun, our lion and zebra, giraffe, our secretary bird, re-located to a buffalo range."

Kethuda was silent, sensing the deep sorrow in her assistant's heart.

Gai roared like a lioness, rattling the windows, gasping, breathing her fury into the air of Ankara. "The women of Africa are not victims, Madam. We could not stop the removal of our animals, but we are sisters, linked through our *yeyos* and ourselves going back to our ancestors. You may not believe me, but we are more 'powerful'—to use your favorite word—than women of the West, who called themselves feminists, in the twentieth century. The power of the Earth is in our blood."

"Humble in spirit, powerful in action?" Kethuda asked.

"Yes, Madam. We monitor our lion, our zebra, on our In-Phones. I go to sleep at night to the *ooik, ooik* of zebra. One day we will bring them back."

"When water returns to the Maasai Mara?" Kethuda took a quick breath, regretting those cruel words.

Gai turned to her mistress, ebony eyes as still as a breathing stone.

"I'm sorry," Kethuda said. "I'm an idiot."

Gai lifted an eyebrow.

Kethuda burst into laughter, "You agree with me!" Gai joined her, their bodies relaxing, the sweet scent of their sweat encircling the room.

A knock on the mock wooden door broke their joy. Gai peered through the peep hole. "Your father, Madam."

Kethuda's belly burned, her arms sweating, her head filled with wild thoughts. She motioned for Gai to help her dress, throwing off her nightgown, sliding her arms into her uniform: white Ataturka gown, blue silk hijab.

Gai breathed slowly, motioning for her mistress to slow down. "You are strong, Madam. Your body knows this. You know this. And I have my e-arrow rifle well in hand."

"Where did you learn to be a markswoman?"

Gai's face radiated warmth, as if she were a child. "My *yeyo*. She taught us the bow as soon as we could walk. So supple in the hand. So satisfying to strike the target. The transition to electronic e-arrow rifle was painful. You do not shoot the arrow. It does."

Kethuda nodded unsteadily. "But, now, you have command of it?"

"Yes, Madam, and all the strategy for war. When the water left our country, tribes who had traded in harmony for a century learned to kill. I learned to kill."

Kethuda brushed away nausea at the thought of this woman leading a charge into battle and swept onto the balcony, seating herself in a fan-backed green chair. The sun shone directly overhead, casting shadows that stretched into the street below. Kethuda was aware that her people could see her perched like a snowy egret looking down at its prey. She straightened her hijab. "Let my father enter."

Hamza paused on the threshold of the balcony, bowing with cynical deference, "Madam President."

"Two coffees, please, Gai."

She was amused to see Gai's nose wrinkle in disapproval: coffee? How de-hydrating to the human body. But she complied, placing a tray of the luxuriant liquid on the balcony table, casting a wary eye at Hamza.

"Thank you, Gai. Leave us, please," Kethuda said, her eyes saying, *Stay close with your weapon. I may not have time to scream.*

Hamza removed his sandals, rubbing his feet together, criticizing the coffee, sharing memories of Ayse, who made the very finest cup, back in the day. "I have a wish," he said, his gray eyes scanning the sky. "You are my beloved. All that is left. And I have little time."

"You are in good health, Papa."

"I am, but at 80, Allah wants me with Him soon. I can feel it."

A boy shouted from his ferry-cycle, "Is your coffee delicious, Madam President?"

"No, it tastes like dirt," Kethuda shouted back. "Pea cactus caffeine."

"We should go in," Hamza said.

"No. I want to be visible to my people, not a sultana hiding like a mole."

She rose and leaned over the balcony railing and waved to the boy. He rang his ferry cycle bell, smiling, as he pedaled by.

"I need your counsel, Papa. Even when I am vexed by you, I respect your opinion."

"After all these years, can't you predict my counsel?"

She cradled her cup in her hands. "I received a call from the Israeli Prime Minister this morning."

"A phone call? Such excess."

"Yes, actual voice to voice. Must have cost him a month's energy quota. He was very upset. The water coming out of Pipe 12 to Jerusalem has become a trickle."

"Some technical malfunction. Have you contacted the engineer?

"All systems are operating normally. No indication on our side of any breech."

Silence. She knew his mind mirrored hers.

"Poachers. ISIS, or Kurd?"

"I don't know. Threat of execution doesn't seem to deter either of them. And, it makes no sense. Pipe 12 goes through the most isolated part of the Rojavan Desert. If they tapped the pipe, they would need a human chain hundreds of miles long to haul it back, bucket by bucket, to the nearest town."

A street vendor called out, "Pea cactus buns! Tastes like baklava."

Hamza pulled out a cigar and sucked on it until a flame emerged. "Allah be stunned," he said with an astonished growl. "It just might be true."

She chuckled. "Papa, no. It's an idiotic rumor that the Kurds have some miracle device that pulls water into air."

He shrugged. "You have a better idea?"

She gulped the bitter grounds in the bottom of the cup. Nothing went to waste these days.

"You know what to do, 'Ataturka.' Stop dragging your feet. You're not the hero of the world, my girl. You have one job, and one alone: water for your people. Only for your people. What did you tell the Israeli Prime Minister?"

"That we would solve his problem."

"And that means—?"

She sighed, a great heaviness mooring in her body. "You know what it means. We find out what is going on with this pipe and fix it. Meantime, consider diverting the Last Gate to water meant for the Euphrates to Jerusalem…."

He rose, joining her at the balcony railing.

Below, ferry-cycles crowded the street, bells jingling, workers and businessmen shuffling by on foot. School children, tied together with a pea cactus cord, were making their way home.

Hamza said, "I knew what I was doing, putting you in power. You have primal instincts. I was in a huff at first, when you got up to dance at the banquet with that naked African, but then I realized it was a stroke of genius. You were telling those men: 'See. I'm one of the boys. I can indulge my appetites, the whole world be damned.'"

"That has nothing to do with it. I was showing solidarity with Gai. A woman of the people, not a toy for you and your cronies."

His voice was loud enough to carry into the street, "Is that what you're telling yourself? Grow up, my dear. Those men were patronizing you, letting you humiliate yourself. Any one of them could squash you like a bug."

Her eyes followed his hands as he slapped the railing. *He could toss me over.* She could envision his lament—"My baby. What a horrible accident—"

She had never hated him so much. —*I could have him murdered, kill him before he kills me.* And yet, as she watched him trot up and down, she wondered if she could she ever kill her father; perhaps not, because she had always seen the frightened boy beneath the man. The night before her Inauguration, he had come to her bed, as he often had since Ayse's death, placing his head on her breast, not a sexual advance, but as a boy seeking refuge with the only woman left in his life who would give him love.

"I've changed my mind," she said, lifting her spine as high as it could go. "I don't require your counsel, Papa. I will make my own decision on the matter of Pipe 12 and the Last Gate."

"You have no choice. You must send the water to Jerusalem and let the Euphrates go dry."

"I am the President. I have the ultimate choice," she said with a tremulous calm.

He spat off the edge of the balcony and stomped out.

Gai emerged. "I was ready to shoot him, Madam."

Kethuda nodded gratefully. "Water, please. I'm ravenously thirsty."

Gai returned with a tall glass. Kethuda drank greedily, the water so fresh and clear, it told its own story. "I see it every day in my mind, Gai: migration across America as cities of the Eastern Seaboard are destroyed by mega-hurricanes; Climate Elevators attempting to raise the land mass of Japan and Florida, to no avail; boat people from the Pacific Islands rocking in small boats with nowhere to land; fire engulfing evacuated cities in Australia, in the American West; our Istanbul, once Constantinople, the greatest city of the Ottoman Empire, flooded with seawater, its people living in tall buildings, commuting on ziplines from roof to roof. Nina in Russia fighting for democracy in a country keeping water-rich Siberia for the elites. Shogofa in Afghanistan, risking death as she leads women in burkas to water poach the Taliban. Everyone has too much water—or too little water—or no water."

"Yes, Madam," Gai said, cradling her e-arrow rifle in the crook of her arm.

"You must teach me how to use that super weapon, Gai, in case I need to be *your* back-up someday."

Gai smiled, her dark skin glowing, "An honor, Madam."

"Good. For now, put that thing down and dance with me. I have an impossible decision to make. Thirsty women, children, and men will go without water in Israel if I don't shut off water to the down-streamers. In both cases, people will die, especially children… If we dance, maybe my body will make the decision for me!"

Gai dug her nail into the top of her forehead, just below her hairline. Music tumbled forth: Nurbanu Sultan, a great sensual Middle Eastern singer from the twenty-first century. They made wide circles with their hips; stomping, singing with Nurbanu, shoving scent shells off the tables to use them for drums.

Kethuda collapsed on the floor, her lungs heaving, her heart knowing that the only way to choose was to find her deepest *hatred*. Did she hate the Israeli's more, or the Kurds? The Kurds were terrorists who had murdered her people, but they were a rag-tag, mostly female army, digging in the desert like rats. Did they deserve her sympathy?

"More water, please, Gai."

"Yes, Madam."

"No, don't bring me water. I need to make this choice when I'm *thirsty*."

16 – Gai

IT had been a long day into night with her mistress. Gai's body was weary from so much dancing, so much listening, so much *Yes, Madam, No, Madam.*

When Kethuda fell asleep at last, Gai put on her veiled black jacket and stole out into the night.

No clouds. A perfect starry night for a city, like all cities of the world, banned from burning electric light. Gai walked past candle-lit houses, into the deserted Square of the People that stretched from beneath Kethuda's balcony to the row of houses beyond.

Gai prided herself on her climbing abilities and, most uniquely, in using starlight to guide her feet up a mountain-side, or, tonight, up the outer rim of a parked ferry-cycle.

She was careful not to jiggle the bells. This was a silent journey into a secret world, best accessed when her body was suspended from the force of gravity, and in motion, allowing the images on the private data-wave of her In-Phone to come in without detection.

The top swing of the ferry-cycle was built for two. Gai slid her leg over the handle bar, climbed in, and leaned back on the fluffy pea cactus cushion to view the scope of stars beaming down on her like the bicycle headlights of old friends.

She swung gently, pressing her finger to the nipple of her right breast, just the right amount of pressure, and the secret In-Phone pathway opened, showing her the shining faces of her beloved African sisters, who were water refugees from every corner of the globe.

Oh, the happiness that flowed from her body to every woman, some young, some old, some nongendered, some from the settlement of New Africa in Greenland, some from a multi-racial community in Canada, all from homes and settlements they had forged as close to fresh water as possible. Though there had been no formal election, Gai was their chosen leader, calling to order the great Sisterhood of African Mothers and Daughters.

There were so many questions. A nongendered veterinarian from Chicago, who got into the country before Sam Boatwright had shut immigration down, wanted to know what it was like to be the personal assistant of the woman President of Turkiye.

"Exhausting," Gai said, taking in their laughter as if stepping into a warm bath from long ago. "She's not a bad woman; she wants to do well."

"What does she fear?" asked a young poet camped out in the Parthenon.

"She fears she is not worthy of love," Gai said.

All the women, thousands of them, moaned and whistled.

"That makes women do crazy things," said a Black water engineer, monitoring mountain run-off in Japan.

"Have you shot her father yet?" asked a young woman helping her mother harvest water from a melting glacier in Antarctica.

"Hard not to," Gai said, swinging out to catch a glimpse of the planet Venus, more brilliant than any star. "Anybody shoots that man, it will be my mistress, but I think she is not comfortable with violence."

"Does she treat you good, Sugar?" asked a round woman on a rooftop settlement in New Orleans. She had been born in America, a water refugee in her own town.

Gai slowed down. It had never occurred to her how odd it was that Kethuda wasn't mean like her father. Her mistress listened well, asked questions, seemed to care about her assistant's welfare. "President Kethuda may call herself 'Ataturka,' but she is a real person, grateful for my care and respect."

"What was her mother like?" asked an elderly woman fanning herself on a porch in Paris.

"Kethuda does not know how much she got from her mother, Ayse. She got the greatest gift a mother can give: love and devotion. Kethuda sees only her mother's faults, that she was submissive to a man who dominated the nation."

The women whistled and sighed in recognition.

"That poor baby don't know a thing," said the woman on the rooftop in New Orleans. "She's got her eyes on you, 'cause she knows you know somethin' about life, and all that jazz."

Gai's eyes followed a shooting star, her body warm with all their love. "Speaking of jazz, how are things in America?"

An answer came from a slender scholar in a rowboat on the shallows of the Great Lakes, "I won't sugarcoat it, water's going down, even in the Northern states, even as it's rising on the coasts. Canada says they are Open. It's not true. Their border's closed, same as the Southern one. Plenty of illegal traffic, but punishment's worse for Africans if we get caught. Canada won't say so, but they don't want Black people."

Women from every corner stomped and wailed and railed against the long arc of justice going backwards.

After some of the feelings had cooled down, Gai started singing an African chant, laced with an American slave spiritual. The women all knew it, adding verses in their own languages.

Gai sang:

> I got my women,
> I got my love,
> I got a place on the Earth,
> No lonesome dove.

Live or die,
Evolved or dumb
My soul is free,
Under no man's thumb.

The voices streaming from Gai's right breast vibrated in every chamber of her heart, far into the night.

17 – Sara

I have a love. Not a thought, a knowing, as she leaned back in the seat of the Sun Shuttle, her leg pressed against Ruqia. Any touch between them quenched a thirst greater than water, a thirst that had, apparently, lived in their bodies before birth, beyond death. To have a love is not to possess. It is to enter a birth-less death-less place, together.

Sara and Ruqia were sad to leave the cave, the precious days they had alone. It had taken longer than expected for YPJ reinforcements to find the cave. Gran had given them careful verbal directions. No one wanted a to store a map to the cave on their In-Phone, leaving it vulnerable to hacking from the Turks and ISIS. "What glory," Ruqia had said, biting Sara's ear. "Let them stumble through the desert, let us make love."

On the Shuttle, Sara and Ruqia gazed at each other for one long, daring moment. Desire for a woman was new to Sara's young body, a desire so strong she wanted nothing more than to be with her beloved.

Ruqia sighed and discreetly turned away. Their love must remain a secret.

They reached the YPJ Camp at dusk, stealing one passionate kiss in the twilight before peeling back the curtain of vines and coming into Camp. What a sight awaited them. The women and men had tossed aside their uniforms and donned traditional Kurdish dress as they swirled in the *Govend*. Shouts of joy confirmed that the Water Thread was filling the reservoir hidden in the dark branches of the Burnt Forest with delicious Turkish water.

YPJ soldiers in dance costumes lifted Sara and Ruqia onto their shoulders. "Hail Pioneers of the Water Thread!"

Squealing with delight, Sara grabbed Ruqia's hand in triumph as they were paraded around Camp.

Sara spotted Gran in a red Kurdish blouse and pantaloons, her face flushed with a hint of a coy maiden. She was dancing the *Govend*, hand over hand around a roaring bonfire. Her partner was a young man in a ceremonial white shirt and black pants with long dark hair, dark beard, his face unmistakable in the firelight.

"Mr. Askay!" Sara called, climbing down from the soldier's shoulder and running to him.

He turned at the sound of her voice, disoriented, squinting into the twilight.

"It's me. Sara. I look different as a soldier."

He stared at her, as if seeing a ghost. "I thought you were locked away in a Saudi palace."

"I'm *here*," she said, her heart racing with joy.

"You know each other?" Gran said, ever suspicious.

"Since I was a child," Sara said, walking toward Mr. Askay as if in a trance.

He stammered, "When you didn't come to school, I went to your stepmother's house. She screamed that she had sold you for a well, and the well was dry. She was swindled."

"She's lying. She got her well. She just wanted you to feel sorry for her."

"I thought I would never see you again."

"You helped me stay alive through hours locked up in the ISIS van. I thought of you, your teaching. What are you doing here, Mr. Askay?"

"Gonul. Please. Call me Gonul. You're my teacher now. I've come to fight with the YPJ."

Sara's body grew heavy. "Gonul? Sounds funny to call you that. You're a scholar, not a soldier."

He stepped closer to her, his voice hoarse, "After what happened to you, I tried to go back to the classroom. I owed it to the other students, but I couldn't stop thinking of what ISIS had done to you. I had to join the fight."

"Mr. Askay, you don't know what it's like?" Tears blurred her vision. "I killed one of my captors—I didn't mean to—I wanted only to wound, but I took a life."

"Sara," he said gently, "you didn't mean for him to die."

"*Her.* It was a her. She looked just like me. I aimed for her shoulder, not her heart..."

He folded her into his chest. She lost breath: his arms were strong, his body warm. Ruqia was staring at them, lips parted in surprise, and something else. Fear?

Gran's badger eyes combed over them. "Sir, you dropped me for a younger woman?"

"Gran, this is my teacher, Mr. Askay."

"I have heard of no one else from Sara," Gran said, shaking his hand.

Sara motioned to Ruqia.

Gonul bowed. "You are The Flying Warrior, the bravest woman since Sakine."

Ruqia extended her hand. "You are the smartest man since Ocalon."

Gonul took her hand. "He was a great leader of the revolution, but he had his dark side."

"We all do," Ruqia said.

Gonul could not stop looking at Sara. He was so tall, she so short. "Sara was my best student. This intellect you speak of was hers, not mine."

"Nonsense," Gran said, grabbing his hand. "I can tell by your dancing, you're a brilliant man, Mr. Gonul. Will you do an old lady the honor to finish the *Govend?*"

Gonul took Gran's hand, and they disappeared into the circle of the dance.

Ruqia twirled Sara, pulling her close, stealing a bite on her ear.

Sara was swept away in the *Govend*, into a place in her heart she had never been before, a place of love so abundant, she vowed to live it with her whole body and heart and soul, even if it outraged Allah or Innana or Jesus Christ Himself.

18 - Ruqia

SHE opened her eyes to a morning like no other. Sara lay beside her in the tent. The air seemed as succulent as Sara's skin, as if it were the first air breathed by the first women at the dawn of time. Ruqia studied Sara's sleeping face, the curve of her cheek, the soft furrow of her brow, the curling chambered nautilus of her ear, her breath slowly rising and releasing beneath her cupped breasts. Ruqia gently placed her fingertips over Sara's heart, over a thrumming so strong, she could hold back no longer, sliding her body on top of Sara's, opening her lips.

"My love, it's raining," Sara said.

Ruqia looked up, A torrent of rain was coming down upon them.

Ruqia woke, looking skyward. Nothing but the roof of the tent billowing in the night's breeze. She reached for Sara; she wasn't there; it was a dream.

But it was so real—I felt her close to me...

She pulled on her uniform, threw her e-arrow-rifle over her shoulder and headed out, knowing exactly where to go.

They were lying fully clothed on an old blanket outside the pea cactus grove hidden in the Burnt Forest. Sara and her Mr. Askay—Gonul—close, but not touching, looking up at the night sky. Ruqia did not attempt to join them or pull Sara away on a pretense of some impending duty. She had done that too many times. This time she would wait, hidden in the grove.

If she loves him, I want to know it.

Gonul took Sara's index finger, pressing it to his forehead. "This just in, from an ornithologist in Arizona. No people live there now, just scientists."

Sara chuckled. "Scientists aren't people?"

He smiled. "Look at it closely."

Sara closed her eyes to focus on the image coming to her from Gonul's In-Phone. "The same bird as my Rexie!" she said. "A world away, and this Arizona bird has a fork at the end of his lizard tongue. The advantages of the forked tongue are clear. Devolving birds are able to coil their tongues around any eatable morsel, and sense moisture with those sensitive double-tongues that a single bird tongue can miss."

"I think you have a slippery hypothesis, but I could be wrong. We should co-author a paper," Gonul said.

"You and him?"

"No. You and me, Sara. Send it to him, with your photo of Rexie. He can review it, add his own data."

Sara moved closer to him.

Ruqia's shoulders tensed as she watched them.

Sara said, "What we just did, Gonul—looking at your colleague's private data—I did it too when I sent you Rexie's tongue—it violates the energy quota. If we keep this up, sending papers back and forth, we'll suck up energy from somebody who needs it to find water."

"We can't stop the flow of knowledge." He turned his body to face hers.

She looked at him, not moving. "Isn't other people's survival more important than bragging that we discovered a devolving species?"

"You always ask the most provocative questions."

This guy is so damn charming. And the way he looks at her...

"You understand the principle I'm arguing from?" Sara said.

"Of course, but it's not about ego, Sara. Honestly. It's about looking at the behavior of other species to see what we can learn about our own capacity to adapt, or lack of it."

"We're going to need more than reptile tongues."

Gonul laughed; Sara laughed, a sound that always went right through Ruqia's body. It threw her off balance, and her toe grazed a pea cactus seedling.

Sara and Gonul looked toward the grove.

Ruqia held her breath.

Gonul sat up, the starlight so bright he could see at night. "Must have been a thin-toed gecko. They come out at night."

Sara sat up, her ears tilted to the grove. "So, if you and I and your Arizona bird guy got the green light from the energy monitors at RAT, we could post our paper on the World Board, and it would help people apply our findings to their own communities?"

"Right, we have this amazing technology, the Water Thread. Why shouldn't we share it with the world, so Arizona can pull water from the Pacific and make an inland sea? You said the Thread filters out salt before transforming air back to water."

"It's what we all want, Gonul. Still sounds funny to call you that."

He dropped his eyes.

He is madly in love with her, and there's not a damn thing I can do about it.

"Our problem is much closer to home," Sara said. "The Turks want to take our Thread to fill their swimming pools, while our people die."

He sighed, his tall frame curving into his chest. "I'm not naïve, just stupidly optimistic. We have the technology to transform the world—"

There's just one obstacle," Sara said.

Gonul's face moved closer to hers.

"Humanity," they said in unison.

Ruqia's breath slowed to a still point. *Dinostrich will inherit the Earth, and I will lose Sara to this smart man she has loved all her life.*

"Sara, I have a question for you." Gonul's voice quivered

"Whatever it is, why would I have the answer?"

"Oh, you will."

A beam of golden light broke on the horizon, graying the sky, banishing the dimmest stars.

Gonul swallowed, sweat pearling on his brow. "I know the chastity law in the YPJ, but has there been, or is there now, a provision allowing—marriage?"

That word was like molten lead pouring into Ruqia's body.

"I don't know the policy," Sara said. "It doesn't matter. I don't believe in marriage."

Gonul looked away. "When I went to your stepmother's house, she screamed at me and called me a lecherous old man. After that, I sat for hours, finally admitting how I feel about you. I am older. Ten years, and there is a power difference, the teacher thing—"

Sara laughed. "You are not old. You're 28. You *give* me power. You never lord it over me, or act like you know everything—well, most of the time."

They giggled like children, their eyes warm on each other. Sara composed herself. "I love you, Mr. Askay—Gonul—I have always loved you, and there is someone else in my heart. She's lurking now, in the shadows."

Sara walked into the grove and took Ruqia's hand, helping her stand, kissing her on the mouth. Ruqia tried to speak, but there were no words. She reached for Sara's heart, as she had in the dream, placing her hand on the scratchy surface of her lover's uniform. Sara's eyes had never been so clear, reflecting the dawn light. Together they walked out of the grove and sat beside Gonul, their arms coiled around each other.

Gonul looked from one to the other. They sat for a long moment in silence.

"This is amazing," Sara said at last. "I used to see those couples on the World Board. They call it the Polydormatory."

"Polyamory," Gonul said. "Many loves. Hardly ok with Lord Mohammed."

"We're already burning in hell," Ruqia said. "Please, Gonul, don't tell anyone, especially Gran."

"Of course not," he said.

Sara reached for his hand. "I love you both."

He took her hand, kissed it, put it to his cheek.

Ruqia tightened her hand on Sara's. *She wants us both. How delightfully greedy of her.*

Footsteps crashed through the pea cactus grove. The three of them broke apart. Gran was barely dressed, her patchwork hijab loose around her neck. "The Euphrates." She was panting. "Water level plummeting. That bitch, Ataturka, is selling our water to Israel. She's sending troops along the Euphrates—"

She turned her fury to Sara. "Ataturka knows something's leeching off water from Pipe 12 that should have gone to Israel. That device, the Fooler—Sara Roxan, your damned dinostrich must have eaten it. If you hadn't made them *pets...*"

"What's done is done," Ruqia said, the excitement of battle growing in her body. "This isn't about that crap. They want the Water Thread. We won't let them have it."

"They have a full army—" Gran said. "We have good intentions."

"We have your Allah on our side," Sara said, seizing Gran's shoulders.

Ruqia roared, "We have the YPJ—the greatest women's army of all time!" This was the way to secure Sara's heart: be the warrior the charming scholar could never be.

The wild strumming of the *oud* called them to arms, as a flock of dino-doves sliced the sunrise into slender ribbons of light.

19 – Sara

YPJ soldiers dashed through Camp, seizing weapons, taking down tents, pouring water rations into flasks, gulping water directly from the reserve tank: one last luxurious guzzle.

Sara guided Gonul to the e-arrow rifle station.

"I don't know what I'm doing," he said, holding the weapon by the wrong end.

"It took me a long time to learn the rifle," she said, turning his weapon around and placing it in his arms, the lethal shaft pointing out. "I practice every day, like people practice the *oud*. Ruqia says the e-arrow is an instrument, and when we fire it, we play it. They say a musician feels at one with their *oud* or piano or violin. I thought this was ridiculous at first, but now, the more I practice shooting it, the more I feel its power. It knows things I don't know, seeks human heat, and when you set it *sleep*, it knows to strike anywhere on the body without doing harm."

"Sounds like magic."

"Science and magic—aren't they side by side in the twenty-second century?"

"What happens when you set it on *kill?*"

"It searches for the center of the body or the head, depending on the position of the target."

"Will the Turks shoot to wound?"

"I doubt it. But I will. It's what the water wants."

He touched her lips, gently. She stared at him, not moving. All around them soldiers were shooting their e-arrow rifles into soft targets. Ruqia dashed around Camp, barking orders. Sara and Gonul were uniquely still.

"Come with me," Sara said, leading Gonul into the Burnt Woods. They reached the entry station for the Water Thread on a platform above them.

Gonul asked, "If the Turks find the origin Thread in the cave, how much longer will the water flow?"

She kissed him. How strange it was, to feel lips that were not Ruqia's. And yet how amazing, to feel his love, his desire. They touched each other's faces, listening to the rumble of duty from the Camp. She knew his thoughts were searching for a way to keep her safe in an unsafe world.

"We should get back," she said.

"Not yet, dearest, please. This is our time, suspended between life and death. No one will miss us, except—

"—The Flying Warrior," Sara combed his beard with her fingers. "We're right beneath it—where the Thread comes out of the air—"

He chuckled, straining his eyes. "It's invisible."

"Close your eyes, Gonul. You can hear it with your whole self."

He closed his eyes. "It's so strange. I *feel* it, not with my ears. It's like a sound that is not sound but a new form of movement, like the beating of a million dragonfly wings."

"You're always the prince of metaphor."

They listened without ears, bodies entwined, until they saw an olive-green cloud bruising the sky. "What could make that color?" he asked.

Sara breathed out, strong as the wind. "The discharge of e-arrows drifting to the sky."

"The residue of war."

They made their way back to Camp, fingertips touching, longing not to be separate.

Ruqia saw them the moment they emerged from the forest. Sara knew that face well: a deadness in the eyes, fierceness in the mouth, all feeling banished.

"A toast," Ruqia said, lifting her flask to Sara. "I researched your goddess of water, Little Mama. Turns out she exists, apart from your imagination. She goes all the way back to ancient Sumer, now my Iraq. She is called *Nammu*, Goddess of Water, unifier of all forms of life. Cool, huh?"

Sara pulled out her flask. "Thank you. I had no idea: Nammu, I drink to you."

"Good as any other god I don't believe in," Ruqia said, watching Sara and Gonul drink from the same flask.

The troops gathered around them, armed and ready for battle.

Sara's body coursed with the terror of possible death and, with it, a love so great, she staggered in its wake. She seized Ruqia's face and kissed her, mouth open, pressing their bodies close. She turned to Gonul, grabbing his beard, planting a kiss that was more like a bite, as if she wanted to eat him whole.

The soldiers could not suppress their shock.

Ruqia laughed like thunder at the sight of their faces, lifting her flask. "May Nammu, Goddess of Water, bring us victory."

"Praise Allah," Gran shouted, horrified at such sacrilege.

"All the gods are with us today," Ruqia said, throwing an arm around Gran. "Our wise elder warrior, take the reserve soldiers to the Reservoir and guard the Water Thread."

Gran objected: she was needed on the front lines.

Ruqia dismissed the plea. "No. Hurry, grand warrior, guard our greatest treasure."

Sara fell in with the troops.

The rest was a blur of sweat and hushed voices as they slipped through the pea-vine doorway, down the mountain to the Sun Shuttle. Sara sat beside Ruqia, not leaning out the window in case they encountered a column of Turkish soldiers. Sara stayed in her seat, sneaking glances at Gonul as he received a last-minute tutorial on the e-arrow rifle from another YPJ soldier.

The Shuttle slid to a stop as it approached the Euphrates. "This is where I ran from ISIS in the flock of dinostrich," Sara said. "The water level—my God, R—it's barely a trickle."

"Disembark," Ruqia said, rage evident in her rasping voice.

Sara pushed her way to Gonul, grabbing his hand. "It's cold," she said.

"So is yours, my love."

The metal of the Turk's rifles blinded them as they stepped off the Shuttle. Ruqia called, "Formation."

Sara squeezed Gonul's hand and stepped forward. A novice, he had been assigned to the rear flank. She was glad. The expanse of Turkish troops spread out into the desert as far as she could see, the black of their uniforms covering the sand like the cloak of night.

In the distance, Sara saw the figure of a woman in white on a white horse, her blue hijab curling gently in the breeze: Ataturka, come to relish in the carnage, come to watch every Kurd that did not die in battle drop from thirst.

Sara's rage was an asset. Her hands grew warm as they hugged her rifle, but she knew this was no *oud*, no piano, and she was no musician. Human life was at stake. She secretly set it to *sleep*.

Ruqia led the first flank into combat, leaping from side to side, her e-arrows hitting their mark. One Turk went down, another, another. But the aim of the enemy was true. YPJ soldiers fell, another, and another.

Sara glanced around. Gonul was too far back for her to find him. She dashed in a zig zag, shooting several soldiers to *sleep*, but the onslaught was too great. She fired wildly, not knowing if she tranquilized a human being or shot hopeless missiles into the ground. There was no smoke, no fire. The e-arrows solved all of that by being as invisible as they were deadly. Only the gossamer flare of golden light as they entered the target.

The wind picked up, lifting the top layer of sand into the air. The battlefield became opaque on both sides.

Sara sought refuge in a dust devil, firing blindly from within its core. She shielded her eyes, searching for Ruqia. A squadron of Turks appeared, surrounding the YPJ, e-arrows sizzling as they met their target.

Ruqia leapt toward the Turkish Commander, striking him down with her boot. A score of Turks fired, their e-arrows glowing as the missiles hit her body. Ruqia screamed and fell.

Sara fought her way to her beloved. Ruqia lay on the banks of the Euphrates, her lower body soaked with blood. Sara held her, sobbing.

Ruqia whispered, "I'm an idiot. I should have kissed you sooner."

"I love you."

"Go."

"How can I leave you?" Sara said.

"You're a soldier, that's how…" Ruqia's voice faded, but she kept her eyes wide open, taking in every last moment with Sara.

Sara kissed her and stood up, gazing out at the battlefield. Turks swarmed down on the YPJ. In the distance, the white woman in blue hijab straddled her white horse, looking down at the carnage.

Beneath the punishing sun, Sara's body grew cold with hatred. She flipped her setting to *kill* and charged into battle.

PART TWO
FIRE

20 – Sara

CHA cha cha cha cha

Sara opened her eyes. The call was distinct, echoed by the flutter of wings.

Could it possibly be? Rexie, or "a" Rexie....here?

She moved with difficulty on the concrete floor, holding her broken ribs to ease the pain. A narrow beam of light fell into her prison cell from the barred window at the top. She saw him up there: speckled black wings, saucy tale flick-flicking, tiny feet dancing along the bars. *cha cha cha cha cha: Sara, where is my water?*

"Rexie, you're here, or your cousin, or brother. I'm so sorry. The Turks give me only 5 cups a day. Fly away to the headwaters. The Kebon Dam will give you all the water you want."

cha cha cha cha cha

Pain forced her to stop talking, but she could still see him up there, bobbing, twittering, waiting for his water.

She surveyed the cell. Its crumbling walls were in such ill repair the bricks were like stepping stones, ready to pop out and land on her head. *A cheap form of execution?* The door of the cell was made of rusted iron bars, a slot cut into the base for the meager ration of water and pea cactus squares. *What prison is this?* Not Diyarbakir, where Sakine Cansiz was tortured. That had been torn down in the twenty-first century. This prison must be even older, its walls reeking of puke, sweat, urine. A horrible place to die.

"You are free, Rexie II. Fly away from here."

brrrr, op op, op

It was a new sound, as if he looked down on her with pity.

"I had a pet T-Rex wren. I called him Rexie. He looked just like you." She rolled gently onto her back to get a better view of the tiny bird. "After the ISIS women took me away, I never saw him again. I hope he found another Kurd to give him water, or maybe he migrated. I'll never know."

brrrrr brrrr

"You're telling me you're sorry. Well, hell, Rexie II, I'm damn sorry too."

Questions from Mr. Askay's classroom flooded into her mind: What does it mean to be free? To know the measure of your own soul? To live with others in peace, valuing the common good?

"I have no answers for you, Mr. Askay," she said, cupping her hands in the air, as if holding Gonul's face. "I know I must look to my soul, as Sakine Cansiz did in Diyarbakir. My name-sake endured ten years of torture by telling her captors, 'You can annihilate my body. You cannot have my soul.'"

There was more to the story. Other women warriors were imprisoned with Sakine Cansiz, up to eighty-five in a single cell. In the freezing winter, they helped each other stay warm by preparing a bath in a small bowl in the toilet that they filled with water from the kettle.

"I am alone," she said to Gonul-in-her-mind. "Without you, my darling, and Ruqia, and Gran, I a small person with no courage. I don't know if you are alive or dead. And Ruqia, my beloved, slain by a Turk...like my Mamoo."

Rexie II cocked his head, *cha cha cha cha.*

"Go away, stupid bird. I can't help you." The pain in her body wiped her mind clean.

She glanced at the barred window above. The bird was gone, the emptiness of the cold cell unbearable. Memories tumbled in from the war. As Ruqia had faded from this world, Sara had charged into battle, vowing that this time, death would not be an accident: she would kill with her own will.

Her e-arrow found its mark in a Turkish soldier. Just a boy, with eyes that shifted from black to gray as he crumpled at her feet. Her body grew numb, her mind like a tiny mole sniffing in some forbidden darkness. *I meant to kill this boy. It is worse than mistakenly killing the ISIS Commander. This I did with my whole soul. Now, I no longer have one...* She had knelt beside him in the hot sand, and he had leaned against her and taken his last breath with his head on her breast. She couldn't move after that. The capture, the imprisonment—all she could remember was the cold void that used to be her loving heart.

Alone on the cold floor of the cell, when sleep did come, she dreamed of Ruqia: her long body, small, tight breasts, the tuft of her chopped dark hair. In the first scene she said to Ruqia, "I will spend tonight with Gonul." Ruqia said, "It is good, that you are honest with me, but I still want you to myself." Sara kissed her and went to meet Gonul in a pea cactus field. They made slow love. It was different from what it had been with Ruqia. Sara was grateful that Gonul taught her the ways of being with a man.

"I can't believe it," he said in the dream scene. "After wanting you so much, after all my fantasies, your heart beats beneath my fingertips."

She giggled, "Now there is no doubt I'm no longer a virgin."

He laughed, "It didn't count with Ruqia?"

"It should have," she said. "Ask Allah."

"Oh, let's not."

They covered each other's mouths, and the dream became a nightmare, with great dino-vultures diving down and tearing them apart.

A groan from a nearby cell brought Sara back to the present: the cold floor, the narrow band of light coming down from the barred window. *Did Rexie II really appear, or did I dream it?*

She reached instinctively for her forehead. Nothing. Just a sweaty patch of skin, her In-Phone was disabled as soon as the

121

Turks had thrown her into their prison wagon. No one in the YPJ knew if she was alive or dead. She stretched her fingers back to the base of her skull, searching for the microscopic portal the Turks had used to disable her. She knew it was futile, but kept pressing anyway. The Disabler was a popular tool of criminals and thieves, what they used to call "hacking" in the twenty-first century, but this had more dire implications. Once disabled, the victim could not re-start her own InPhone without an Enabler device installed by another person.

Sara slapped her brow, wailing for Ruqia, for Gonul, for Gran. Their loving images dissolved into mental mist.

"God damn you, Ataturka," she shouted. "Whatever God you pretend to pray to, I hope He drives you down to Hell."

"Shut up," called a prisoner down the row. "They'll beat us all."

Sara curled into a ball, remembering Ruqia's breasts pressed against her back, Gonul's eyes. The longing for them was so great that she screamed, even if it meant torture, or death.

In the silence that followed, she sensed something very strange: *water* cradling her body, as if the cold stone floor were no longer solid, but a shallow stream, rocking her gently to sleep.

21 - Kethuda

CITIZENS of Turkiye crowded into the street below Kethuda's balcony, some arriving from across the country in an array of resplendent red photosynthetic-autos. Others piled off the Ottoman Sun Shuttle, others on ferry-cycles filled to capacity, their gentle bells lost in the shouts of triumph: "Ataturka. Savior. Goddess. Queen."

In the relative safety of her bedroom, she shielded her eyes from the undulating flags, each brazen red with a white crescent moon encircling a white star. Such a beautiful design, people said, dating back to the Empire. She turned away, nauseated. And something more, something she did not want to see or name or feel.

"You must eat." Gai's voice was close.

Kethuda could smell the milky soup. "Take it away, please. It would be unseemly for me to throw up in front of the World Board."

"May I have your soup?"

"Of course. Eat here beside me. Please."

Gai nodded, pulling her vintage ottoman beside Kethuda's stiff pea-wooden chair

"How long has it been?" Kethuda asked.

"Since I ate goat's milk soup?"

Kethuda smiled. "You must have had it as a child in the Maasai Mara."

Gai's eyes grew large, "In the old days, we drank cow's milk and, according to my brother, blood. He said it made him humble to drink blood from the side of a cow."

"Eng drank blood? Did it make him ferocious?"

Gai swallowed a spoonful of soup, her eyes closing with pleasure. "My brother did not find the fury of his manhood until the water went away. A starving lioness came into our village, as many animals did toward the end. He speared her, and we stood over her body. A magnificent creature, though she was mostly bone by then."

"Did you eat her?"

Gai looked directly into her mistress's eyes. "When you are starving, you must eat. Eng made a prayer to Engai, in gratitude for the little meat that was left on the suffering lioness."

Memories of bones flooded Kethuda's mind, the bones beneath the skin of dying Turkish soldiers. "How long since the end of the Five Day War?"

"Two days, Madam. You've eating nothing."

Kethuda reached for her blue silk hijab. "How can I eat? Damn the World Board for showing close-ups of wounded Turkish soldiers, blood pouring from their heads, their bellies, their hearts."

"The Kurds are good marks-people."

"The Kurds are damned to hell for killing my young warriors—for hoarding their mythical Water Thread. I think it was a ruse to lure us into battle."

"I worry for your health, Madam. Your belly is tight from so much hatred."

Kethuda held her belly with both hands, like a woman carrying a child. "My belly is tight from the clamor of nations. It's easy for other leaders of RAT to find fault when they haven't faced a moral dilemma of this magnitude. Only that idiot Sam Boatwright sounded off his approval, 'Good for you, Babe,' he babbled. Only in America would they call a President 'Babe.'" She felt a weight in her body, a sadness in every cell. "Nina in Russia did not call me 'Babe.' She called me a heartless dictator. Ironic, coming from a Russian. She's smart. She thinks my goal is to colonize the down-streamers for my Empire. That's my father's goal, not mine."

Kethuda closed her eyes, grasping for one moment of peace. Instead, she saw the veiled face of Shogofa of Afghanistan proclaiming with sadness, "Ataturka does not serve only the Turks. She has no wisdom to see how her water war will bring ruin to our entire continent."

Gai stirred the milk in her bowl. "You question your decision to divert the water in the Last Gate to your customers? The moisture level in the Euphrates recedes very quickly."

Kethuda said nothing, staring down at her new white gown, shimmering like a waterfall. A victory gift from her father.

Gai put down her spoon and drank from the bowl. "Or perhaps you question the timing of marching troops down the Euphrates?"

"Hush," Kethuda said brusquely. "Must I hear this from *you*?"

"It was not only our boys who died in their own blood."

"You think I don't question my choices? I question them every day. Every hour. Every minute. I am Ataturka, the President of Turkiye, a living legend of the Ottoman Empire. I cannot care about the blood of our enemy when I cannot eat or sleep from hearing the sons of Turkiye call for their mothers as they died...." She glanced at the statue of the Seated Woman of Catalhoyuk, those stone eyes watching her, judging her.

Someone pounded on the door.

Gai quickly drank the last of the soup and placed the empty bowl on her mistress's plate.

"Clever," Kethuda said.

Gai smiled. "Shall I allow them to enter?"

Kethuda nodded, looking out the window at the red river of flags. "Savior," shouted the people. "Speech! Speech!"

The door opened with a smack. Hamza hurried in, followed by the three Ministers, the three State Scientists, the Prime Minister of Israel, and the King of Saudi Arabia.

Kethuda did not turn around. In the reflection of the glass door, she could see them bowing to her, presenting red sky-rocket lilies, jars of Myrrh, a necklace of black pearls.

"Madam President, it is rumored you have taken Kurdish prisoners," the Saudi King said. "They say you have one here in Ankara, a young girl. She is my property."

Kethuda looked at his reflection. "Your property?"

"She was on her way to me, bought and paid for. She escaped and joined the terrorist YPJ. A fierce warrior, they say. She killed your men."

"She should be executed, not rewarded with the luxuries of your palace."

His voice was not gentle. "I paid a high price. She is mine."

Kethuda turned around, meeting his eyes. She had trapped a vulture once. That bird had looked at her with a kinder eye than the Saudi King's. "The girl is my prisoner, and her whereabouts remain strictly confidential. No leaks to the press. If she is who I think she is, she is needed for questioning regarding the device that turns water into air."

The King laughed. "You believe that myth?"

"Something sucked the water out of Pipe 12 and transported it to a Reservoir in Rojava. We have seen nothing but a couple of holes, a large one made by some sort of human tool on the lip of the Reservoir, and a smaller one, on Pipe 12, possibly made by an animal."

Hamza's hands clasped the King's shoulders. "Find yourself another virgin. This Kurd—probably no longer a virgin—is a water poacher and will pay with her life." He leaned close to his daughter, "I knew you would drink the goat's milk soup. Your Mama cooked it whenever you had a tummy ache."

"I remember," Kethuda said. If Ayse were here, she would whisper to her daughter to honor the desires of the Saudi King, to never incur the wrath of a powerful male.

The King chuckled with steel in his cheeks. "Interrogate her, but do not mar her beauty. I expect her to be brought to me, cleaned, perfumed, and moistened."

Kethuda's intestines turned like a snake bent at a right angle. She threw back the sheer white curtains and stepped onto the balcony. Her father, the Ministers, the State Scientists followed. The Israeli Prime Minister and the Saudi King stayed out of sight.

The lights of the World Board were brighter than the sun. Kethuda pulled the corner of her blue silk hijab down over her brow until all she could see were the people just below her: babies clutching their mamas, boys waving tiny flags, old men straining to get a glimpse of her.

She delivered her memorized speech, producing one solitary tear aimed into the enormous eye of the World Board, lamenting the impact on the down-streamers in Rojava, Syria, Iraq, Iran. They would survive. She had decreed that they be relocated to water refugee camps along the Mediterranean, declaring, "It is what the water wants!"

The crowd loved it, throwing up sprays of pea cactus lavender, shouting, "Ataturka! Goddess of Water!"

She looked into the all-seeing eye of the World Board, "We offer one million dollars, in the currency of your choice to anyone, in any country on our embattled globe, who can bring me the Water Thread."

Someone shouted, "What if it's a myth?"

"Fine. Bring me this myth."

There was laughter, cheering, and applause. Many believed her, and they all liked the idea of a million lira.

Afterwards, she sent her father and the men away, peeled off her gown, and crawled into bed. Her belly continued to twist in knots. Gai brought her mistress clear water and hot pea-lime tea until she fell into a fitful sleep.

In the night Kethuda woke, wiping her damp face on the bed sheet, grateful she couldn't remember the dream that had rattled her to the core.

Moonlight streamed in through the sheer white curtains, making a pattern of ocean waves across the floor.

Kethuda slid out of bed, dug into her closet for a dark shirt, pantaloons, and the black hijab she wore to her mother's funeral. "Gai?" she said, tapping on the inside of her assistant's door.

"Yes, Madam?"

"Dress, please. In black. Bring your e-arrow rifle."

They stole through the streets of the city, past revelers in cafes, boys racing ferry-cycles, soldiers standing in circles, smoking. High above, Turkish flags whipped across the face of the full moon.

They reached the back door of Ankara Prison and swore the guards to secrecy with gold coins.

"They could still rat on you, Madam," Gai said.

"They do so at their own peril," Kethuda said, as they followed a sleepy guard up the narrow stairway to the top.

Death row.

"Leave us." The guard peeled away, and Kethuda and Gai walked past the cells. Men slept on cots that bowed with their weight. One large woman stared at them as if her face would be the same whether asleep or awake.

At the end of the row, they found a girl curled on the stone floor, moonlight from a high window casting shadows of bars across her body.

"How small she is," Kethuda said.

The sound was enough to wake the girl. She blinked.

"Why do you sleep on the floor?" Kethuda asked.

The girl squinted, moving her eyes toward the sound of the voice. She held her rib cage, breathing heavily. "What?"

"The cot is more comfortable," Kethuda said.

"I will not sleep in a Turkish bed."

"You have such hatred in your heart?"

The girl shivered, dragging her body toward the sound of the voice. When she reached the cell door, she pulled herself up, peering into the darkness. Her face was illuminated by moonlight: broad Kurdish cheeks smeared with sweat and blood, a dark braid mangled with dirt and sweat; black almond-shaped eyes so clear they seemed to lead all the way down to the darkest corners of her soul.

"I need information from you," Kethuda said, her voice horse in the thick prison air.

"Who are you?"

Kethuda had expected a meek child begging for her life. Instead, there was a forthright energy coming from the Kurd very different from the swaggering aggression of Hamza, or his ministers, or the Saudi King. This was the voice of a girl with nothing to lose and, seemingly, nothing to hide. Kethuda straightened her spine. "I am your imprisoner."

The girl grabbed her ribs and laughed, cruel, mocking, "Ataturka? Should I be flattered? You want me to grovel? Praise your beauty?" Her laughter dissipated, her voice hard as rare Earth metals under ice. "Thrash me, burn me, boil my bones, you will get nothing from me, *bitch*."

Kethuda stared into the cell. The girl felt rage, of course, and defiance, but there was something else, something in the looseness of the child's body, the tilt of her head that Kethuda had longed for all her life.

This child knows what it is to be something, *where I am nothing*. She held this thought for a split second, then it dissolved, and she saw only the enemy.

They stood, for countless moments, the girl holding onto the bars, her dirty bare feet solid on the stone floor, her eyes looking past Kethuda for something in the darkness. What could she be searching for?

"Where do you come from?" Kethuda said, shocked at her own question.

The girl cocked her head, "I fight with the YPJ. You know this. Why am I the only one imprisoned here? Where are the other soldiers of Rojava?"

"You are to be handed over to the Saudi King." Kethuda noted the hitch in the girl's breath and her attempt to hide it. *This kid would rather be tortured and executed than go to bed with the slimy king. Good to know.* "I will not hand you over. Not yet. I am curious to know what you know. To know who you are."

"Where are the surviving YPJ?"

"Relocated. Now, you tell me what you know about the mythical device that turns water into air and back to water."

"Go to hell." The girl turned away and crawled onto the floor, her back barely visible in the moonlight.

Kethuda called out. The girl did not move. "Do you want me to have you tortured?"

No response.

"Whatever you imagine, it will be much worse. You will beg for death."

Silence.

Kethuda's stomach recoiled from the smell of urine and spit.

Gai's gentle voice coaxed her mistress to abandon the interview.

Kethuda returned to her room. But she could not sleep. She watched the patterns of moonlight move across the floor, the memory of the girl's face swimming beneath it.

22 – Ruqia

SOMETHING cool and smooth touched the lips of The Flying Warrior.

"Drink." The voice was male. She closed her mouth. A Turk? Giving her poison?

"It's water. Tastes like shit, but it'll keep you alive." A familiar voice.

Ruqia opened her eyes slowly. Gonul's face was near, his eyes red, his lips cracked, his shoulders hunched as if carrying a heavy load. She gulped the water, gritty but wet, her eyes searching past his face.

"I'm sorry," he said. "Sara's not here."

Ruqia breathed slowly, her heart thrumming. "Where is 'here'?"

"Medical tent. The Turks are shipping us out to an encampment on the shore of the desalinization plant."

"Christ."

"He's not coming with us."

She chuckled, "Bastard, it hurts to laugh." She felt pain all over her body, the worst in her left leg.

"I'll try to find some morphine."

"Where is Sara?" The pain in her heart was deeper than the pain in her body.

"We don't know. Gran and I have looked for that long black braid everywhere, among the living, among the dead." His eyes closed.

"They've got her," Ruqia said.

They looked at each other in simple anguish: Sara in a Turkish prison, a fate worse than death.

"Did they find the Thread?"

"Not that we know of. But somebody has it. Gran was with the soldiers guarding it at the Reservoir in the Burnt Forest. She glanced away for a split second, turned back, and it had disappeared. When the Turks found Pipe 12, there was no sign of the Thread. Nothing but a puddle and a few dinostriches."

"The Turks've got it. They're giving the world the run around."

"I don't think so. Their monster, Ataturka, advertised a million bucks reward." A crease appeared in the corner of each of Gonul's eyes, as if the sun had entered the tent, and he could not bear its brightness. "They say the Turks crashed into the secret mountain laboratory where the Water Thread was made. If that's true, my friend, Joseph, and the Scientists for Humanity had already cleared everything out. All the Turks found was a *paper clip*. They didn't know what it was."

A fireball of pain radiated through Ruqia's left leg. She tried to sit up.

"Don't," he said, his voice gentle but firm.

She recovered her breath, "What happened to me?"

"The e-arrow landed in your femur. It shattered the bone, all the way down through the knee."

Breath abandoned her body. Death she was prepared for. Death she had rehearsed many times: darkness, then a slide into some void on her way to becoming a micro-atom in the night sky. When they had lain naked in the desert in those precious early days, Sara had taught her all the constellations. Ruqia loved Cassiopeia, the queen lounging on the horizon in a W pattern. She told Little Mama she wanted to go there when she died.

This was worse than death. The shattering of her *self*, the Flying Warrior. She re-lived it in her mind, the moment she felt the e-arrow sizzle into her body, the stench of burning flesh: the end of her. If Mama and Papa were here now, Mama would weep. Papa would shake his head, looking into her with those gray eyes that saw truth. He would quote the Quran. He would say, "You promised you would not kill. You lied."

A coil of shame settled in Ruqia's body. She could not bear it, so, slowly, a part of her mind moved away, looking back at herself from a distance. From this place, it seemed a violation of nature for a foreign missile to burn into the soft flesh of a mammal. Any mammal. A human, a dinostrich, an owl.... Such carnage goes back to our species' first appearance on Earth, and yet, now, as humanity boils and drowns, violence seems an evolutionary throw-back, like a baby toe.

A soft shriveled hand touched Ruqia's damp forehead. Gran's eyes were tender, her patchwork hijab so frayed, it hung around her weary face like witch's hair.

Ruqia pressed Gran's hand. "Lame for life. Not what I put in for. You've got that pea-morphine, right? Put me to sleep, Gran. For good."

Gran slipped her hand away. "Don't be an ingrate. Allah watched over you. Cherish your life."

"Double dose should do it. I'll make your apologies to the Man Upstairs."

Gran turned to Gonul. "Help me." They each took an arm, rolling Ruqia out of bed, careful of her leg in its heavy pea cactus cast. She bit her lip against the pain as they guided her out of the tent into the dusk, where thousands of people were gathered on both banks of what had been the mighty Euphrates.

The sun appeared on the horizon, shining in all its majesty as the last drop of water from the riverbed evaporated into the air.

A great cry came up from the crowd.

Ruqia leaned against her friends, her limbs heavy with grief. "Sara, I'm glad you are not here to see this."

The wail of the mourners reverberated upward, through dust and air and outer atmosphere, into the hearts of the stars.

23 – Sara

THE bruises on Sara's rib cage were fading, the bones slowly healing. *If only I could banish these pictures from my mind: the fighting, the blood, Ruqia dying, my comrades, the men who laughed at me for loving a baby dinostrich, so many, watching them die....*

"I must be brave. Braver than I am," she said out loud, looking up at the high barred window, hoping Rexie II might be there. "Remember Sakine? She could have faced execution at any time. She didn't think of that. She thought only of the people in the cell with her, protecting them, helping them."

I can't do that. There is no one here but me.

Yesterday, the other prisoners on her floor were taken away. No one was left to yell "Shut Up!" when she screamed. Was this part of the punishment? A silence so isolating it would drive her insane? She already suspected there were tiny cameras and microphones hidden in the crumbling bricks. Was she being spied on, or was she being paranoid?

She had one delicious respite: sitting on the stone floor cross-legged, remembering Mamoo, Papoo, Gonul pulling her into his arms, Ruqia touching her in the dark cave...

The door squealed open. She stood up, breathing slowly. *I am named for Sakine Cansiz. I can bear torture as bravely as she did.* But her legs trembled, and her mind? Would it hold fast—as she had sworn when Ruqia inducted her into the YPJ—or would the agony in her body weaken her resolve and make her betray everyone she loved?

Two male guards entered her cell, clamping cuffs on her wrists and ankles, forcing her to sit on the cot. They clipped the chains to iron circles on the floor and left without a word.

Now comes the torture.

Minutes passed. Sara screamed, the echo bouncing throughout the empty hallway. No answering sound.

When she was very little, she had sobbed over a broken toy. Mamoo said, "No tears, you must be brave." Papoo said, "There is no shame in weeping. Sometimes the bravest people are the ones who cry the most." Good old Papoo.

The door squealed. A figure in black entered, followed by a Black woman. Ataturka and her entourage. *Come to watch the torture?* The Black woman placed a small table and chair in the center of the cell with a carafe of water, cups, and a bowl of fresh figs. Sara noted an e-arrow rifle tucked into the black folds of the servant's gown. *Will I be murdered outright? If so, why the show of water and figs?* She clasped her knees tightly together to keep them from shaking, the smell of her sweat mingling with the sweetness of the ripe figs.

Ataturka settled into the chair on the other side of the little table. Sara hated to admit it, but she was hypnotized by this woman's graceful movements, her strength, her poised authority. Moonlight from the high barred window spilled onto Ataturka's face, highlighting her square jawbone, high cheeks, her eyes dark and unmoving as she stared at Sara.

The Black woman poured water from the carafe into two tin cups. She handed one cup to Sara. Sara curled her hands around it: a mug, so much water—unrationed. Sara gulped the water, and long tears slid down her dirty face as she swallowed.

"More?" the Black woman asked in round tones: an African, perhaps a recent water refugee.

Sara nodded, wiping her face with the back of her sleeve. Another full cup appeared in her hands. She drank more slowly, savoring every sip, the cool liquid sliding down the back of her throat. As she held out her cup for more, Ataturka lurched back in her chair, breathing as if an elephant had sat on her lungs. The Black woman was alarmed, but not surprised. She offered her mistress water.

"No, no water for me." Ataturka turned to Sara. "You mock me, Kurd, drinking like a pig—throwing it in my face that I have never been thirsty in my whole life!" She rose from her chair, swaying, gasping as if her lungs were on fire.

The Black woman uncuffed Sara, leaving everything on the table as she hurried out with her swooning mistress.

Sara bit into a fig, moaning in rapture at its sweet, gritty taste. She knew the figs were brought in from some country at a high cost to the ruling elites. Sara thought for a moment that she should refuse them, but it was too late. The starving animal of her being was enrapt to taste and swallow such a treasure.

Why did Ataturka think I was mocking her? I was weeping with joy to drink the clear, delicious water. Oh…she's never been so close to a Kurd before. She could smell the filth of me, choke on the scent of my salty tears. I hope I drove her insane.

She smiled, savoring the possibility that she had some power over this Turkish monster. If Gonul were here he would say, "Too fanciful, Sara, bring your hypothesis down to Earth." But Ruqia would say, "Trust yourself, Little Mama. Who knows what festers in the heart of the queen of darkness?"

24 - Kethuda

SHE hurried into her room, gasping for air, crawling into her canopy bed.

"I will call a doctor," Gai said.

"No."

"These attacks have become more frequent, Madam. Tonight, the worst."

"I can't give my father ammunition."

Gai spoke in the African language of her birth, clicking her tongue at the end of each phrase.

"Don't bother to translate. You think I'm a weak woman."

"No, Madam."

"Do you think I have epilepsy?"

"I think not, Madam. I think you have anxiety. These are panic attacks."

"I can barely breathe. It feels like I'm dying,"

Gai pressed a cold cloth to her mistress's face. "You come by these fits honestly, Madam. You have a great deal to be anxious about."

"The girl haunts me. She acted like she doesn't care who I am, what I could do to her—"

"She is a child of 18, totally unschooled in the ways of the world, probably severely dehydrated—"

"Don't use that word in my presence!"

They were both startled. Gai said quietly, "I know that word is upsetting, for all of us in the arid countries. I apologize."

Kethuda breathed more slowly, her mind moving very fast. "I've never been so close to a person like that Kurd. She should have been terrified of me. Instead, that first meeting, she called me a bitch. Just now, she sobbed like a baby, as if I wasn't even in the room. No fear. I have never known someone with no fear. Even my father—no, especially my father. He must control us all, or he is terrified that we will annihilate him." She rolled over, looking up at Gai, "Show it to me again."

"No, Madam. Not until you are calm."

"Show me!"

"If you want to see it, you must do it yourself."

Kethuda glared at Gai in defiance, pushing the cold cloth off of her forehead and pressing her fingertip to the portal of her In-Phone. The replay on the World Board bled into view: thousands of people—Iraqis, Arabs, Syrians, Kurds—water refugees from every down-stream nation, standing together on either side of the Euphrates, their mournful cry heard round the world. Kethuda shivered, the volume of the wailing echoing through her skull, new images dancing in it: a cartoon in *The New Yorker* showing Kethuda as the Grim Reaper, marching down the barren Euphrates, beheading down-streamers in her path. The author of the cartoon? Elena Maria Juarez, the journalist who had praised Kethuda at her Inauguration, now condemned her, calling for her to resign her Presidency and her seat on the RAT team, writing, "The woman has no concept of human Water Rights as a moral imperative outstripping the petty ambitions of Imperialism."

News clips of world leaders announced sanctions against Turkiye from all RAT countries except old Mr. Boatwright in America, who said, "My buddy, Ataturka, is acting in the American tradition of national best interest." Russia and China sent compliments, with veiled offers to partner with a new RAT alliance of the East, including the Turkish expansion into Rojava, Syria, Iraq, and Iran.

Kethuda had expected these responses. She had nursed the absurd hope that the women of the world would still support her, would understand that she had to honor contracts with her customers while conserving water for her own people. Instead, they expressed sadness and rage, saying they had been betrayed. Shogofa in Afghanistan said, "Ataturka is a trans-woman with the penis of her New Ottoman Empire." Nina Navalny reached for a reference to the man who had persecuted Alexei Navalny, calling Ataturka, "Putin in drag."

Gai pulled her mistress's finger off her forehead. Kethuda did not resist, but the images lingered in her memory with no mercy.

Voices rose from street vendors beyond the balcony: "Pea cactus olive oil, half-price." "Turkish flags you can cook in your soup. Tastes like gobble-gobble turkey"… "Pea cactus water bottles in three colors."

"Shall I close the balcony door?" Gai asked.

"No. I need to hear the voices of my people. I made this choice for them."

"Of course, Madam." Gai's voice betrayed two minds: approval, and a carefully modulated disapproval. *What is going on beneath the surface of this African woman who tends my body so lovingly?*

Sleep came to Kethuda, and with it a dream: she stood with the water refugees in the dry riverbed of the Euphrates. A great cavern opened at her feet, spiraling down into the Earth; many fell into it, disappearing into the darkness. Kethuda held on to the rim as a rivulet of water flowed up, absurdly, against the force of gravity, filling the empty riverbed.

25 - Hamza

HE was hidden in the alcove outside his daughter's door, surmising that Kethuda and Gai were asleep at last, for he had been listening to every word, and now they were silent. His sight might have been failing, but his ears were those of a night owl searching for prey. His soldiers followed Ataturka wherever she went and did their own surveillance. From their reports, Hamza knew that his daughter was visiting the Kurdish teenager. This was a bad thing, Kethuda was obsessed with the girl, instead of making speeches across Turkiye, as they had planned, to "seal the deal" on her policy: Keep Turkiye Flush (in water and Israeli gold).

His soldiers reported that Kethuda had had a fit in the girl's presence, trembled, raged, and collapsed. Hamza couldn't begin to understand it. He could squash the callow Kurd with one blow. But then, he was Hamza the Great, descended from Ottoman Sultans. His daughter was a creation of his own imagination. Even her name, Ataturka, was his idea.

And this Black African. He could never look at her without picturing her in the Ballroom, half-naked, swirling her hips toward the men. But there was something about her that disquieted him. An influence on his daughter that could be dangerous. Her opinions were always reasonable, often protective, but with a tilt toward Universalism, a love for all mankind. Even her name, "Gai," half of some weird hermaphrodite god. This "Gai," a water refugee from the dark continent, no doubt, must have a misplaced empathy for the down-streamers, calling the terrorist Kurd, "only a child."

A child. He recalled another child, a baby in Ayse's arms. Such beauty; such betrayal. From the moment of Kethuda's birth, Ayse's affections had shifted to her baby girl. All the spoiling and back rubs and fawning she had lavished on Hamza evaporated, like mist from a shallow pond. He grew to resent, even to hate, both mother and child, turning to other women to shame his wife, making his daughter a son in his own image. And yet he also loved them both with an obsession that only increased with the years. When Ayse died from the horrible cancer, he could not weep, but turned his grief into sculpting his daughter into an evolutionary leap in the alchemy of monarchy. Even her sexuality would be his. He would train her to love her own power more than she would love any mortal man. He made her a goddess, a chaste one with a metaphorical penis used only to assault the enemy, never to penetrate loving flesh of woman or man.

"Did I create a monster?" he said out loud, as if Ayse were standing beside him. "After you died, I denied your daughter girlish feelings. Is that why she is dumbfounded by this Kurd awash in nothing *but* feelings?"

A noise came from within the apartment. Had Kethuda heard his voice? He pressed his ear to the wall. A sigh came from the bedroom. Did she turn in her sleep? He pictured her lying in the canopy bed, and with this came a longing for her love so strong, it turned to hatred. If it weren't for her, he would never have become a needy little boy, clawing at his mommy's breast. He always made her pay for it. Whenever he slapped her or choked her, he feigned remorse, but he was secretly proud: violence is love aborted.

It came to him in a stroke of brilliance: a bold new strategy to control his daughter, while pretending to protect her from the she-devil-Kurd. Ataturka would stay tucked under his wing, fearing him, needing him, loving him.

26 – Gonul

HE woke in the night, his pea-sand mat moistened by the rising tide of the Mediterranean Sea. Moonlight caught the tips of the towers of Beirut, rising like ancient ruins offshore. There was nothing ancient about these buildings. They were contemporary climate ruins, like buildings buried by the swelling seas of coastal cities around the world.

Gonul closed his eyes. He could hear the different languages, different dialects of the thousands of water refugees camped on the beach behind him. Sleep eluded most of them. The desalinization plant, perched on the shoreline, roared like a bear, day and night. Mothers murmured words of comfort to their fussy children. Gonul found their voices comforting, but the children fretted, unable to adapt to such a strange place, so far from home.

A cooling breeze came off the sea. He removed his turban, its Kurdish pattern of orange and blue shimmering slightly beneath the stars. The gentle wind felt good on his damp head. In this moment of reprieve, he imagined Sara locked away in a dark cell, deprived of light, or touch, or love…. Maybe she was dead? If so, he would look for her in the stars. He tried, but a mournful sadness overtook him. What use was his love when she was so far away?

He returned to what he could see and touch and know: Ruqia lying beside him. It seemed both strange and inevitable that he grew closer to her each day. Whenever he held Ruqia's leg to clean her wound, he pictured Sara's leg pressed against it in an erotic embrace. He cleaned carefully, as if holding something sacred.

Ruqia moved onto her back, every muscle braced against the pain. Her eyes were closed, but he knew she was not asleep.

Gran, on the other hand, could sleep through a hurricane and was doing so, nestled beside them, *wheezing* breath in, *gurgling* breath out. The lines of her face were softer in moonlight, but Gonul knew this proud warrior was dying inside, to be reduced to a refugee.

He dipped the end of his turban into his water cup and placed it on Ruqia's face.

"You're stupid," she said.

He smiled. "No back-talk. You're the patient."

"No one wastes water like this."

"Hush and enjoy it." He glanced at the expanse of the bodies camped beneath the stars. First light, the Turks would herd them in line at the desal Kiss-Off station. No one believed there could be enough water for so many people for very long. The nightly growl of the desal plant was becoming more of a shrill whine. Gonul's old friend, anxiety, made its way into his throat. He stroked Ruqia's face. "Tell me about ecstasy."

Her eyes grew wide. "Are you trying to distract me from the pain, or are you a sleezy old man?"

"Shut up," he said gently.

"Someone might overhear. If my breech of chastity is discovered, the Turks might put me out of my misery. Their bitch President wears a hijab now. Praise Allah and all that crap."

"Use your indoor voice. Tell me what it's like to make love to 'Little Mama.'"

"Was."

"We don't know that. For now, ecstasy *is*."

"You're a stubborn bastard," she chuckled. "I'm not giving you graphic details. Sara told me about a guy in Greek mythology, Tire-something, a blind clairvoyant, who lived as a woman for seven years. Somebody asked him whether he had more fun as a man or a woman, and he said something like, 'A man's pleasure is great, a woman's is over the moon.'"

Gonul slapped her playfully with the turban. "Fair enough. Women rule."

Ruqia smiled, falling silent.

They listened to the ocean waves move in, move out.

Ruqia said, "After making love, Sara would sometimes go on and on about the totally scientific (and also divine) force in water."

"Totally scientific," he said, closing his eyes happily.

"I told her I thought she was nuts, and she said, 'What do you believe, R? You must believe in something?' I told her no God watches over us. No God ever stopped me from killing a ton of people in the battlefield—"

"I asked for ecstasy."

"Yeah, so, Sara and I, we were babbling about my arid atheism, and she started running her fingertips down my arm, and I felt this shudder of pleasure…"

"Go on."

"I'm breaking my own rule here. It does get graphic."

"I can do graphic."

She sighed, "It took hours, each of us touching every inch of the other's body with our hands, our lips, until there was a state of being that came over us, our bodies pressed together, like we were one. For me, *that* was the divine…"

He sighed, remembering the moment in Camp, soldiers dashing all around, when he stood completely still, looking at Sara.

Ruqia's eyes rested on his face.

"Thank you," he said.

She reached for his hand, surrendering to her grief with sobs that shook her body. He wrapped his arms around her.

They held each other, for uncounted moments, until Ruqia's tears dissipated into a deep sleep.

Gonul gently put her down and walked along the water's edge, past families sleeping on the sand or in makeshift tents. There was not a lot of movement; everyone was instinctively conserving energy because rations were so slim.

The corner of Gonul's turban was still damp. He wiped his face, recalling his grandfather taking the bright blue and orange turban off his bald head every night, hanging it on a hook above their beds. "Can you see the shadow of the turban on the wall?" he asked his little grandson. "Like an angel guarding us through the night."

The stars seemed to grow brighter as Gonul approached the sea, their light refracting onto the surface of the buried buildings of Beirut. It had all happened sooner than anyone predicted, especially in this part of the world. Where did they go, the inhabitants of Beirut? Some poured into Syria. Others migrated north, only to be turned away by a Europe dealing with their own crises. It was easy to lose track of entire populations fleeing from consequences no one could control. In the mountains of Rojava, Gonul and his grandfather had watched the perma-drought kill the grasslands and melt the snow from their mountain home. A popular design on Kurdish clothing was taken from the pattern of melting snow on the mountains. With snow receding, the pattern was gone. One night, Grandpapa went out to the mountain and lay down with his sheep. The next morning Gonul found him, curled on the Earth, the sheep bleating beside him. Gonul took the turban off Grandpapa's head and put it on his own. As he carried his grandfather's body down the mountain, workers passed with seeds and shovels, ready to dig up the parched grassland and plant the new genetically engineered miracle, the pea cactus.

Gonul had no memory of his parents. They were said to be modest folk, his father a great cook, his mother a gifted engineer. They had had a lovely home in Damascus, but found themselves on the wrong side of the Syrian dictator. After his parents were executed, Grandfather snuck the boy out of the city and took him to the mountains of Rojava. Gonul grew up tending sheep, but thanks to the In-Phone, he schooled himself at a very young age on everything that seized his curiosity. And what a "seizing" it was. Grandpapa used to laugh, "You cannot know *everything!*" "Why not?" Gonul had said. He discovered an ally in his quest, a boy named Joseph who lived on a hill nearby. During the day they signaled each other with brightly colored kites. At night, they spent hours on the In-Phone together, throwing each other questions about the nature of the Universe. Those were good years for the curious. The quota system on In-Phone energy was not enforced until after Gonul had become a teacher, but even the quota did not quell what Sara dubbed his "obsession with knowledge." He saved his energy quota points like rare jewels, using them to search for the cause and motivation behind everything natural or human made. "Mr. Askay, if you're not trying to discover something," Sara had said to him, "you have no idea who you are."

At the waterline Gonul took off his boots, tossing them onto his shoulder as he walked into the surf. How sublime, to feel water on his skin. *I will have salty pants. I don't care.*

He touched his forehead, knowing he was about to use a year's worth of energy quota. It didn't matter. *Let them come after me. I have to learn what I can about the Water Thread. Who took it? Does Joseph know where it is?*

Five years ago, Gonul was allowed to visit the secret lab in Rojava. Joseph had become a Transformation Scientist: one who studies ways to make one form of matter transform into another. Joseph joked that his team was like the ancient alchemists, not turning lead into gold, but trying to turn water into air, and air into water.

Joseph was taller than Gonul, with wild black hair and a long beard he never combed. His colleagues called him "the wooliest Kurd of them all"; his purple-marine eyes shone brilliantly beneath his forested eyebrows.

Joseph had blindfolded Gonul and led him somewhere high in the mountains where an international team of scientists and engineers, the Scientists for Humanity, worked in a hidden university with a re-imagined atom-smasher. Some of SFH's members were descended from the scientists at Los Alamos, New Mexico, where the atomic bomb that leveled Hiroshima and Nagasaki had been built. Their descendants abhorred this legacy, creating a team of people who were ethical humanists first, scientists second. They wanted to reconfigure the chemistry of water, to allow it to travel in the form of air, returning to water when pulled by an energy force on the receiving end. They chose Rojava as a secluded site, much like Los Alamos, but, unlike the heroes of the atomic bomb, these scientists were prohibited from seeking individual glory. The device, later called the Water Thread, was to be credited "authorship anonymous." Early in the program, some scientists had been asked to leave when they demanded their own publicity, and the team had been pared down to those who were uninterested in the spoils of ego.

The visit to the secret lab had been the most thrilling day of Gonul's life. He loved the light-hearted integrity of the team. No one knew if they would live to see the results. Joseph said that the greatest challenge would be how to bring the invention into the world so that it was used equally, not for the benefit of any one country or regime, which had led to a discussion of morals and values and political theory that lasted until dawn.

Since the Five Day War, Gonul had tried to contact Joseph. All messages come back, *Recipient Not Found*. Not a good sign. Had the Scientist for Humanity been captured by the Turks? The Saudis? The Israelis? The Russians? The Chinese? Or were they in another, even more remote, secret location, hiding the Water Thread until the world could meet their ethical standard?

Gonul did not find any In-Phone data on the Water Thread. Which was good news. At least the Turks didn't have it, but—what was this—incoming data on the World Board: a photo of Sara behind bars, her head held high. Over her picture, the voice of Hamza. "This woman, calling herself 'Sara,' murdered our soldiers, poached our water, and refuses to divulge the whereabouts of the supposed Water Thread. She is an enemy of the people and will suffer the justice of public execution."

27 – Kethuda

"Is there a special place in hell for daughters who murder their fathers?" Kethuda sat naked in a shallow bath of ice water. Anything to quell her rage. A throb from her In-Phone signaled in-coming thought-messages: Elena Maria Juarez wrote in *The New Yorker*, "After 324 years, America is still searching for her soul, but we have never yanked an 18-year-old girl out of prison and executed her without due process. Sara Roxan is a soldier of the famous YPJ, protected under the RAT-sanctified Geneva Convention. Ataturka! Are you listening? Has your father eaten your balls? Or just your soul? Make him spit them up, or resign your masquerade."

Shogofa in Afghanistan called Sara Roxan "sister" and begged Ataturka to release her so she could come to Afghanistan and lead women against the Taliban.

The worst came from Nina Navalny, calling Hamza "worse than Rasputin," and Ataturka his "political whore."

Kethuda took her hand from her forehead.

Gai sponged her mistress's back. "I do not indulge in thoughts of hell."

Kethuda's laugh was bitter. "If there is a Maasai god, isn't there a Maasai hell?"

"I think you are there, Madam."

Kethuda massaged her tight jaw with an ice cube. "The Kurd is my prisoner. The Saudi bastard wants to bed her; my father wants to kill her. She is *mine.*"

It was obvious by the crinkle in Gai's tattoo that the notion of owning a human being was distasteful to her.

Kethuda looked upward, addressing unseen spirits. "I see you, laughing down at me, Boudica, Benazir Bhutto, Joan of Arc—"

"Not all women heroes were murdered, Madam. You pick tragic examples to justify your claim to the Kurd. You are no better than the men."

Kethuda rose from the bath. If she had been her father, she would have struck Gai. Instead, she stood naked in front of her. "I'm freezing. Bring me a robe."

Gai brought a finely crafted pea-cactus towel and dried her mistress's body and wrapped it in a soft sea-green robe.

Kethuda drank clear water tea, the most coveted beverage throughout the arid countries. "You took quite a risk, Ms. Gai."

"Yes, Madam."

"Why?"

Gai sat across the room, her dark eyes showing no fear. "I think you want me to, Madam."

"Who are you?"

"What you see, Madam."

"No, you are a fox, you just don't want me to know it."

Gai smiled, the black lines of her tattoo spreading on her forehead. "You also travel in many burrows, Madam."

Kethuda lifted her spine, ready to attack. Instead she leaned back, laughing until she cried. Gai joined her, pouring more clear water tea.

"I want to know more about your African sisterhood," Kethuda said. "Who are these women?"

"Oh, Madam, they are water refugees from my continent, scattered all over the world. They are mothers, sisters, wives, priestesses, engineers, scientists, traders, oracles, business-women, artists."

"What strategy do they all use?" Kethuda asked, leaning forward.

Gai sighed. "A white woman's question."

Kethuda sat back. "How would you ask it?"

"I would want to know how each woman brought her own complex personality to the task of leadership. I would want to know how each woman experiences courage. The very courage I am using at this moment. Not the courage of a lion tearing into a baby rhino, but the courage of a human saying, 'Whether I live or die, I am guided by something larger than myself.'"

Kethuda's head ached, and her eyes fogged over. "You burden me with too much philosophy."

"It is not philosophy, Madam. It is the truth."

Kethuda's voice had the echo of a woman shouting from within a coat of armor, "Your sisters and mothers are so high and mighty? No compromise, no shenanigans, no evil? Where are they now, scattered across the world, begging for water!"

Sunlight stole through the sheer white curtains onto the Seated Woman of Catalhoyuk. The light on the glass dome obscured the statue, as if the goddess had tucked her leopards under her arms and trotted away. Kethuda peered through the glass. Seated Woman was still there. Kethuda lifted the protective shell and touched the goddess's head, reconstructed from the headless figure discovered in the ruins. What did the original head look like? Was she beautiful? Her people worshiped her, even as the crowd outside the window worshiped "Ataturka" (or gave a good show of it). "Should I go to the ruins of Catalhoyuk, Gai? Hold the bones of the people who worshipped our goddess?"

"What do you seek, Madam?" Gai dutifully scooped water from the bath, pouring it into a metal container to be sterilized for drinking.

How could Kethuda confide the truth to her assistant? *I seek to fill up my empty self. I pretend at power. In fact, I am nothing.*

As if in answer to her mistress's unspoken thoughts, Gai said, "never mind that your father threatens to execute the Kurd. You are the President."

She is so naïve. Once Hamza announced his intent to the world, nothing will stop him.

"Should I go to the Kurd, watch her grovel in her cell."

"She does not grovel, Madam."

Kethuda replaced the glass over the statue. She did not need to hold bones, she needed something *alive* to give her the courage to face the Kurd. To face her father. To face herself.

The tiny bells of ferry cycles chimed in the street below.

Kethuda fell silent, listening. "You often walk in the streets, among the people, right, Gai?"

"Yes, Madam."

Kethuda's heart seemed to skip a beat. She swallowed, feigning confidence, "Take me with you."

"Where, Madam?"

"You know the city. Where will I find the people who need me the most, who hate me the most?"

Gai suppressed a smile, but not before Kethuda caught it. *Why would it give Gai pleasure to see my fear?*

"I know such a place, Madam, if you are ready for it."

"I'm not, but take me anyway."

They waited until nightfall. Gai found what she called "peasant pea cactus attire." Kethuda had never worn anything so scratchy. It was the beginning of her education in how everyone else lived.

They wrapped the burlap-style hijabs around their heads and covered their faces. "Tickles my nose," Kethuda said.

"The secret is not minding that it tickles," Gai said.

They went stealthily down the back stairs of the Presidential Apartment and onto the street. Kethuda was accustomed to sliding into her Ataturka-mobile. Instead, they set out on foot past pea-fig vendors, squealing children, young boys and girls selling their bodies for water.

Kethuda had never walked these streets before. She had had no idea the cobblestones were so hard, the smell of human sweat so rancid, the coughing from dry throats so unrelenting.

The full moon illuminated a man walking toward them, a Black man so tall and lean and proud, he seemed to have dropped in from another world. Kethuda thought that the men of Catalhoyuk must have looked like him, human bodies so fluid they were an integral part of the natural world. Gai ran to him, kissing his cheek. He folded her into his arms and held her.

"Madam President, my twin brother, Eng."

He bowed.

Kethuda walked toward him with a sense of ease, extending her hand. He looked at it, asking his sister, "Do I kiss it or shake it?"

Gai giggled, glancing at her mistress.

"I would be honored if you would shake my hand," Kethuda said. "I've heard so much about you."

His long Black hand encircled her small white one. "I am deeply honored to meet you, Madam President. How do I thank you for the good judgment to employ my sister?"

"I am the one who benefits from the arrangement. She has taught me many things."

"She has taught me since we came from the womb," he said with a wink to his sister. "I am honored to guard you this night."

"You don't have a weapon?" Kethuda asked.

Eng lifted a corner of his dusty green pea cactus robe to reveal an e-arrow rifle, its tiny red light primed for action.

They hurried through the streets, crossing into the section of Ankara beyond the vendors, the ferry-cycles, the prostitutes, to the Water Square. Low-income apartment buildings rose so high, the sky was a slender band of starry night between the tops of the steel buildings. Torches on high poles gave the illusion of a Medieval courtyard, the scratchy pea cactus coats of the people like the wool smocks of serfs. The air was infested with thornies jabbing the bare arms of children. A mother wailed, "Allah, make it rain. Bring back the butterfly; send the thornies to hell."

The line of people at the Kiss-Off station stretched to the horizon. Kethuda had seen this on the World Board, but never in person. Gai put a firm hand on her mistress's shoulder. "Be calm, Madam. There is enough water for all. So far. It just takes a long time. The people are used to it."

The *so far* resonated with Kethuda as she made her way into the throng of her citizens. It felt like a gathering that had become so routine, no one thought it odd that they had to wait hours for a meager ration, only to return the following night, and do it again. People chattered among themselves; a street mime entertained; children played with hoops. Each family carried bowls, pitchers, or vintage plastic buckets once used for picnics at the lake. They pressed their lips to the metal button and collected their rations for the next day. Many complained their rations were dwindling, as there never seemed to be enough *salties* or real food in the city to sustain a healthy weight, especially for children.

Kethuda breathed slowly. *Not a time to have a panic attack. I am here to learn the truth.* A boy toddled up to her and grabbed her legs. She was shocked, not by his gentle squeeze, but by her reaction: *what joy to feel the touch of a child.* The mother hurried to pull the boy off, hefting him onto her hip.

"He looks heavy," Kethuda said. "How do you manage?"

"He makes me strong."

"I want to know how you feel about things," Kethuda said, glancing at Gai and Eng.

"Things?" said the mom, allowing her boy to suck on her dry finger.

"The water."

"What water? Are you from abroad that you don't see how little we get?"

"I *am* from, another country," Kethuda said, squirming under her itchy clothes. "At least you have a daily ration."

"Are you blind?" The mom turned to the horizon. "The bright moon tonight shows you how barren our mountains are. Last year we had at least a dusting of snow."

"I see," Kethuda said, her body heavy at the sight of the moonlight on a few barren peaks.

"There is no future. Hamza will make his daughter kill the Kurd—the only person who knows the whereabouts of this Water Thread—"

"You believe in it?"

The mom put her boy down, resting a hand on his thick black hair. "What else do we have? No help from Ataturka, her father's doll on a string. She does not have the balls to save the Kurd and bring us the Water Thread."

"She will not defy her father?"

The mom laughed. "She has nothing to fight *with*. They say Hamza has his own soldiers out looking for the Thread, soldiers loyal only to him. He will find it and keep it for himself and his rich friends. He doesn't care if we dehydrate. And his daughter? She cares only for her gowns and her glory."

Kethuda's belly rumbled so loudly the mom could hear it. Mistaking it for hunger, she offered Kethuda a *saltie*. "No, thank you," Kethuda said. "Keep it for you and your boy. Excuse my stomach. It is hard to hear that you have so little hope."

The boy cried and tugged on his mom's skirt. She gave him the *saltie*. "Go back to wherever you came from and tell them there is no hope in Ankara. Not for ordinary people."

All night Kethuda listened to her people. She stood beside them, smelling the sweat of their bodies, of her own. Everyone had the same fears, the same loathing for Hamza, the same bitter assessment of the false President, Ataturka.

"She may think she's trying her best," said a young woman in a bright white and green patterned hijab. "We see Ataturka tossing lavender seeds from her balcony, oblivious to the fact that nobody wants to grow her stupid pea-cactus lavender? Why doesn't she throw us bottles of water?" The young woman's face hardened with despair. "We are all doomed without the Water Thread. If Ataturka truly cared about us, she would stand up to her father, make her own war against him, and find the Thread for all of her people."

"What fashion is her scarf?' Kethuda asked Eng as the young woman stepped away to get her ration.

"A re-imaging of an ancient Kurdish design of snow melting on the mountains," Gai said. "A pattern called *belekevi.*"

"Kurdish?" Kethuda asked, her belly rumbling at the thought of Sara, slated for execution.

"There are still Kurds in Turkiye," Eng said. "In spite of how many of them your father murdered."

Shuuuush, shuuuush came the relentless sound of the pump doling out water.

"Have you had enough, Madam?" Gai asked.

"No." Kethuda said, turning to the next person in line.

28 – Sara

SHE woke from a dreamless sleep, her body damp with sweat.

cha cha cha cha cha

Rexie II flapped his wings on the barred window high above.

Sara wiped the pooled sweat from her eyes. Something strange was happening. She kept hearing footsteps on the stairs, but no one came to see her. Voices, but no information. Worst: no food or water for 18 hours. She was running out of *salties*, her mouth sandpaper dry.

"I don't have water for you," she said to Rexie II. "Go to the dam, or the mountains. There's nothing for you here."

Silence. A flutter of wings.

"No. Don't go. Stay. Be with me, whatever comes next."

She could hear the click of his little lizard feet moving along the bars: *stay or go?* The suspense was more than she could bear. All feeling went out of her body, leaving a strange, yawning emptiness. "Go, if you must, Rexie II. If the divine is in the water, She is in my sweat. She came to me the first night I was here. She rocked me, stench and sweat and all. She will be with me, to the end."

cha cha cha cha cha

"You always want me to be happy. If that's what you want, I'll do it. Stay and we'll 'cut a rug,' as the Americans used to say. Not much dancing in the world today; it depletes energy…"

cha cha cha cha cha

She stood up, singing the *Goren*, pretending that Gonul, Ruqia, and Gran were beside her, dancing. "Come down, Rexie II. Perch on my shoulder. Dance with me."

cha cha cha worr mop

The door at the end of the hall squealed open, followed by angry voices, "Outrageous." "We have our orders." "I will take this to your father."

"Hamza is not the President."

The door squealed shut as Ataturka swept in, her sandals clicking on the pea-concrete floor.

Sara continued her song, her dry throat making sounds like a rusty *oud*, but still proud. She noted that something was different in the Turkish queen. Ataturka wore the same outlandish white gown and blue hijab, but her body was rounder, less stiff, as if she had gained weight, not in pounds, but in some puncture of the mind that brought her closer to Earth.

"What is your song?" Ataturka said.

A tall Black man appeared, placing a chair outside the cell. The queen thanked him and descended into it, her white silks brushing the dirty pea-concrete floor.

"I haven't had water or food in a day and a night," Sara said. "Your form of torture?"

Ataturka glanced at the Black man, a shared look of disgust. "I am sorry," she said. "You will now be served by different soldiers."

"What happened?"

"It's resolved." My father is no longer dictating the terms of your imprisonment."

"Does he know that?" Sara said.

The queen's eyes searched the floor. The Black man slid water and pea cactus bread into Sara's cell. She drank and ate, taking her time. The bread smelled like avocado, masking, for a few precious moments, the stench of sweat and urine. Sara wondered where they got the avocado to flavor the bread. Shipped in from high-rise farms in Florida? More privilege shoved under her nose to lure her into their world of consumption. *How ignorant these people are. They don't know me at all.*

Ataturka watched Sara closely, oddly curious that her prisoner was eating and drinking so slowly.

"You grew up in Rojava?" Ataturka asked.

"Why?"

"I've made a study of political structures. When the Syrian government pulled out of your country in the twenty-first century, Rojava created their own form of democracy. I have read accounts. I want to know your experience."

Sara glanced down at the last slice of the pea cactus bread, its green color laced with streaks of purple. She pushed it out through the slot in the cell, offering it to the queen.

"No thank you," Ataturka said with a hint of surprise.

"It is very good." Sara pushed the plate closer.

"I think you are hungrier than I."

"Really? You look very hungry to me, your Majesty."

The queen blinked, a subtle movement, betraying some hidden vulnerability. She glanced at the Black man, held the look for a moment, then motioned for him to leave. He bowed and obeyed, his dignity palpable. The virgin queen liked him. Even more, respected him: ammunition Sara might need.

"Depriving you of food and water was not my idea."

"Whose idea was it?" Sara's voice was strong, her throat no longer as dry.

The queen was motionless, but for the drumming of her left toe.

Sara chuckled, calling to Rexie II, "She plays with me like a toy."

nah nah nah nah nah

"He doesn't like you." Sara's voice mirrored the mockery of the bird.

"Murderer. *Kurd*. How dare you make fun of me. Do you want torture? Death? I can make it happen, little girl, with the flick of my fingernail."

Sara's body tensed with terror, but she held her head in proud defiance.

Ataturka rose with studied magnificence, pacing, breathing hard. She paused, close to the cell bars, her hand over her nose to hide the stench. "Cyrus the great, of ancient Persia, created a society on the principles of chastity, openness, humanity, and liberality."

Sara could hear Gonul's teaching in her mind. She cleared her throat: "If I remember, Cyrus came to power when Persia needed new leadership after years of war and deprivation. He reached out to the people, walked among them, and garnered their loyalty by creating a just and economically viable state."

Ataturka lifted her eyebrows.

Sara laughed. "You thought me a country bumpkin."

"I admit I didn't expect a command of history from one so young."

"I had a very good teacher," Sara said with a catch in her voice, Gonul's face in her mind.

Ataturka moved her chair closer to the bars, sitting with her legs apart, as if astride a mighty horse. "You may be eager to follow your namesake as a martyr, but in truth, you can better serve your people by staying alive and being true to your real name, Fatima Roxan."

Sara clasped her hands on the cold iron bars. "Kethuda—that's your real name. Why should I tell you anything?"

Ataturka sighed and pulled off her blue hijab. "It's hot in here."

"You noticed."

"How can you bear the smell?"

Sara gripped the bars tighter. "The piss and filth in here are perfume compared to the smell of my mother's burning flesh. Your bombs wiped out our Equal Voice Council. It's too late for you to be curious about our form of local democracy."

Ataturka lowered her eyes. "I didn't know it was your family that was hit that day. The target was terrorists, not ordinary Kurds. I was a young woman at the time, with no power, at home, nursing my dying mother."

"*You* are the terrorists," Sara said, searching for Ataturka's eyes. "My Mamoo was an ordinary Kurd. The army of women—the YPJ—who could have defended them were miles away, chased down like dogs by your soldiers."

Ataturka took small breaths, like a woman in labor. "Mama and me, we heard of the massacre. Mama wept, whispering a Sufi prayer for Allah to receive the dead. She reached out to me with all her strength. 'Kethuda, you must change this,' she said; then she died."

"You took our water. Is that how you honor your mother?"

"I had to choose: water for my people or your people. What would you have done?"

"Your *rich* people, or my people. Your Israeli customers, or my people, your *power*, or my people—"

Ataturka threw her chair against the iron bars. The Black man hurried in, glancing in at Sara, his calm presence betraying curiosity. In the next moment, he turned his full empathy to the queen, escorting her out with whispers of tender support.

Sara stared at the chair resting upside down, her mind swimming with thoughts of impending torture and death, and something else: *I spoke truth to power. I deserve to call myself Sara, a woman of substance at home with the brave.*

29 - Ruqia

SHE pressed her lips to the steel button and stared at the gray water filling her tiny tin bucket. No cups, just a gross quantity of de-salted water, based on body weight. Ruqia grimaced at the taste of chemicals and salt: this stuff was wet, but it certainly wasn't water. She walked past the dull faces of the people in line behind her. Some recognized her, uttered words of praise for the Flying Warrior. Ruqia did not thank them. She had not spoken a word since Hamza announced his plan for Sara's execution. Words were distant memories, like feelings.

The smell of brine burned her nose. Great towers of processed salt surrounded the long, flat, steel desalinization plant. Scientists reported that all viable marine life had fled to cooler waters, but International Law, enforced by RAT, kept the brine from being dumped back into the Mediterranean. Ruqia fantasized jumping into the sea and swimming to find the fish far from the searing sun of the coast. She had forgotten: she could never swim again.

The creature calling herself "Ataturka" was on the World Board, claiming that the Kurd needed to be kept alive so she could confess the whereabouts of the Water Thread. Ataturka spoke of a split between her and her father, with the majority of the Turkish military pledging loyalty to her. No one believed it. Ataturka had no power to defy her father. She was his puppet-doll. Sara might already be dead.

A new shipment of water refugees disembarked from the Sun Shuttle.

Great, more mouths.

An older woman stumbled toward Ruqia in gaudy robes and cheap American jewelry. "My child! My Fatima," she wailed. "I promised her father I would find her a good husband. Now the Turks will cut off her head!" She flailed her arms in the air and would have fallen in the sand, but a young woman, jangling in her own garish garb, scurried to catch her.

"Mama, do not blame yourself. It is the *Turks,*" said the daughter as they knelt together, praying.

Gonul charged at the wailing women, his voice quivering with rage, "Fidan, you are not Sara's mother. *You* are the one who should lose her head, selling your step-daughter to ISIS."

Gran pulled him away. "Cool yourself, Mr. Askay. Don't waste time with these wretches." He listened to her, but his fury and grief grew like wild roses in a dark swamp.

Something stirred in Ruqia. Now that Sara was famous, these deplorable women were using it to grab the attention of refugees and Turks alike: anyone curious enough to watch the show. Ruqia stared at the heavy cast on her leg with a numbness beyond feeling, but not beyond self-pity. She forced herself to look at Sara's sobbing step-family. *Am I so different? Haven't I been pining for the glory of The Flying Warrior, instead of asking myself, "if I can't fly at the enemy, what kind of warrior can I be?"*

She watched Gonul turn away from Fidan and Nazan, Gran rubbing his shoulders, whispering comfort. *It is time for me to speak. I cannot hide in my grief any longer.* "Teacher Askay, and the one I call Grandmother," she said with more breath than voice.

Gran and Gonul were amazed to hear words coming from Ruqia's lips. They hurried to her side.

"The night before the battle with the Turks," Ruqia said in the voice of a child learning how to talk. "YPJ sat together, knowing we faced death or capture. Sara said, 'let's talk about democracy.'"

"I remember," Gonul said.

"The very word seems a joke now," Gran said.

Ruqia cleared her throat, "That night Sara looked at you, Gonul, and she said, 'In class, we used to discuss what makes democracy fail.'"

Gran said dryly, "Not adhering to the principles of Equal Voice."

Gonul touched Ruqia's hand. She let him. He said, "What holds a democracy together? Tolerance, but more than that, respect for the other person, even their different points of view. Sara's mother, Gita Roxan, led Council brilliantly. She read our Constitution at every meeting. When conflict arose, she addressed it, moving to consensus."

Ruqia said, "I'm done feeling sorry for myself. Look around us." She gestured to the line of refugees stretching to the horizon. "What if we attempt Equal Voice here?"

Gran and Gonul stared at her, blinking away the sand on their eyelashes.

"Many of these people are from Rojava. They could help us form Councils."

"Equal Voice, Equal Justice," Gran said, the lines in her face deepening. "Could anyone here care about those words?" She looked at the people holding their cups, their minds on one thing: water.

"We must try," Ruqia said. "What else are we going to do, sit here and wait—for what?"

They split up, Gonul clearing a space for a Council Circle, Gran off to recruit people she had befriended in line. Ruqia seized her e-arrow rifle and her pea cactus cane as if charging into battle. Pain shot through her leg with every step. The medics had run out of drugs. That was good. Her head must be clear. She walked through the sand, the cane sinking with every step.

At last she found the people on the outskirts of the Beirut Camp. The women of ISIS huddled together: water poachers, thieves, sex traffickers. Some were simply wives of imprisoned or killed ISIS men, trying to nurse their babies with dry teats. *Why have I come here? Why seek to know my enemy? To please Sara? To answer a question dawning in my own heart?*

A woman with one leg recognized Ruqia, "You—you know the girl they will execute—the girl that murdered our Commander!" She spat in the sand. "The Turks will draw and quarter her. Allah will dance."

Ruqia pressed her good leg into the sand, standing her ground, "Sara didn't mean to kill your Commander."

"She did. And you shot *me*."

"Look at me now. Crippled like you. Allah's justice?"

"Go away."

The ISIS women hissed, throwing sand in Ruqia's face. She turned away, coughing, calling over her shoulder, "We're starting a democratic Council. You're welcome to join."

Mocking laughter followed her as she made her way back, cursing herself for trying to make peace with women who hated her as much as she hated them. And yet, the question inside of her did not go away.

She came upon Fidan and the daughter, slumped together, swaying and praying.

"I can't kneel," Ruqia said. "If I could I would get down beside you so you could see my face. I'm inviting you to join our Council. You're from Rojava, you know home rule."

The daughter shielded her eyes from the sun. "You are the lover of Sara?"

Ruqia touched her heart. "I'm not sure how you know that, but, yes. I am proud to say it."

"You don't hate us?" Fidan said.

All breath left Ruqia's body. "Oh, I hate you. That's why I want you to come to Council."

The garish women looked at each other, eyes narrowed.

"Most people who come to Equal Voice have strong feelings," Ruqia said. "But Gran is skilled at bringing us to common ground. I will be her lieutenant."

"What's in it for us?" Fidan asked, one eye peering up from her glittery gold hijab.

A deep sadness filled Ruqia's heart: her beloved Sara was forced to scrub floors and wash toilets for this horrible woman. A Turkish prison, or imminent death, might be better than enslavement to this she-devil.

Ruqia walked away, pulling her cane out of the sand, step by step until she came upon the Council space that Gonul had prepared. Kurdish women sat in a circle, dotted with a few men. Gran had done a fine job of bringing people to this circle in the sand that was their new table of democracy.

The meeting was difficult, everyone distracted by hunger and thirst, no one getting enough water in the daily ration, or enough pea cactus squares. Children were getting sick, old people losing the light in their eyes. Everyone could taste the salt in the de-salinized water, often more dehydrating than quenching.

The slightest mention of the word *dehydration* was reported to make Ataturka turn bright red and whirl like a top. This brought a united cheer from everyone on the Council. Gran used this every time she needed to get attention, or remind participants that they were united against one enemy.

The meeting lasted for days as people came and went from the ration line. After many ideas had been debated, rejected, resurrected, and put to a vote, a plan was devised to approach the Beirut Regional Desalinization Project with an offer of volunteer labor, in hopes of tripling the capacity of the plant.

"There may be no way out of this exile," Gran said. "But we must move forward together, hoping eventually to immigrate to northern countries." No one believed this, but they didn't say so, and shook Gran's hand in gratitude for the glimmer of self-determination. Ruqia noticed that the women in the Council all wore brightly colored, handsome hijabs. Gran looked like a waif in her mother's old scarf.

At sunset, Ruqia dug deep into her pack to find a treasure buried at the bottom: Sara's lemon-yellow silk hijab. Ruqia had touched it in the darkness of the cave, before she knew the woman who wore it. It was time for it to be re-purposed. She knew Sara would approve.

That night, a full resplendent moon rose over the masses of refugees sleeping in clumps along the beach. Ruqia and Gonul led Gran into the surf, ceremoniously peeling the threadbare hijab from her silver hair. Gran folded it, kissed it, and set it afloat in the sea. They watched as the waves rocked it, until it disappeared.

Ruqia took out Sara's lemon-yellow hijab and curled it around Gran's silver hair, the very hijab that Gita Roxan had worn to unify people in Rojava at the Council of Equal Voice.

Gran's face shone, bright as the moon. She held out one arm to the sky, the other to the Earth. "Twirl with me," she said. "This night we thank Allah, for our lives, for our love." She spun slowly, her bare feet moving along the tide line, one foot on sand, the other in the shallows.

Ruqia felt tenderness, watching her old friend twirl, Sara's hijab white in the light of the full moon. Gran had suffered great loss in her life, but she was settled in her heart and in her faith.

Ruqia longed to be like Gran, to know such sturdiness in herself. Ruqia knew only a perpetual restlessness that calmed only in the heat of battle or the passion of love. Bereft of both, her soul was out to sea, like Gran's discarded hijab.

Gonul lifted one hand to the sky, the other to the Earth, rotating awkwardly, "I'm getting dizzy."

"Keep your eyes on the hand pointing down," Gran said.

Gonul obeyed, turning with more ease, "Come on, R—"

"I don't believe in God, and who wants a gimp Dervish?"

"Your mind can spin all the bullshit it wants," Gran said, pulling Ruqia into the surf. "God loves your soul, Ruqia. He doesn't bother with the rest."

Gonul took Ruqia's arm, spinning her slowly, "Tonight, we dance the Sufi swirl," he said. "It's what the water wants."

Ruqia pulled away from him, struggled, fell, and came to standing on her own. After many attempts, Ruqia relaxed into her own "gimp version" of the whirling Dervish.

The three friends felt a quiet joy as they twirled side by side in the ebbing tide.

30 – Kethuda

HER father's footsteps shuffled in the hall outside her door. Kethuda touched her finger to her temple: In-Phone reading, 12:10 AM.

"May I help you, sir?" Eng's voice was calm, professional. He must have relieved his sister on watch. Kethuda slipped out of bed, one ear to the door.

"Stand aside, man. I need to see my daughter." Hamza's voice was gruff. She had not seen him since the split in the Turkish military, the old soldiers pledging fidelity to her father, the newer ones, mostly women and young men, pledging loyalty to their President, Ataturka. She was secretly amazed, determined to live up to their trust and hope.

"The President is sleeping, sir." Eng's voice was gentle but firm.

"No need to wake her. I just want to…." his voice trailed off.

Kethuda knew exactly what he wanted. There were many nights when she woke with her father's head on her breast, her gown soaked with his tears. Compassion and revulsion moved through her body, like mighty trade winds blowing in opposite directions.

"You are welcome to make an appointment, sir."

"An appointment? Who the hell are you?"

"My name is Eng, sir."

"I am her father."

Eng did not reply. Kethuda imagined his ancestors, the Maasai warriors, contemplating how to handle an old crocodile.

"Sir, you have the right granted to all citizens to request an appointment."

"Stand aside, man. You have no authority over me."

"With respect, sir. I am in the service of the President. Are you questioning her authority?"

Hamza's voice was like a termite, boring in, "Do you have children?"

Kethuda pressed her ear closer to the door.

"I have not been blessed with wife and child," Eng said. "I understand you had a wife of legendary beauty and devotion, and now your daughter rules the land. You are truly blessed among men."

Why am I relieved he has no family? Kethuda rested her head against the door.

"Since her mother's passing, my daughter is all I have."

"Yes, sir."

"So. Let me in."

"I cannot, sir. Please, do not pressure me to use force."

"I know what you're doing, you and your sister and the ruffians guarding the Kurd. I could have you and your sister executed on either side of that girl, like the thieves and Jesus. How about that?"

"Do you want a revolution, sir?" Eng's voice was as sharp as rubies dropping on a silver plate.

Hamza spat and stomped, and, pulling his last card, wept like a wounded child.

"I am sorry, sir. Your pain must be very great, but you cannot see the President. Not tonight."

"I'll have your head in the morning."

Eng was silent. Kethuda held her breath.

Hamza stomped away, muttering threats under his breath. She exhaled, "Is he gone?"

"Yes, Madam. Are you alright?"

"You knew I was here?"

"I could feel you, behind the door." His voice was gentle.

She wanted to be close to him, to break her vow. *What did Cyrus the Great build his success upon? Openness, humanity, liberality…chastity…*

"I won't sleep tonight," she said, opening the door. Aware that he was seeing her in her sheer white nightgown. "Follow me—" She pulled on a black cloak, and they walked quietly down the secret fire escape into the street.

The Kurd's prison cell was gray, the air steamy. When Kethuda's eyes adjusted to the light, she could see the prisoner, wide awake, having pulled her mattress onto the floor: a compromise to her moral stance never to lie down in a Turkish bed. A hopeful sign.

Kethuda's chair rested upside down like a cockeyed skeleton. Eng set it aright, testing it for sturdiness. He nodded, holding it for her as she sat, staring at his long strong hands.

"A good chair," he said. "You could not break it, Madam." She smiled.

The Kurd stared at them, not moving.

"We thought you might be hungry," Eng said, sliding a tray of olives, pea cactus bread, and water into the cell. He leaned close to his mistress, "Shall I stay, Madam?"

Kethuda felt the warmth of his body, but this was not the time to give way to unbidden desire. "No, Eng, thank you. Please leave us."

He paused, walking over to a crack in the wall behind her, pulling out his opal-handled Maasai knife. He dug a tiny e-camera out of the stone, tossing it to the ground and smashing it with his feet.

Such strong, elegant feet.

"Thank you, Eng," she said. He bowed and walked away, her eyes following the line of his back, his legs. When she glanced up, the Kurd darted her eyes away: *the little bitch has been watching me.*

Kethuda peeled off her black robe, revealing her sheer white nightgown. She was determined not to speak first.

The Kurd walked to the tray, looking at the food and water as if it were a work of art. She drank, licking her lips, savoring every swallow; picked up an olive, holding it to the moonlight, turning it like a rare jewel. She bit it, closing her eyes to dam her tears. She ate each olive in this way, sipping the water slowly. When she finished, she returned to the mattress, putting the bread beside her pillow.

Kethuda leaned back, breathing slowly.

The two women remained in silence for some time, the only sound the clicking of some random bird's toenails on the barred window high above.

"Where am I?" the Kurd asked. "This isn't where Sakine Cansiz was imprisoned. I'll bet you've never seen pictures of her. Not what you might call beautiful, but I would. She was so *alive*: thin face, wild hennaed hair, her mouth tight with defiance. Am I in some rotten tower in Istanbul?"

Kethuda suppressed a smile: *the girl spoke; this is progress.* "No. Istanbul is being dismantled and reassembled inland. You are in the ancient prison of Murad, in the capital city of Ankara."

"So dark and stinky, it must be death row."

Kethuda lifted an eyebrow: *the girl is brave.* "That depends entirely on you, Fatima Roxan."

The Kurd laughed, mocking, and bitter, "My stepmother, the lovely woman who sold me for a well called me 'Fato'. Always trying to make me feel ugly."

"I'm sorry."

"Why?" the Kurd said.

Kethuda lifted her feet and propped them on the bottom rung of the chair. She didn't want the soles of her gilded sandals to touch the filth of the cold pea-concrete floor. "I was blessed to have a mother who thought I was the most beautiful creature in the world."

"My mother thought that too. She was a very great, and courageous woman, a super loving mom." Kethuda glanced down, a wave of sadness welling in her eyes as she recalled the scent of wild violets in her mother's long dark hair as Ayse carried her on her shoulders across the meadow.

The Kurd sat up, crossing her legs. "What are you thinking?"

"Just now?" Kethuda said. "You stare at me, Kurd, like I'm a specimen under glass."

"Don't people stare at you like that all the time?"

Kethuda sighed, "The way you talked about your mother. I was thinking of mine."

"You said you were nursing your dying mother when mine was killed. Who killed your mother?"

"Why do you want to know?"

The Kurd looked down, "It doesn't matter. None of this does. I was just trying to imagine how much you hate me."

"Kurds didn't murder my mother, so we are not tit for tat on that score. My Ayse died from the last strain of cancer in the twenty-first century."

The Kurd looked into the darkness, searching for Kethuda's eyes, "That sucks."

"Yes," Kethuda stood up, pulling her robe up to keep it off the floor. "It's not so much that I hate *you*, you're a symbol."

The Kurd laughed. "Do me a favor. Don't lie. I may be a clever symbol for your political gain, but let's be honest: you hate *me*, and you'll have me tortured if I don't tell you a bunch of shit."

Kethuda stared, "What if we drop the topic of death and torture, just for tonight?"

The Kurd's eyes seemed to darken with a hint of surprise.

Kethuda wiped sweat from her chin, "When I come here, I always find you awake. Do you ever sleep?"

The Kurd stared at the remaining water in her cup. "Not since that day your bombs killed my mother. I must sleep sometimes. I dream."

Kethuda straightened her spine. "I don't sleep through the night either. Not since my mother died, and my father started…." She stopped.

"What?"

"My father never got over the loss." She knew the Kurd saw underneath this tepid answer: those damn unmoving eyes. "So, do you catch up on your sleep in the day time?"

The Kurd answered as if flipping a coin toss, "All the time. A friend jokes that I'm the only soldier she knows who can fall asleep waiting for the war to start."

"What friend?"

The Kurd laughed, "You know better than that. Go ahead, pull out my fingernails."

"I just happened to bring my torture tweezers—" Kethuda reached into her pocket and pulled out an empty hand, waving it, laughing.

The Kurd's laughter went up a notch.

Kethuda combed her mind for other ways to get to this mysterious child. Kurds were said to be a bizarre race, one foot in the ordinary world, one foot in some hazy half-forgotten realm of spirit. "What do you dream about, Fatima?"

"Why would I tell you?"

Kethuda lounged across one arm of her chair, "No reason I can think of, unless it could be to your advantage to show me something that challenges my view of you as a terrorist."

The Kurd glanced into her tin cup. "I dream of water. I'm standing on the shore of an extraordinary ocean, not the Mediterranean, something much larger that swells all the way up to the sky. All the stars are out, shining so bright I have to shade my eyes. Then the sun comes out, moving across the water until every wave pulses with light—and the stars?—*They're still there*—in broad daylight, shining as bright as the sun."

Kethuda closed her eyes, seeing the vision so clearly, she put out her hand as if to touch the sun, the sea, the stars.

"You see it?" the Kurd said. "Or are you pretending?"

Kethuda was surprised at her answer. "I see it."

"For real?"

"For real."

"I don't know what that dream means," the Kurd said, "but it haunts me, like somebody's trying to show me another universe, larger and wider and deeper than I ever imagined."

"Yes," Kethuda said. "I felt that once, a long time ago, when Mama took me to the mosque and we swirled in the circle with other Sufi. I got dizzy, but I felt it for a moment, what you said, something bigger... Mama said we were dancing with God."

The Kurd seemed surprised, her eyes wide in disbelief, but she did not criticize or make a snap judgment. She said nothing at all.

Kethuda was confused. She had not thought of that moment in the mosque in many years. The Kurd was sending black magic: watch out.

They sat in silence, sensing each other's presence.

The Kurd took a sip of water, "What do you dream, Madam President?"

My own dreams—oh, my God... Kethuda held onto the bars, trying to control her panic. *I must not reveal myself to this child...*

The Kurd rose and moved closer in the muted moonlight. "I told you my dream. Tell me yours."

Kethuda paced, visions from her dreams pouring forth.

"What you see is horrible, right?" the Kurd said, with no mockery.

Kethuda's belly contracted, as if in childbirth.

The Kurd said, "Tell me. What have you got to lose? My life is a throw-away."

"Why do you want to know?" Kethuda said, struggling for breath.

The Kurd moved into shadow. "I don't always dream of water and sun and stars."

"You're ashamed of something," Kethuda said, panting. "I know about shame. I dream of Turkish soldiers ripped to pieces, rivers of blood in the sand. Kurds advancing only to be blown into the air, their bodies falling in pieces, like rain. I did not hide in my Ankara apartment. I was *there*, on the battlefield."

"I saw you on your white horse above the troops."

"You saw me?"

The Kurd sighed. "I thought, 'we cannot beat them. They have a goddess on their side.'"

"You really thought that?"

"I did. I hate you for it."

Kethuda closed her eyes, "I had to see it for myself. The soldiers were grateful that I showed up. They protected me from being killed, but they could not protect me from what I saw, what I *still* see." Kethuda had not spoken these words, even to Gai. She felt liberated to say them to her enemy. "What do you see, Sara Sakine Cansiz?"

"I don't have to tell you."

Kethuda smiled: *now we're getting somewhere.* "You're a coward, Ms. YPJ. You can slaughter my soldiers, but you can't tell me your nightmares."

The Kurd slammed her palm onto the bars. "Shut up! What do you know? Did you shoot somebody? No. *You're* the coward. You let your soldiers do all the murdering for you. I dream of blood on my body, on my hands. I accidentally killed an ISIS Commander. I see her face every night in my dreams."

"To hell with ISIS; did you kill my Turks?"

"Yes, you bitch. I killed a boy. His black uniform was too big for his skinny frame. He died on my breast. Every night I dream I push his heart back into his body and breathe in his mouth, but he still dies."

A sadness swept over Kethuda's heart.

The Kurd said, "I dream of your soldiers killing my beloved. I watched it happen. I couldn't do anything. She was a great warrior. All my loves may be dead. At your command." She crawled back to the mattress, her small body heaving with rage and grief.

Kethuda wanted to shout in triumph, but all she could do was stare at the sobbing Kurd. She had no more words. No more feelings, only exhaustion. She crawled down onto the filthy floor, oddly not caring. *I will rest, just for a moment.*

As the beams of the traveling moon came down from the high window, Kethuda and the Kurd fell asleep on opposite sides of the cell.

31 – Ruqia

THE Equal Voice Council got what they wanted. Refugee volunteers were conscripted by the Beirut Desalinization Project to increase fresh water production. This brought no increase in rations for the refugees. Gonul and Ruqia did night reconnaissance, discovering that the surplus water was being loaded onto Moon Shuttles and sent to an encampment of rich squatters in the dry Dead Sea.

The next day Gran went with them through the towering castles of brine, to the office of the top executive. After waiting eight hours with no rations, they were finally admitted to his office, sculpted in mahogany pea cactus to resemble a twentieth-century boardroom.

Gran spoke diplomatically. Ruqia was blunt: "Our people are volunteering their labor, increasing the output of your plant, and you're using us for your own profit."

The executive was a slender Turk with a mustache like a raven's beak, "We can't just give our extra water to you people. We have a bottom line. If we make no profit, we will have to close down altogether, and where would that leave your tired, your thirsty, your huddled masses?"

"You dare to use those words," Ruqia said, her face burning with rage. "Where is your beacon of hope? Your Lady Liberty?"

"Ahhh," the executive said with a droll sigh. "She's right outside the window, sculpted in salt."

"One day they will bury you in your own brine," Gonul said.

"We could go on strike," said Gran.

The executive rose, indicating the meeting was over, "If you do that, I will suspend rations, and your Equal Voice Council can bury the dead."

"We screwed ourselves," Gran said, walking out.

Ruqia stared at the Turk's bullet-train mustache, contemplating her signature *double-sole*. Ooh, what glory to fly through the air and smack her enemy in the face with both boots.

Gonul whispered, "You can probably still do it, R, but they would kill you."

She limped out, away from Gonul, away from Gran, finding respite that night, alone, at the shore. *I am not Sara. I can't sacrifice my life for democracy. If I stay here, I will die.* It was simple truth. The rising tide slapped her ankles. Darkness stretched over the ocean, the water reflecting the brilliance of the stars. She noted its beauty, but nothing could soothe the grinding energy in her body. *I was not made for this prison of passivity, waiting, waiting, for a deliverance that will never come.*

Strength left her body. She bent over, sliding her leg onto the sand, holding her cast, picturing the reality of the wound beneath the hard shell. A wave of tenderness came over her for this body destroyed by a force outside of nature. "Dear Crumbled Leg, I've been mean to you. Cussing you out for being smashed up and not serving me the way you used to. Like your whole job was taking me where I wanted to go. Sorry about that."

"You're talking to your leg?"

She smiled, catching the humor in Gonul's voice.

"Why not? Should I name it?"

"Why not?" He sat in the sand beside her. She noticed new lines in his face, a tightness in his fierce brown eyes, his long hair tangled as if reflecting the landscape of his heart.

"How long have you known you had to leave?" he asked.

She smiled, "You know me well. A warrior, even a damaged one, doesn't sit on the beach."

"I've been waiting for you."

"This is my deal, not yours."

"That's why I've been stalking you," he said. "Afraid you would hop on the Moon Shuttle in the middle of the night."

She snorted, "You don't have to tell me I'm crazy. I am. I have no idea how to shoot a rifle with one hand while holding this infernal cane with the other."

"If it comes to that."

"It will."

The ocean lapped higher against their feet.

"I need to learn how to shoot with one hand."

His face was all business. "I'll make a sling for your arm, to hold the rifle in place while you fire."

"You can do that?"

"Wherever you're going, I'm coming with you."

"You're a scholar, not a warrior. Why do you want to do this?"

"I can't sit here and rot any more than you can. I need your warrior mind; your warrior heart."

She looked far out to sea, her eyes moist, "Thank you."

"Of course, General R."

She smirked, "General Cripple."

"History tells us otherwise: Lord Nelson lost an arm. He did all right."

"You and your damned enthusiasm. Bad as Gran."

"What about her?"

Sadness filled Ruqia's chest, "She'll be mad at me."

He whistled in agreement. "She's too old for this mission. And, she's needed here, to teach people Equal Voice democracy."

"What if they can never use it?" Ruqia said.

"Then they need it even more." Gonul's face was soft in starlight, his eyes resting on her with gentleness. *He is looking at me, not as a lover, but, what?* Her mind stopped, her eyes looking down at her toes, hidden momentarily by sea foam. "Mr. Askay, Gonul, I may need to ask you…"

"Yes?"

Her mouth was so dry she could barely speak, and yet she did: "I may need to ask you for *help*, not just making the sling so I can shoot, but also other stuff…"

"It's so hard for you to ask?"

"Impossible."

He suddenly pulled away her cane. She reached for it, struggled to get up, and then—as if reaching from Venus to Earth—reached her hand out and let him take it and pull her up. She fell into his chest, breathing hard, laughing at herself.

"Not so terrible, was it?" he asked, holding the pea cactus cane on the surface of the incoming tide. "The pea cactus was engineered to absorb liquid from a body of water."

"Even salt water?"

"More so. It filters out the salt. I'm not sure how."

"You don't know the how? You know everything."

They giggled, watching the cane grow thick as it absorbed water from the sea. They packed up a few *salties* and pea cactus squares and stole out past the ghoulish towers of brine to the Moon Shuttle, its photosynthetic panels tucked underneath, like a great snoozing beetle. The Shuttle did not absorb energy from the moon, but ran at night on stored sun-thesis. This Shuttle, apparently, was out of commission until dawn.

Three Turkish soldiers sat beside it, smoking, laughing, polishing the metal handles of their e-arrow rifles.

"What's going on?" Gran said, coming up beside them.

"We have to find Sara," Ruqia said in a horse whisper.

"We'll free her and find the Water Thread," said Gonul.

"You're out of your minds," Gran said. "Your friend, Joseph, and those other Scientists for Humanity, they have the Water Thread. They don't want to be found—not by you—certainly not by the Turks, who will be on your ass."

Ruqia placed a hand firmly on Gran's furrowed forehead. "The Thread is our only bargaining chip. Without it, we're forever at the mercy of the Turks."

"You'll dehydrate out there."

"I'd rather die in the desert than wait for the Turks to drive us into the sea."

Gran turned to Gonul, "You'll take the cripple with you, but not a senior warrior?"

He took Gran's hands. "This community needs you to run Equal Voice."

She hissed softly, "I knew after I left Aleppo, I would never have a partner, or children. I couldn't bear the loss. But you two, and Little Mama, opened my heart, damn you. You're my family."

"Then Allah will bring us back to you," Ruqia said, astonished at her own words.

Gonul glanced at the soldiers lounging by the Shuttle. "Tonight, we ask one last service from you, Gran." She laughed wickedly when she heard the plan. They embraced with muffled tears.

Gran went back to camp and shook Fidan and Nazan out of snoring slumber, "You stole pea cactus from the ration bin!" she screamed, dragging them by the ears toward the Turkish soldiers. The startled women howled. The soldiers scrambled, tossing away their cigarettes.

Ruqia and Gonul snuck past the racket to the back door of the Shuttle. "Tickle the great beast's belly," Ruqia said as Gonul shot a silent e-arrow into the crack of the door. It would not open.

"It won't budge without sunlight," he said, cursing, pulling Ruqia beneath the snoozing Shuttle. "We'll wait 'til dawn."

Soon he fell asleep, his face close to hers. A peaceful, beautiful face, his dark beard catching a sliver of moonlight. *A face Sara loves.*

Sleep did not come to Ruqia. The soldiers returned to their post. She choked on the smell of their sweat and tobacco, shivering with fear and excitement. Whatever was to come: death, discovery, saving the world or ending it, she had the sensation of sailing out on a dark sea in a boat she did not command. Someone else was at the helm, but the fog was so dense, she couldn't see who it was, if anyone was there at all.

She lay beside Gonul, her eyes wide open, until the warming of dawn opened the Shuttle door. They crawled in and hid under the seats as the giant wings awakened, stretching toward the sun, propelling them at lightning speed into the desert.

32 – Kethuda

SHE stirred, unsure if she was awake or in a luxurious state of dreamless sleep. Her eyes blinked at the white brilliance of the afternoon sun. She was in her canopy bed, the sheer white curtains billowing in the window. *I feel like a character in a fable who has slept a hundred years.* Her body was sticky, her hair matted to her neck. Then she remembered: her sleep had come on the pea-concrete floor outside the Kurd's prison cell. As Kethuda had fallen asleep, she heard the Kurd softly snoring.

Gai extended a tall glass of water.

"What time is it?"

"Two o'clock, Madam."

"In the afternoon?"

"Yes, Madam. My brother carried you here from the prison. He was very careful not to wake you. It is a blessing from Engai, that you slept so long."

Kethuda drank the tall glass of fresh water, "Do you know of the Temple of Asclepius?"

"The Greek god of medicine? I did not know he had a temple."

"A Temple of Dreams. People came, scholars and slaves alike, to sleep together and tap into the healing property of dreams."

"Did you dream, sleeping with the Kurd?"

"I did. I was burrowing through hidden passageways. I was not alone, but I couldn't see who was beside me....Where is your brother?"

"On guard outside the door."

There was a stirring in Kethuda's breast, in her loins. How strange to think that this man, a warrior among warriors in his own country, was reduced to standing guard outside a door. "Tell me more about your brother."

Gai's ebony eyes followed the movement of the sheer curtains in the window. "In the years before the perma-drought, Eng was a soldier in the great Chino-African war. Kenya and Tanzania led the insurrection against our colonizers. Eng was gifted, not only as a soldier, but with the pen. He wrote many essays and posted them on the old Internet. There was no RAT back then, no energy quota, so he was free to write of the rights of native Africans, of justice, and the need for a universal code defining the common good. The International Court in the Haag had attempted to assert this back in the twentieth century, but global consensus never happened, even as climate change swept the world."

Kethuda was entranced. "And now?"

Gai filled Kethuda's water glass, "Since the end of African habitation, my brother and I are like all other African water refugees, dancing for our supper. My brother is a much better dancer than I."

Kethuda blushed, "Promise me that one day I will see him dance. If he is anything like his sister—"

Gai cocked her head, with an impish smile, "Shall I have Eng come in?"

Kethuda nodded, rising from her bed, reaching for her black cloak.

He entered, bowing. "Your father has been here three times."

"He's in a frenzy?"

"No, Madam, oddly, he seems quite calm."

"My father is only calm when he's plotting something. How is recruitment for my army?"

Eng's face was calm, a shadow of sadness in his dark eyes. "It is not robust, Madam. It is a great happiness that some young women and men of the Turkish army have stayed with you, but we must recruit from the common people if we are to be any match for the soldiers loyal to your father."

"I need to go among my people."

He looked at her without blinking. "I believe they know who you are. They also believe your free will is the property of your father."

Kethuda paced the room, pausing to touch the glass dome covering the statue of the Seated Woman of Catalhoyuk, "They get mixed signals from me: Earth Goddess one minute, Catherine the Great the next."

Eng and Gai exchanged a glance of amusement, but the tone in Eng's voice was serious, "Yes, Madam. Something must be done to clear up this confusion in your image."

"My father's soldiers are idiots. They found the laboratory of the Water Thread, but couldn't identify a paper clip."

"It is an ancient artifact, Madam," Gai and Eng said in unison. She poked him in the belly; he grabbed her hand. She tickled him behind the ears. He giggled, "Please, little sister, no more!"

Kethuda wanted to tickle them both: to cut loose, to be so close, so silly, so loving.

"Oh, Madam, I am sorry. We forgot ourselves," Eng said.

Gai straightened her posture, shooting an impish glance at her brother. He smiled back warmly.

Kethuda remembered the Turkish people in the Water Square. They were not giggling or tickling each other. There was no energy for simple joy when they were worried about having enough water. "We have offered the citizens good money to join our army. They don't care. They want a guarantee of rations. I'm selling too much water to the Israelis and the Saudis. I will draft letters closing their accounts, saving all the water for our own people."

"Madam, can you do that?" Gai asked.

"I can. I am the President." Her heart stopped for a beat. *Where did this courage come from?* When she was with Sara, the rest of the world went away. No anxiety over alienating Nina Navalny, or what Elena Maria Juarez would write in *The New Yorker*, or if the secretive Chinese would find a way to poach Turkiye's water. The time with Sara had an energy all its own. *Am I poaching courage from my enemy? If so, so be it!*

"Gai, would you help me write the 'dear John,' letters? Eng, if you would spread the word among the people that I am prioritizing their water supply. No more selling to foreign customers. Ask them to join my army to fight my father."

Eng reached for his sister's hand. "It is very dangerous, what you propose, Madam President. My sister could be in harm's way for helping you compose such letters to powerful allies of your father."

Gai withdrew her hand. "Do not protect me, brother. We both know how much courage it takes for our Madam President to make this choice. It is more dangerous than for you to share this information with the people. If you like, I will do that and you can stay here and help her write the letters."

"We are all in danger," Eng said. "I will go. Your work is here, sister."

Gai reached for her brother, held him close. He touched her nose. "I will be careful." With a bow to Kethuda, he left. She watched him disappear, her body warm with longing, "Let's get this over with, Gai."

They made quick work of it, composing the letters and sending them swiftly over the In-Phone to Israel and Saudi Arabia.

A familiar fist pounded on the door.

"Ready your weapon, Gai. And bring strong coffee."

She went onto the balcony. A haze covered the buildings of Ankara, voices echoing up from the street: "Mommy, wait for me," a little girl called, the *click click* of her tiny feet running on the stones. Bells jingled on a ferry-cycle. Far in the distance, an *oud* player wailed a ballad.

"What is that song?" Kethuda asked.

"Kurdish, Madam. The *Goren,* a song in the rhythm of the heart." Gai opened the door and retreated into the shadows as Hamza stormed into the room.

"You sent the Black man away?" Hamza said, striding onto the balcony.

She did not look up. "Coffee?"

"You look like Hell."

"I love you too, Papa."

"Don't be mean."

She forced herself to look at the creases around his mouth, a deeper dull brown. "Can you think of one reason why I should be kind, Papa?"

He splashed coffee from the carafe into his cup. "I took *charge.* You wallowed in your women's crap, being so *nice* to the Kurd, dancing with your naked Gai, making googly eyes at that Egyptian male."

"He is not Egyptian, Papa. He is Maasai, like his sister, who no longer has to dance naked for anyone."

"That's irrelevant. Our people want a strong leader who is not afraid to execute terrorists."

Rage swept over her. "*My* people. I've been out among them. They want water, and they want the sustainability of the Water Thread. I need the Kurd alive, to tell me where it is. You would execute our only hope just to prove you're more powerful than I?"

"I don't have to prove anything. I *am* more powerful than you. If you must, have the girl tortured to find out if this mythical device exists. Put those pictures on the World Board. Then people will know how tough you are, and they will relax."

She stood completely still, taking solace in the far distant *shuuuush* of the pump in Water Square, remembering her long night with the people: *without the Water Thread, we are doomed.* "I will find out what the Kurd knows. It is what my people want." She added under her breath, "It is what the water wants."

He leaned toward her, the fleshy skin under his watery eyes baby pink in the sunlight. "You don't have the balls to torture her."

Kethuda lurched away from him, revolted by the smell of his aging skin and rancid breath. "She is my prisoner. Stay away from her, or my soldiers will come after you." Her heart fluttered, her palms sweating. *He knows that fewer soldiers have taken my side. But that will change. I have used my power to cancel the contract with his customer-chums.*

His laugh was like a donkey coughing up phlegm. "Your soldiers? What a child you are. When it comes down to it, not one man in all Turkiye would raise a hand against me."

"I am no child, and you are an old man, full of delusions."

He called to the heavens, "Ayse, did you have an affair? This kid did not come from my seed."

Kethuda breathed more easily: *if he's calling for Mama, he is deeply rattled.* "Mother is proud of me, watching us in this very moment from some distant star."

He leapt from his chair, seized her, pulled her breast to his face, sobbing. Her body stiffened. Gai moved toward the balcony with her rifle. Kethuda motioned for her to stay back, and yet, something was changing in the heart of the President. In the past she would have felt empathy for her father as he wept like a baby on her breast. In this moment, she felt *nothing.* Neither revulsion nor rage, nor love; just a quiet, yawning emptiness.

Sensing it, he pulled away and searched her face for a morsel of sympathy. He found none. "You will pay for this," he said, angrily wiping away tears. "You always *pay.*" He left quickly.

Silence settled in, even in the street below.

"Shall I draw your dry bath, Madam?"

"Yes, thank you."

The reflection of the sun on the glass dome of Seated Woman filled the room with brilliant shards of light. Kethuda stared, letting it sear her eyes. If she didn't feel sorry for her father, did she need him at all? And what of this pinnacle—or was it a chasm—of emptiness? Who would understand her deepest feelings and how they were changing, not from her own will, but from some mysterious source guiding her from within?

The answer was surprising: the same person she might choose to torture, to put to death, not to please her father, but for all the Turkish soldiers who died at the hands of the Kurds; and to secure her reign in the eyes of her people, as Turkiye's Virgin Queen.

33 – Gai

THIS night she traded her black hoodie for one of Kethuda's light hooded gowns. If she was caught, she would use the excuse that it needed to be laundered with dry pea-powder. The hoodie was too warm to wear, now that the temperature had warmed again. A spike that had not been expected until a decade into the twenty-second century. Many scientists said the Earth could actually be cooling, due to the abundance of synthetic photosynthetic energy. No one wanted to talk about how much the burning of fossil fuels had played into the population explosion in the twentieth and twenty-first centuries, and what a wound it had made in Mother Earth, and how long it would take to heal.

Gai dismissed these thoughts as she hurried through the street. Clouds hung over the city, cloaking it in a sticky humidity. And rain? Not the wispy things in the sky this night. Rain clouds were a distant memory: dark, monstrous, belching thunder and lightning and rain, torrents of rain. People ran out into it, mouths open, laughing, crying, made whole, body and soul.

Gai smiled at the memory of her *yeyo*, putting out buckets to catch the rain. Maybe the warming temperature was on the minds of the Sisterhood of African Mothers and Daughters? She had been getting signals that they needed to talk.

Gai scaled the parked ferry-cycle and curled into the lover's swing at the top of the wheel, wiping her sweating face on the tail of Kethuda's gown. She brushed her breast, stopping abruptly at the left nipple. *Not the left one!! Not yet.* Her finger found the right nipple. *Close call.* Voices and faces of her beloved women crowded into her private In-Phone.

The round woman on the roof in New Orleans was playing the trumpet, the water level sloshing at her feet.

"What are you doing, sister?" Gai shouted over the rapturous notes. "Playing a farewell like the orchestra on the Titanic?"

"It's happening too fast," said the horn player. "Our President, that gnarly ole Mr. Boatwright, is coming to us on a Sun Show Boat that's gonna take us up the dry Mississippi Riverbed to higher ground. General Gai, I'm in a powerful grief. I thought I'd live and die in New Orleans, the only home I've ever known." She played a mournful riff, the other women on the In-Phone shouting "We are with you, sister." "Love you, precious," and so much wailing. The ferry cycle vibrated, and Gai grabbed a bell to keep it from ringing.

A stylish woman from a boarding house in Ireland said, "Sister, you have to take New Orleans with you. I had to vacate my home in San Francisco, once the most beautiful city on Earth. Every night, I rub my chest and say, 'You're with me, San Francisco!'"

Gai wrestled with her conscience. Should she tell the women about the Water Thread? It was in the World Board Press, but most people outside Turkiye laughed it off as a cruel joke. Should she give her women hope that one day, there could be technology that would take the water flooding New Orleans and San Francisco, deprive it of its salt, and fill reservoirs in Arizona, Texas, California.... Of course, she would have to confess that she knew about the Water Thread by eavesdropping on her mistress and the Kurd. The Sisters might be curious about her motives, and this would open a can of worms Gai was not ready to touch.

"You are quiet, General," said the elderly woman, fanning herself more slowly on her porch in Paris. "It's getting hotter here. Have you noticed where you are?"

Murmurs of agreement flooded in.

The woman and daughter harvesting water from melting glaciers in Antarctica complained that the pace of the melting had increased.

The women in the colony of New Africa in Greenland reported the opposite: the temperature in their pocket of the world was getting colder.

The water engineer in Japan said that her lab was working on a fantastic new technology, but it would be years before it was finalized.

Gai's heart drummed in counterpoint to the swaying of the lover's swing. *I should tell them about the reality of the Water Thread. I should give them hope!*

The young poet at the Parthenon was optimistic. "They said it would take a century to perfect synthetic photosynthesis. It only took fifty years."

This inspired a cheer and calls for a song. "Lead us, General," said the woman on the roof with her trumpet. "You got them pretty soprano pipes will lift our spirits and hearts— Oh, here it comes," she said suddenly, as a mighty Sun Showboat docked on her roof, its photosynthetic panels painted to look like paddlewheels. Old Southern music played, "Swing low, sweet chariot...."

Sam Boatwright himself stepped out onto the roof in his white pea cactus suit and broad-brimmed hat, took her hand and guided her away.

The African Sisterhood cheered her on as the New Orleans feed faded to black.

Gai picked up the sorrowful mood, announcing in a rousing voice, "Ms. San Francisco, out there in Ireland, will you sing us that famous song, handed down through the centuries, 'I Left My Heart in San Francisco'?"

The stylish woman took up the challenge, belting out the song as thousands of others joined in.

Gai did not sing with them. She listened, feeling their pain and grief and, wonderfully, the sliver of hope in every voice. Did she dare believe that one day, she could call them and shout, "Sisters, Mothers, Africans, we have a Water Thread that will heal the world"?

34 – Sara

SHE climbed slowly up the back wall of her cell, brick, by brick. *I can make it to the top, and if I fall…a coward's way out?*

She took a deep breath, hefted the toe of her boot onto the brick above. The workmanship on the wall was so clumsy, it provided a climbing wall for the insane. She grabbed onto sharp corners as her feet found one more jutting brick, another, and then she seized the iron bar and reached the window.

She found no moon in the night sky, no pulse of light from a star, only a milky haze. But being near the window, the ringing of little bells made her think of her old tricycle, and the scent of pea-paprika stew was like Mamoo's chicken-in-a-pot.

"Cha cha cha cha," she called into the night.

Silence, broken by the distant laughter of children singing rhymes.

Rexie II did not come.

The thump of footsteps echoed in the stairwell. Her heart quickened, her palms moistening. She climbed down quickly. *Wait too long and my hands will be too slippery to get down safely.* She scoffed. "Safely?" This could be soldiers coming to torture her to death. If so, wouldn't she hear the sound of boots? Could it be Ataturka, her face hidden behind a mask so thick she would fall over from its weight? Sara giggled with hysterical anxiety, imagining the queen crashing forward onto the floor.

Ataturka entered, followed by the Black woman.

Sara muffled her giggle: time to put on her own equally heavy mask.

The Black woman slid a tray bearing a cup and small pot into the cell. Sara inhaled the scent of Turkish coffee. *Could there be any better lure than this?*

The Black woman bowed to her mistress and left.

Holding her own cup, Ataturka sank into the chair. A column of lazy steam rose into the musty air. "Please. It tastes better if you drink it when it's hot. I know it is dehydrating. But there's plenty of water to compensate."

Sara glanced at her cup, the scent like a drug. She picked it up, sipped, the dark liquid caressing her mouth, her throat. Nothing had ever tasted so rich, so smooth. *If the divine lives in water, her soul-mate lives in Turkish coffee.*

She studied the woman before her, her square features, her snake eyes on either side of the mountainous nose. A strong face. A beautiful one. A lonely one.

"Where is he?" Sara asked.

"Who?"

"The Black man. The one you want."

Something twitched in the queen's face, just below her left eye. "Drink your coffee, Kurd."

Sara smiled: *a point for my side.* "You can talk about him to me. I know about desire. Besides, who am I going to tell?"

"There is nothing to tell," Ataturka said, unable to conceal a note of bitterness, perhaps for a father who had forced her to remain a virgin these 40 years.

Silence entered the room and, with it, a sadness not even the queen could hide. Sara sat cross-legged on the cold stone floor, the caffeine helping her hide the well of her own sadness.

Ataturka's eyes seemed to darken, and her voice spoke in a higher register, "Sara, what happened to your father?"

A hard knot of grief, tempered by rage, swelled in Sara's belly. *She wants to get at my heart. Is there some advantage I can find in giving her what she wants?* "He didn't die from your father's attack."

"I'm glad you acknowledge it wasn't me who sent the bombs to your village."

Sara said nothing. The coffee had grown bitter. She put it aside. "My father died of heart failure; his heart could not bear the loss of my mother."

"Were you close to him?"

"Why do you want to know?"

The queen looked away. "I want to know if it exists, a love of father and daughter that is not confused."

"What do you mean?"

"A confusion over where father ends and daughter begins. If that 'confusion' is shattered, what is left?"

Sara sensed that this was very vulnerable ground, and that the queen was asking it for her own personal reasons. How odd. "I don't know anything about this 'confusion.' Papa never looked to me to act like a wife or a mother to him, if that's what you mean. He was my Papa. He loved me fiercely, but his deepest, sacred bond was with his wife."

Ataturka's body seemed to slump in the chair, as if she had just witnessed a miracle. "Really? You don't know about this blurring of father and daughter? This place of intense love and violence?"

Sara held her breath. *My answer must be careful. Political, yet honest. She has an infernal nose for falseness.* "I think I know what you mean," she said, her mouth dry from the caffeine. "When my father died, I was left at the mercy of my step-mother and her daughter. I was nothing in their eyes. That was violence."

"Did you believe that? That you were nothing?"

Sara exhaled. *I must tell the truth.* "No. I remembered the love of my father and my mother, but I was so lonely I wanted to die. As lonely as I feel here. But I have never felt I am nothing. I don't know what that is."

Ataturka's shoulders curled inward. She stared at Sara, taking in the shape of the child's almond-eyes, the grime of her gnarled black hair, the dirt obscuring the camouflage pattern on her uniform.

"What do you see?" Sara asked.

"A dirty girl on the outside," Kethuda said, "on the inside, a young woman who knows who she is, a woman who was deeply loved. I hate you for it. Your father never expected you to make his grief go away with your love."

Sara sensed a great longing in the queen. *She wants* me *to make her grief go away, even as her father wants it from her.* "Papoo never let me into his grief. He held it to his heart like a precious jewel. To me he made a happy face. A false one."

"Your father didn't want you to suffer. And yet, he died and left you alone."

Sara's anger was quick, "His heart gave out because Mamoo died. Your father killed mine."

Ataturka turned away, her voice a puppet song, "The bombs of my father were meant for terrorists. Now, he has one. You. He has announced your upcoming execution before the World Board."

The room swayed, Sara's body grew weak, her mind picturing the horrified faces of Ruqia, Gonul, and Gran.

"Sorry," said the queen, her voice light as a feather.

"Monster."

"It wasn't my idea. My father wants to use your execution to make an obvious grab for power. Only I can say what happens to you, Fatima Roxan. Your fate is up to you."

Sara's heart burned, "I will tell you nothing."

Ataturka took off her vintage gold leather sandals, holding them up to the bars, her voice shaking, "Imagine your feet in my shoes. I am responsible for keeping my people in *water*—"

"While my people die."

"I don't like it, but I live in these shoes, not yours. I just cut off our water to Israel and Saudi Arabia to bring more water to my people. Those men hound me day and night—begging me to change my mind. I've blocked their In-Phone channel to Hamza, but he will find out soon and come after me. The Saudi King wants our water back, and he wants you delivered to his bedroom immediately."

Sara wrapped her arms around her belly, longing for Gonul, for R...

"I've said no to him, because I know time is running out, for all of us." She panted as if running uphill. "I need to know if it exists, your Water Thread—"

Sara gasped. "So you can poach it?"

A look of hope scampered across Ataturka's face. She leaned closer to the bars. "It is *true*.... You have it, a device that carries water through the air!"

"No. No—there is no such thing." Sara heard the false note in her voice. *Oh my God, what have I done?*

Ataturka leaned as close as she could get. "The break in Pipe 12, you know about it. You installed the Water Thread and pulled our water out of that pipe all the way to a reservoir in Rojava—"

"No! We hacked into your pipe and let it drain into the sand. Just for spite."

Ataturka's voice was oddly gentle. "Fatima Roxan, you were not born under a deceitful star."

Sara turned away, her body convulsing with shame. "You will never find it."

The queen's voice was triumphant, "Oh yes I will. You're going to lead me to it."

35 – Ruqia

As the sun descended beneath the purple sky, Ruqia allowed Gonul to help her out of the Shuttle. They were at the end of the line, the desert spread before them so flat, so dry, that no life stirred.

"Is this Rojava?" she asked.

Gonul touched his forehead. "Just below it. The Syria nobody knows."

They walked north, toward Rojava, sucking water from Ruqia's water-soaked cane and crunching *salties*. It was hard for General R, her caste sinking into the sand, her leg throbbing each time she lifted it.

Gonul looked back.

"Shut up," she said.

He nodded and went on ahead, stopping from time to time to wait for her, in spite of her fussing.

She spotted a low structure through the veil of dust. "What's that, a village?"

They walked toward it. Gonul hurried back to her. "We need to go the other way," he said, blocking her view with his body.

"Buzz off," she said, spitting dust. "You are not my superior, Mr. Askay."

"You don't want to see it, R. Trust me, please."

She stopped. "What is it?"

He opened his mouth, but no words came out. All he could do was shake his head.

She moved forward. He let her. The wind died down. In the stillness, she heard sounds coming from a long house made with dead pea cactus fronds, the roof slanted toward an opening at the top.

Ruqia heard breathing. She stepped into the doorway and pulled back a curtain of dry pea vines. People lay on the ground, close together, naked, their bodies becoming bones. A little girl was curled in her mother's arms, holding a little brown bird. No breath came from the mother or the father. The bird was still, but the child breathed very slowly, pressing her lips to the feathers of the bird.

Ruqia knelt beside the child. She stayed for a long time, as the breathing of the little girl grow slower and slower, until it stopped. She touched the thin hair of the child, the soft feathers of the bird.

Ruqia looked out across the bodies. No movement. No breath, yet a sense of peace in this Temple of Return.

After a time, she made her way back to Gonul. They sat in the sand in silence.

"Let's send these folks to wherever they think they're going," Ruqia said.

Gonul lighted the walls of the Temple. They watched the flames turn to ashes that fell across the desert in the windless sky.

Afterwards, they combed the ashes into the sand until the only remnant of the Temple and its people was a soft gray tint of the desert floor.

They walked north, saying nothing, eating the last of their *salties,* sucking out the last of their water.

At dawn the next day, they came to a cooler zone, bordered by pea cactus fields. They ate raw seedlings, squeezing out paltry moisture from new green shoots.

Gonul sent a thought message to Joseph. "Where are you?" It came back, marked "undeliverable."

"He's not going to answer you, or anybody," Ruqia said between swallows. "They're in deep hiding, maybe in outer space."

"Joseph wouldn't take the Thread into space." But his eyes were uncertain as he reached across Ruqia for another fistful of pea cactus.

They heard voices. She pushed him to the ground. They were as still as bones.

Turkish soldiers came toward them, smoking, chuckling, as boys do. One tossed his cigarette butt into the dirt beside them. They held their breaths. The Turk walked away, moaning that he needed a woman.

Ooooogle, oooogle

A dinostrich thrashed in the pea cactus.

The Turkish soldiers perked up at the sound of fresh meat, grabbing their e-arrow rifles. "Dinner!" cried one of them, running straight toward Gonul and Ruqia.

She seized her rifle: no way to avoid combat with these kids. She looked at her gun as if she had never seen it before, its smooth, elegant design suddenly grotesque. She glanced at the setting: *kill*. What happened next seemed to take a long time, but it could only have been seconds: the memory of the little girl and her bird—her parents curled beside her—all the bodies becoming bones in the Temple of Return: death, the quiet finality of it.

She flipped the setting on her rifle to *sleep*, attacking the young soldiers, one after another, until they all fell, unbloodied, at her feet.

She gasped, grabbed her cane, leaned on it like a roaring fire slowly going out. The wind came up, dust collecting on the sleeping boys.

Gonul pulled her into his chest. She fought him. He pulled harder until she lost all resistance and leaned against him, sobbing.

"I love you like the sister I never had."

"Bastard."

He chuckled.

She wailed, her body jerking.

"Welcome home," he said.

She pulled away suddenly and looked into his calm brown eyes. "Don't say that. You think I can get fixed all at once, like some miracle cure. Make my leg strong again, and all I'll want is to be the Flying Warrior, loving the smell of blood!"

"Shut up."

She slapped him, hard, across the face.

He held his cheek, looking at her with those damn wise eyes.

She stared down at the bloodless boys, her mind a swirl.

36 – Hamza

"SHE'S recruiting enough nut cases for an *army*?" He stared at his top intelligence officer, a tall pale man with blue eyes and graying hair.

"See for yourself, sir," he said, touching his forehead and putting his other finger on Hamza's brow.

"I don't want your sneaky films. Take me there."

The officer's pale eyebrows wrinkled. "Is it wise, sir?"

Hamza's skull burned. "You would defy me?"

They hurried through the streets, dressed as pea cactus vendors, satchels of produce on their backs, tabs on their fingers for quick transactions with customers. Beneath the disguise they carried gold-hilted swords that doubled as e-arrow rifles.

The stench of the city reminded Hamza why he hated the common people—the acrid smell of fake rubber from the ferry-cycle tires; dust blown in from the snowless hillsides that no amount of sweeping with pea-brooms could clean away; the black smoke of fires burning in doorways where electric lamps used to be.

The officer led him down a narrow alleyway. When they heard the *shuuuush* of the Kiss-Off station in Water Square, they hid in a doorway, peering through a recently installed two-way mirror knot hole. At first everything looked ordinary: women and men in line with pails and bottles. A child slept in a mother's arms. A grandfather told stories to a circle of children awaiting their rations.

Hamza spotted Ataturka's Egyptian man in the shadows, showing the people something on his In-Phone. Apparently,

Ataturka had canceled the contact with the Israelis and the Saudis.

"What? Why?"

"The Turkish people want water. They want to be special. See, sir. It appears the African is showing people the voided contract with our customers."

"I will kill her."

"Yes, sir."

"How many troops has the gigolo recruited?"

"We don't know, sir. It has increased many-fold. There is no data to confirm that the African man is having a sexual relationship with your daughter."

Hamza scoffed. He had seen it in her eyes: a quality of desire for the Egyptian she had never shown for other men, certainly not for her father.

Women joined the Egyptian, showing the voided contract to other women.

"Who are they?" Hamza asked.

"The women wearing green hijabs with egg-shaped white forms in the design? They are called the *belekevi*," the officer said.

Not those bitches! "I thought we killed all the Kurds in Turkiye. I personally raped hundreds of them in our last offensive. I had to rip off their spotted-green head gear every time."

"Yes, sir. Many of them bore children after the Cleansing of the Kurds. These girls could be your daughters."

Hamza struck the man with the hilt of his sword. The officer fell, blood streaming from his forehead. Hamza looked away; the man could bleed to death: he deserved it. To suggest that these *belekevi* traitors were the product of the seed of Hamza the Great was blasphemy worthy of death.

A desire swelled in him, no, a call, worthy of Allah Himself: *to crush my daughter before her rebellion even begins.*

37 – Sara

CHA cha cha cha cha

Sara stirred, still dreaming: Mamoo and Papoo helping their little girl into a row boat. Summer on Lake Van, the sun so warm. Mamoo sharing her umbrella, cuddling Sara as Papoo told a fairy tale of a brave girl kidnapped by gypsies, who found her way home.

The dream faded, and the world came into focus: the smell of rats and urine, the hard, stone floor under the mattress, the shadows of the bars on the jagged wall, and most horribly, Sara's shame: the truth she had let fly out of her mouth like a moth from an open fire. "You want to poach it," she had told the queen. A confession that the Water Thread was real.

I am guilty as charged, for I betrayed my own.

cha cha cha cha cha!

"Rexie II, what's the matter? Are you thirsty?"

He flapped his wings against the bars at the top of the cell. Sara glanced at the tray. No food or water left for her during the night. Odd. Of course, the queen had not returned. Even more strange since Ataturka knew Sara had more information about the Thread. Was Ataturka instructing her torture team, or was she laughing with confidence now that she knew Sara was a bad liar?

Footsteps echoed on the lower level of the prison. Someone was coming, but not only Ataturka and her small entourage. It sounded like an army.

Rexie II screamed, *reeep, reep, reep!*

A tiny bit of water was left in Sara's tin cup. She took a sip, then held the rim in her teeth as she climbed up the bricks.

"You always know more than me, Rexie II. What's up, my little dinosaur? Are you devolving faster?"

She reached the top and, holding on tight, extended the cup through the iron bars. Rexie II's slithery tongue reached down, lapping greedily until all the water was gone. How well she remembered sending the image of the first Rexie's lizard tongue to Mr. Askay. Her heart hurt. "Rexie II, if only you could speak Kurdish. Why are you so alarmed?"

He flicked his head to one side, his intelligent eye catching the morning light as it shifted from peach to gold.

A door slammed in the stairwell.

Sara dropped the tin cup and gripped the bricks with both hands, climbing down, her heart drumming.

kkkeeek, kkkeeek, kkeeeekkk!

The door opened with a *crash*. Soldiers marched in, opening her cell door with the flick of a wrist. They wore different uniforms, the color of bronze statues poured straight from the mold. A tall old man swept past them, his white hair not moving, as if painted on. His eyes went up and down Sara's body, assessing her round parts.

"Who are you? Where is Ataturka?" She was surprised at the strength of her voice.

"No wonder our Saudi friend paid a King's ransom for you. Cleaned up and scented, you'd be quite the morsel." He leaned closer. "You smell like a rancid whore. Your kind always does." He spat on the floor. "Kurd."

"We could clean her up, sir," said one of the soldiers. "Each take our turn."

Sara's heart skipped a beat; her hands were cold.

"Sorry, boys. No time for that. I think the way she is will do. Tie her hair back, so the World Board gets a good shot of the face of a water poacher."

This horrid old man is Ataturka's father. No wonder she knows nothing of love.

"What about the smell, sir?"

"Leave it. People with those full sensory In-Phones can smell her. One of its best features."

A soldier with big hands grabbed Sara's arms. Another slid his hand between her legs. She tried to bite him, but he was out of reach.

breeeek, brreeeek, ggreeeeeeekkk!

"A little birdie," cried a soldier, pulling out his e-arrow rifle. With the strength of ten warriors, Sara knocked the gun away with her boot.

Rexie II screamed and flew off.

He got away. He got away. She experienced a moment of joy, before she felt the smack of a rifle on her face.

Darkness followed, then, gradually, a sensation of being dragged down stairs, across a bumpy street, onto a platform. She opened her eyes to the brilliance of the sun. *I am outside.* Her head pounded; she tasted blood on lips, her mouth dry as cotton, her arms and legs clamped in chains so heavy she could not move.

She inhaled the clean air of Ankara, so unlike the perpetual dust of Rojava. High above, something white, each tuft connected to the next, moved gracefully across a blue sky. *Clouds.* How long had it been? Papoo had still been alive. Tears moistened her face as loud voices and blinding lights assaulted her.

"And now for the Main Event on the World Board!" Hamza's rasping voice greeted the crowd to sounds of cheers, but it was peculiar. Hundreds of people lined the street, but their mouths were closed. The sound came from a tall black box, pre-recorded.

A flock of great blue heron glided beneath the clouds. Rough hands shoved Sara across the platform to a large bowl of water: the punishment for water poaching was death by drowning.

All feeling flushed out of Sara's body, but her mind was suddenly clearer than it had ever been. In an instant she recalled the faces of Ruqia, Gonul, Gran, the YPJ, the people of Rojava, Mamoo, Papoo.

She screamed, "Liberty, Equality, Water for All!"

Hands gripped her by the neck and plunged her head into the water. She held her breath, eyes wide open. *How strange, to be learning about myself to the very end: I want to see the color of the water. To feel its silken fingers on my face.*

Her lungs ached. Her eyes searched the water, as if looking for a divine presence that would be with her on her way out. In the moment when she could hold her breath no longer, the platform shook; the hands on her neck fell away, and another hand reached across her breast and pulled her out of the water.

She gasped, her lungs expanding greedily, her eyes blinking wildly in the bright sunlight. Loud noises thundered across the platform, the singing of e-arrows, the screams of woman and men, the sound of bodies falling.

Belekevi seized Hamza, spitting on him, jeering at him. His bronze soldiers stormed down upon them, seized Hamza and hauled him away.

"Are you all right?" A voice Sara knew well: Ataturka. Their eyes met for the first time with no bars between them. "By the heart of the divine," Sara said. "I can see your eyes. They have seen too much."

Ataturka stared back. "Not as much as you." She turned her prisoner around so they could both face the all-seeing Eye of the World Board. "Citizens of my country and all other countries: my father acted on his own today. His eagerness for justice belies the fact that this girl has a wealth of information. She has already given up a great deal. The Water Thread is *real*. No myth! She knows a great deal more. I cannot execute her until I have milked her dry."

The clamoring of artificial cheering mingled with the screams of the violence in the street. Sara's legs collapsed. Ataturka's strong grip held her up to face the Eye.

"Ataturka lies. There is no Water Thread," Sara said. "She saves me only to torture me."

Sara believed this, but, there was more. Ataturka would not kill her until she had milked Sara, not only for information, but for wisdom only a woman knows.

PART THREE
EARTH

38 – Ruqia

HOW do you go on living when part of yourself has died? The thought came to her as she lay next to Gonul in a desert sand cave. He slept, cuddled against her. A surprise. Most nights he walked the desert, planning their next move. His slumber allowed her to pay attention to what had been running through her mind like a team of wild horses every night and every day since she changed her rifle setting to *sleep*. Staring at those unbloodied Turkish soldiers, she felt the depth of her crimes: all the murder she had done in the name of fighting for her people's rights, for her people's water—and that was *true*, but even before she had been wounded, she had been *tired*. Tired of being the best. Tired of murder.

There is a new Ruqia. No longer The Flying Warrior; I am becoming plain Ruqia, a wandering shell of a person, knowing only one thing: I can no longer kill.

She turned away from the sleeping Gonul, her tears mixing with dust to make a dirty paste on her face. *Until I know who I am, I will move forward. No self. No self-pity.*

There was great urgency. They had to find the Water Thread. The Turkish queen had saved Sara only to tell the world that "the Kurd" had divulged that the Thread was real. How could this happen? Sara would never have betrayed the YPJ. Tortured unto death, she would have stayed true. Was it all staged by Ataturka and her father, so they could pretend they held the secret of the Water Thread?

A familiar hand reached to cradle Ruqia's head, and a canteen touched her lips. She drank, looking up at Gonul. "Your face, it's weirdly peaceful," she said. "Did you see Sara in the patterns of the moonlight?"

He smiled, but there was pain in it. "A dino wren followed me all night."

"They're nocturnal?"

He drank from the same canteen. "Not when they were birds. Now, as tiny T-Rexes, they must be feeding at night, like their ancestors."

She rose to her elbows. "Dinosaurs hunted at night? You know this for a fact?"

His large dark eyes settled on her lips, no doubt thinking that Sara had kissed them.

"One day you will look at me and see *me*," she said, without offense.

His eyes found hers. "I see you, Ruqia. The willow beneath the barbed wire."

"What's a willow?"

He smiled. "A tree with lacey branches that sway in the breeze. Graceful, but strong."

"You're hopeless."

He looked down at the sand in the cave around them. The wind had sculpted patterns like waves on the shore. "I'll laugh again when we find the Water Thread." He stood up, offering his hand.

"You're no fun," she said, taking his hand. It was still embarrassing to accept help. "Let's get the hell out of here. Those soldiers I couldn't kill are tracking us."

He touched her chest, just below her collarbone. She could feel her heart beating against his fingertips; a tear of gratitude formed in her eyes.

"You fear living from your heart," he said. "It must be hard. You loved war for so long."

"Damn you," she said, but beside the angry humiliation, was a distant memory: the scent of the Earth in her mother's garden.

Gonul seemed to read her mind. "I love you too."

She swatted his arm, and they headed toward the horizon, dust swirling behind them.

39 - Kethuda

THE sun streamed through the white lace curtains, forming delicate patterns on Kethuda's face, her thoughts like tiny jewels perched on the rim of her soul.

Something happened to me when I pulled the Kurd from the water. I felt her body in my arms, her lungs swelling, her mouth sucking the air like a newborn bird in the nest.

Feeling Sara's body, rescued from death, has given birth to something in me, a new way of seeing life in others: the pain in face of an old man driving a ferry-cycle down the street, a child licking a pea-cherry tomato in the market, holding it out to her brother; non-gendered lovers kissing as they stand in line for water.... Life, connected.

At this moment I have the power to save life...or end it. But I am no Earth Goddess, no daughter of Allah. I am Kethuda, daughter of Ayse. What I do next is critical. A quick flip of fate, and I will be the one looking into the water bowl of the executioner.

"Madam?"

"Yes, Gai. I'm here."

"You seem very far away." Gai pulled back the sheer white curtains. The sun brightened. She shielded her mistress's eyes with her body. "My Gramma told me that before the perma-drought, when hunters returned to the village, they were met by someone who would say, 'I see you.' And the hunter would say, 'I am here.' Are you 'here,' Madam?"

"I am more 'here' than I have ever been."

Gai's eyes moved sideways. "I see two of you, Madam. One 'here', one somewhere I cannot reach."

"Too early in the day for philosophy, my friend."

"Check your In-Phone, Madam. There is strong reaction to your rescue of the Kurd."

Kethuda touched her forehead and smiled. Elena Maria Juarez from *The New Yorker* wrote, "While the true motives of Ataturka remain a quagmire, the moment when she seized the drowning body of Sara Roxan and pulled her back into the air will go down in history. A woman of power using it to save another woman, an enemy. My colleagues are making art from it: truly a moment frozen in time."

Shogofa in Afghanistan was more circumspect: "Did Ataurka save the girl only to torture her? I fear a replication of the worst tactics of the Taliban."

Nina Navalny, underground in Russia, wrote, "If only someone like Ataturka had been on the scene when the Bolsheviks slaughtered the last Czar and his family. The water went away not only because of a warming climate, but because we murder our enemies. Survival, you say? We are beasts, you say? Ataturka did not say that. She said, "My enemy will not die." Are you listening, Ataturka? What you do next will echo in the chambered heart of God."

There was much more. Sam Boatwright in America praised Ataturka for "manning up to her daddy."

"We will be here all day if you read them all," said Gai.

"Yes, General."

Gai smiled and helped her mistress dress, and they were met in the street by a new honor guard of women soldiers wearing hijabs of green and white Kurdish design.

One young woman walked boldly up to Kethuda. We are *belekevi!*" she said, with fire in her very being. "We are proud to support your army, but we have our own war to fight."

Kethuda stepped back. "Your own war?"

Gai smiled gently. "She is saying it is time for you to know this, Madam. These women are Turkish Kurds, *belekevi*, their fabric the traditional pattern of the melting snow on the mountains. They are members of the Resistance."

"The Resistance?"

"Yes, Madam. We are water refugees: Africans, Arabs, Indians, Jews, also many native Turks who line up at the Kiss-Off stations, even as wealthy Turks consume more than their quota every day."

"It was not always so divided," Kethuda said, a plea in her voice. "People think it's all about privilege and greed. Our country used to be much more democratic."

"Perhaps," Gai said with steady eyes. "That was before the water went away. Now, all people hold tight to what they have. Swimming pools are not used for sport, but to horde water. It does not help those who had no swimming pools in the first place."

"Why do they want to guard me?" Kethuda said, studying the stoic faces of the *belekevi*.

"You will help us. You have no choice if you want to maintain hegemony over your father."

Kethuda held her breath, seeing it for the first time. Her belly grew cold with fear, even as her mind reached out in excitement. "You didn't dance naked in my father's house because you had no other option."

Gai had never seemed so tall, one blink affirming everything.

"You pretended to be an object of sexual desire, all the while learning what you could to benefit—what did you call it?"

Gai's voice hummed with pride. "The Resistance."

"You did not expect me to hire you, but when I did, it was a bonus."

"Yes, Madam, but I have not been disingenuous. It has been a great honor to serve you, to watch you struggle with the possibility of being a woman of conscience, rather than a woman of self-glory." Gai's eyes went to the faces of the *belekevi*. "We hope you will make the right choices, Madam."

"And what is that?"

"Not only to defy your father, but to join the Resistance and help us create a true, democratic society."

Kethuda was motionless, her mind spinning: *Will I be the Marie Antoinette of this Resistance? I would never say "Let them eat cake!" But what if they demand water for all the down-streamers? Or a complete restructuring of Turkish law? How do I keep water flowing for the Turkish people and make room for thousands of water refugees?*

She banished these thoughts and turned to Gai and the *belekevi*. "Thank you. I see my options with fresh eyes."

"Yes, Madam."

They reached the outer gate of the prison, heavily guarded by Kethuda's troops. Eng was their commander. Recent battle had not aged him. He was as quietly alive as ever.

"These troops serve the Resistance?" she asked.

Eng glanced at his sister with surprise.

"I wasn't going to tell her yet," Gai said. "A *belekevi* spilled the beans."

Eng poked his sister in the ribs.

Kethuda wondered how they could be so playful at such a serious moment. She burned with envy.

"How does this sit with you, Madam?" Eng asked.

Kethuda shrugged, "'I am here.'"

The brightness of his smile was like the sun, "I see you," he said.

She turned away, crossing her arms around her body, to keep his smile from penetrating her heart.

Gai moved close to her mistress, taking her hand, bowing. "I must take my leave, Madam."

"Where are you going?"

"I entrust you to my brother, Madam. I must go with a division of the *belekevi* to find the Water Thread."

Kethuda felt a great sadness and a tremor of dread, "I need you."

"It is your own fault," Gai said tenderly. "You made the boldest possible grab for power, saving the Kurdish girl and claiming that you, and she, have special knowledge of the whereabouts of the Water Thread. Your father is banished with his bronze soldiers. They comb the desert, the mountains, looking for the Thread. And here, in the city, the bronzies lie in wait, undercover, amassing numbers. We must find the Water Thread before they do."

"You could come under fire," Kethuda said, her heart trembling.

Gai looked at her brother.

"My sister is a great leader," he said, looking only at Gai. "She has studied the art of warfare with our *yeyo* since she was a child."

Kethuda cupped Gai's face in her hands. "I can't bear to lose you."

"Madam, I will take you with me in my soul. I will continue to serve you by knowing the goodness you aspire to, the goodness that eludes you, the pain that lives in your heart."

Eng folded his sister in his arms, his chin on the top of her head. Kethuda suspected they had been like this in the womb: separate, but one. He tapped the tip of her nose. She laughed softly and hurried away, fighting back tears.

Silence settled over the cold stones of the street.

40 – Ruqia

SHE pressed down on her wounded leg, surveying the barren hillside once covered in feathery green grass: nothing but dirt blowing away in the wind.

Gonul had gone ahead but returned and, taking her arm, guided her up the hill, where a tiny village rose out of the barren mound. "A place to rest," he said. "Maybe water." She was giddy with relief at the prospect of water and, even more, knowing he was here, helping her climb.

They entered a circle of cracked mud houses in an empty market square. Threadbare pea cactus banners flapped flaccidly over vacated stalls, their faded signs advertising Apricot-Flavored Pea-Squares, Pea-Fabric Soft as Silk, Pea Cactus Butterfly Kites in Four Bright Colors.

"Equal Rights Council" was carved over the doorway of an empty circular meeting house. A skinny baby goat bleated. Gonul scooped him up and carried him on his shoulders. They went from house to house, searching for signs of life.

Ruqia touched the hoof of the goat. What a joy, to touch an animal! She nudged Gonul: at the far edge of the village, a family huddled around a well, the father and son pulling up a cylinder of water. The family was wary at the sight of strangers.

"Friends," Gonul said.

A little girl ran up to him, reaching up for the goat.

"Yours?"

She nodded.

He handed it to her.

Ruqia pulled something from her pack: a great delicacy taken from the sleeping Turkish soldiers she had shot with her weapon on *sleep*. "We haven't much to give. Have you tried dried dinostrich?"

The girl shook her head. The mother frowned, eyeing the shriveled meat with caution. She pulled off a small piece, tasted it. "Pig."

Ruqia smiled, "You know what pig tastes like? I'm jealous. I grew up on snake."

"Pig for water?" Gonul asked.

The son took a bite of dinostrich, looked back at his father.

"Not too much water," the father said.

"We're grateful for whatever you can spare."

The interior of the family home was draped with colorful Kurdish cloth in a pattern of turquoise and orange as bright as the sunrise. The rugs and cushions were well-worn.

Little Mama and me, we could have a place like this one day. Sara could go to Gonul's home to love him and make babies. The three of us could raise them together…and—what a surprise: I will want time alone with Gonul, to laugh, to share our thoughts and hearts, not as lovers, but as beloved friends, as close as a sister to her brother.

Ruqia noticed Gonul watching her from across the room. Was he thinking the same thing? Impossible to tell, yet his eyes rested on her with protection and love.

The banquet was humble: tea with goat's milk, pea cactus chips, Ruqia's dried dinostrich, and cool, milky water. Everyone sat on the floor around a cloth, eating from the same plate. "A feast," Ruqia said. "We are in your debt."

"We will stay here as long as the well runs," the father said. "Then we will move on. You come from the coast?"

Ruqia told them of the lines that formed for water every day by the desalinization plant near what had been Beirut. She told them about Gran, staying behind to bring Rojavan democracy to the water refugees, in spite of everything.

"What have you heard, about the whereabouts of the Water Thread?" Gonul, asked, slowly sipping his tea.

The father looked away. The mother cleared her throat, looking at him over thick spectacles.

"I was there when we first plugged in the Water Thread," Ruqia said, moving her eyes from Gonul to the mother. "It is the wonder of our modern world and the only thing of value we can use as a bargaining chip with the Turks."

"You were *there*?" the little girl said. "What does it look like?"

"About the size of your dinner platter, but thicker, like a big egg with tiny black feet. It has the power to pull water into the air, carry it very far, and turn it back into water. We could bring water from the Arctic all the way to your well."

The eyes of the child grew large. She looked at her mother.

"People told us things," the mother said. "We did not ask, but gave water to those migrating down from the villages of Rojava."

The father said, "People wanted to give us something, "as we filled their canteens."

"The stories went on through the night," the son said. "A Hidden University, somewhere in the mountains."

"The Turks stumbled upon it, searched through everything."

"They only found one thing."

"The paper clip?" Gonul asked.

"We were told it was a tiny spiral," the father said.

"A spiral?"

"An odd one. It had the appearance of metal, but when touched, it became a spiral of water, like a fountain. Then it became air. It disappeared before their very eyes. The Turkish soldiers were angry, for there was no evidence to bring back."

"How do you know this?" Ruqia asked.

The father said, "The Turkish soldiers came through, demanding water from our well. As they drank, I overheard them puzzling over what they had seen, fearing that no one would believe them... I said, 'It sounds like you found an eccentric paper clip.' Their leader liked it, so the fiction was born."

At the end of the meal there was much gratitude and a warning from Gonul that the Turks could come back in their search for the Water Thread. He took off his grandfather's turban and gave it to the little girl, "For you to make a dress of bright colors." She hugged his neck, and he draped it around her shoulders.

The family offered them a warm place to stay the night, but Ruqia was out the door faster than Gonul. "I will walk all night," she said, stealthily soaking her cane in the family's well, watching it swell.

"Yes, R," he said, shielding her crime with his body, "we will find the Hidden University and this 'spiral.'"

They hurried higher up the mountain, the dust covering their tracks.

41 – Sara

SHE woke in her prison cell from a half-remembered dream: Gonul's long hair falling across her body, Ruqia's teeth glowing as she laughed under desert stars.

With the morning light, it all came back to her: Ataturka pulling her from the execution bowl.

I am alive. Here. Now.

Her fingers stirred dust particles dancing in the shaft of sunlight.

I must not accidentally give up any more secrets!

A familiar sensation rippled across her forehead: *my In-Phone?* The queen must have enabled it! As she reached for her forehead, something in her belly warned her to stop. *The queen knows I will contact my people. I could bring imprisonment or death to my beloveds.*

She lowered her fingers and reached for her morning water. She drank slowly, calming herself.

Without warning, Ataturka swept in. The African man followed, opening the cell door and placing two chairs inside. A young woman in *belekevi* hijab carried a pot of black coffee, two cups, a small plate of pea cactus layer cake, and fresh grapes. This woman, barely a girl, looked at Sara with cautious eyes.

"Educate us, Eng," the queen said, swooping into one of the chairs. "What is it the African warrior says when he comes out of the bush?"

The Black man stepped close to Sara, his voice as low as the base string on the *oud:* "I am here."

The queen responded, looking at Sara. "Then what, Eng?"

"Then the person from the village says, 'I see you.'"

"I see you," the queen said. "That is your cue, woman warrior of the YPJ."

Sara squirmed, "I am not your toy."

The queen's eyes narrowed. She motioned to the Black man and the *belekevi* to leave.

"Where is your African woman?" Sara asked.

"The world has changed," the queen said, pouring coffee. "For me. For you. I am surrounded by your people, like that girl, a Kurdish Turk. Also by water refugees—Arabs, Africans, but also what they call 'common' Turks, civilians loyal only to me in gratitude for cancelling my contract with the Israelis and Saudis. Together they form an army."

Sara savored the dark sweet flavor of a grape exploding in her mouth. "Is that why you saved me, the revolutionaries put a knife to your throat?"

The queen studied the surface of her coffee. "I am not my father."

Sara was completely still, experiencing a new sensation, as if she stood barefoot on the Earth, dust swirling, but it didn't matter, as if the Earth Herself had entered Sara's body, her mind momentarily cleared of despair.

Silence beat her tiny wings.

The queen took a slice of cake, bit into it. "I made a statement on the World Board that you will lead me to the Water Thread. Don't make me a liar."

Sara sipped her coffee. "It must have been a disappointment to discover that your Black bodyguard works for the Resistance. But, actually, now that he's no longer your lackey, he must be even more attractive to you."

A strange melancholy clouded the queen's eyes. "You must know something about love, Fatima Roxan. Who holds your heart?"

Sara let out a bemused chuckle. "Nice try, your highness."

Kethuda was not amused, "Your YPJ shot down Turkish soldiers with stun rifles in a pea grove at the end of the Shuttle line. No explanation for why they weren't shot dead. Very strange. And your people are crafty at covering prints, though it seems the stun-gunners were a male and a female with some sort of foot drag. We will find them. You could shorten the agony by telling me who they are and what they know."

"One has a foot drag?"

"Some sort of injury. Uses a cane, it seems. Why would the man take her with him?"

Sara breathed out slowly. Ruqia was alive, injured, and Gonul was taking care of her. They were out there, looking for the Thread, working side by side, stun-gunning Turks, not killing them. A wellspring of longing flowed through her body into her heart.

The queen watched.

Sara desperately tried to contain her feelings, but it was no use. She wiped her tears with her sleeve.

The queen poured water, handed it to Sara. This act of tenderness, or pure manipulation, only made Sara weep harder.

"These are the people you love," Kethuda said with wistful envy.

Sara glanced at the queen through moist eyes. Suddenly, here, in the midst of such longing, a rocket of a thought landed in her brain: *this is* my *power, that I know how to love and she doesn't.*

Sara's voice was steady as a large bolder at the bottom of a rushing torrent, "I have feelings. I have loves. You know this already. Something happened to me after you pulled me from death. Resurrected, by your hand, into a second life, I am no longer a quaking girl. I have the opportunity to become who I really am, not only now, but for eternity."

The queen's spine curled upward. "I have changed as well," she said, pulling back her hijab, to reveal her own dark, moist hair. "My skull is split in two. Half of me sees the game I must play to stay in power. Half of me sees the unbroken connection in all people, all creatures, the Earth Herself. My In-Phone is driving me mad, streaming pictures of the water refugees, the down-streamers, those across the globe who are flooded with water, countries who think I have the Water Thread begging *hourly* for me to syphon water from their flood zones. All those people could be helped, if only you will help me."

Sara stood up from her chair, towering over the queen.

Ataturka's voice trembled, "I mean to use the Water Thread for the good of *all*."

Sara laughed.

The queen rose, now the taller of the two. "Sara, I'm telling the truth. I want you to know me, not as a ruler, but as a human being."

"You want me to *know* you?"

"Yes. What will it take for you to let me in?"

Sara exhaled. A stillness entered her body, clearing a pathway in her mind, a voice within whispering, *What have you got to lose?*

"Madam President, if you want me to know you, you must show me all of you, not this mask you concoct for the world, but what you *feel*, what you really care about. And…" She took a breath, "you must go on the World Board and take responsibility for the carnage of your ancestors: the genocide of the Armenians, the slaughter of the Kurds, the murder of my mother—all of it."

The queen stared at Sara with tears of humiliation so deep, her body could not hold it. She lost her ability to breathe and slammed her fist against the cell bars. "Eng!" she called, sliding onto the floor.

Sara heard footsteps. The Black man came running, lifted the queen into his arms. Sara offered water. Ataturka drank.

"If you confess your country's crimes to the world, I will speak for the Kurds."

"It will be my death sentence," Kethuda said. "It makes no difference to you, Sara, if I live or die. It makes little difference to me, except I have a duty to my people."

"Do not say such things," Eng said, lifting her in his arms and carrying her away.

When they were gone, Sara wrapped her palms around the bars, listening to his footsteps fade down the stairs, the murmur of their voices. *Is it true, that it makes no difference to me if the queen lives or dies? Why would I care? Do I owe her my life?*

It was an unanswered question that hung like a rice paper moon in Sara's sleepless night.

42 - Gonul

HE hated to leave Ruqia on the cliff below, but his mind was racing fast, his body leaping like a great horned sheep up the rocky cliff, each hand-hold opening a memory in his mind—the feel of the dusty rock ledges, Joseph's steady voice, leading him up, blindfolded, and once there, the blindfold removed, the glory of the tiny prototype sucking molecules from the air, the towering vats of water, the digital data on every wall. And the people of the Scientists for Humanity: women and men and nongendered humans from across the globe—Asians, Africans, Jews, Arabs, Ukrainians, Russians…. Joseph was proud to be the only Kurd. "There is no hierarchy," he explained. "We work as a creative team. Sometimes we disagree." "Often," chirped in a nongendered Israeli, their prayer shawl hanging from their waist. Joseph laughed, "Right. It's not easy, but in the end, we have one goal that aligns us more than it draws us apart."

"I see it," Gonul called down to Ruqia.

"Watch out for soldiers!"

"They won't be here."

"How do you know?"

"Why would they still be guarding the Hidden University when they found no trace of the Thread?"

"Your logic will be the death of you," she said, a touch of panic in her voice.

He approached with caution. The outer shell of the Hidden University was a rough cluster of rocks so ugly that any discerning eye would turn away.

Gonul wrestled with himself. Go forward quickly, quench his curiosity, or go back for R?

Satisfy myself, or care for another?

He chuckled. This was the debate running through the history of humanity. He had said to Ruqia that she was the sister he never had. The other truth was that this whole thing could be a wild goose chase, the Hidden University as barren of clues for them as it had been for the Turks.

If I am to be different from my enemy, I must be congruent with my deepest values.

He turned around and made his way down the mountain. Ruqia was straining to climb; her wounded leg was soaked in blood. He placed her cane across her chest and put her on his back.

"You're insane," she said, but did not struggle.

"Hang on. Grasp the ledges as we climb."

Soon they stood before a massive rock door with broken hinges. Turkish cigarette butts scattered like breadcrumbs showed the way.

Inside, tables and chairs were tossed asunder. Sunlight streamed in through windows that looked like solid rock from the outside but were active photosynthetic cells.

Gonul was drawn to a glass case in the center of the room containing a dissected wren, its parts laid out, carefully labeled. "R, look at his luminous, speckled feathers—"

"Eyes black as midnight, tail like a tiny sword," Ruqia said.

"The label says, 'a slightly elongated tongue'—"

"Little Mama's T-Rex Wren!"

"Right: a 'Rexie,'" Gonul said, bending closer. "According to the description, he's not evolving into a dinosaur. It says, 'There is no evidence of de-evolution of the wren to ancestors possessing adaptive qualities in arid zones of the Cretaceous.'"

"But I can see it," Ruqia said. "The tongue is forked, and extra long."

"They call it a 'bird's adaptation to the perma-drought, stretching the muscle of the tongue to access hard-to-reach water sources."

"Sara will be so disappointed," Ruqia said, brandishing her cane as if to fight off bad feelings.

Gonul stared, not at Ruqia, but at the air around her, "Do that again."

"Move my cane?"

"Yeah, faster this time."

She twirled it as fast as she could.

"Keep doing it," Gonul said, watching the air swirling around her, some of it dust, some of it something else.

"The 'paper clip,'" he said. "It appears to be one thing, but when touched, becomes a spiral of water, then air."

"Things are not what they seem..." Ruqia stared at the wren. "What if this is a clue, seemingly about a bird, so that it was passed over by Turkish soldiers looking for obvious evidence of the Water Thread?"

"A clue meant only for the curious."

"For those who would question a conclusion based only on the appearance of, what do you call it?"

"An outlier," he said, his heart quickening. "Without DNA analysis, it's a shallow conclusion that this bird is not devolving."

They looked up in the same moment. The air was churning with millions of tiny particles. Gonul scooped a handful of air particles and patted them onto his forehead. His In-Phone pulsed with energy.

"What do you see?"

"Nothing. Random static."

"Maybe it needs a circle of energy to complete the charge." She took his hands and pressed her forehead to his, creating a tremor of energy.

Electric words appeared in the air: *The Thread Will Bare When the Earth Flows Like Water.*

"You see it?" he said.

"Yes!"

"It's written in Joseph's own hand. They have it somewhere, the Water Thread, but they won't give it to the world—"

"Until the Earth flows like water."

They held their hands together, barely breathing.

"It's a riddle," she said.

"A prophesy. What does it mean?"

"I don't know. But Sara might." Ruqia put her thumb on Gonul's forehead and placed her other fingers on her own forehead and pressed down hard.

His heart thrummed. "R, if you're doing what I think you're doing, it could blow your whole In-Phone—your whole body.

"Yeah, yeah, if I explode, tell her about the riddle and tell her how much I love her."

A holograph of Sara came into the room. She was sitting in a prison cell with Ataturka, a small table between them, cups of dark coffee, plates of cake and grapes.

Ruqia wept and Gonul knelt, his legs weak with joy.

Sara turned at the *whooshing* sound of the hologram. Her face was thinner. Her leaf-shaped eyes grew round as she saw Ruqia and Gonul. "My darlings!"

Ruqia reached her arms into the air, embracing Sara's visage.

Gonul put his arm around Ruqia, holding her steady, extending a hand to touch Sara's gossamer face.

Ruqia's voice was cruel, "Sara, you break bread with this butcher?"

"The Kurd has no choice," Ataturka said, studying something in the air, behind them. 'The Thread Will Bare When the Earth Flows Like Water?' Did one of you write this?"

Gonul gripped Ruqia's arm. *Say nothing.*

"What does it mean?" Ataturka asked.

Sara closed her arms around Ruqia as she reached for Gonul. "I remember what it felt like, my loves, when we touched flesh to flesh."

Ruqia sobbed with strategy, whispering to Sara's form, "We came to you in holograph because there is no trace of the Thread in the Hidden U. Do you know the answer to the riddle?"

Sara buried her face to divert Ataturka's attention. "Your leg is seriously hurt."

"He is caring for me," Ruqia said. "We are best friends. Who would have thought?"

"I would," Sara said, stroking the insubstantial projection of Ruqia's feathery hair.

Gonul could see Ataturka staring at the three of them, her head cocked like a great bird of prey looking down at a nest of strange, loving mammals she could neither devour nor join.

Ruqia looked up. "Ms. Turkish President, have you visited the refugee camp in Beirut?"

Ataturka's voice was tight, "I get daily written reports. I know of their suffering."

"But you haven't *been there*, smelled the human decay, watched the starving babies stagger into the ocean and drown."

Ataturka opened her mouth but could not speak.

"Have you ever been thirsty, Ms. President?" Ruqia asked.

"My mother, Ayse, used to say never ask questions if you already know the answer."

"You know nothing of suffering." Ruqia stepped toward Ataturka, bringing their holographic eyes close.

"Show me," Ataturka said.

Gonul could not bear to leave Sara's side, but he nodded to Ruqia, pressing his fingers to his forehead, thumb to temple, pressing down very hard. Behind him, a vast double-hologram came into focus: Gran, sitting at council, her lemon-yellow hijab whipping in the wind. "My family!" she cried, hands on her heart.

"Gran," Gonul said, "so good to see you." He glanced at Ruqia: how thin Gran looked, and all those around her. Gonul forced his voice to be all-business: "How much water did they give you today, Gran?"

"Is that Ataturka behind you, with Sara, in a *cell*?"

"Yes," Ruqia said. "The President of Turkiye is serving Sara her special Turkish coffee. Can you smell it?"

Gran inhaled, "I smell something much stronger: Ataturka, you monster, you think to bribe our Sara with *coffee*?" She moved a bony arm to those sitting in the circle beside her. "May I introduce our council: Rojava democracy in exile: Fidan, Sara's stepmother, and her daughter, Nazan. They sold Sara into slavery, and in spite of our bitterness toward them, we have extended compassion and forgiveness and included them in our council of Equal Voice."

"Equal Voice? You sound like a throwback to that gutless body from the last century," Ataturka said.

"The United Nations?" Gran's voice saddened. "A noble effort. They did some good, but had little power. In Rojava, Equal Voice Councils are local, independent. Power rests with the whole. We do not claim to be a body devoid of corruption. As humans we do our best, but we have the power of united, democratic will."

Ruqia asked, "Gran, you forget who you're talking to. Tell the Turk the ration you get as a refugee."

Gran said, "Nazan, at the age of 19, is given five cups of water a day. RAT favors the young. We old ones will die soon, so, some days, like today, we go with no water at all. For food we get a raw pea cactus to chew on every few days."

"I wish I could give you my water," Sara said.

Gran stretched an arm to touch Sara's airy fingertips. "You *survive,* my dear Sara-bird. That joy I will take with me to the Afterlife. You will be gratified to know we have recruited two ISIS women to our council. They were comrades of the

Commander you accidentally killed. They have seen it in their hearts to renounce their ISIS affiliation and join us."

Gran placed a hand on the heads of the two young women in black hijabs. One of them stared up into the hologram, "The Thread Will Bare When the Earth Flows Like Water."

"What does it mean?" Gran said.

"We were hoping you would ask Allah," Ruqia said. "Perhaps He knows."

"You are asking us to pray?"

"Yes," Ruqia said, "This atheist needs all the help she can get."

"I think we can manage that. We have not been able to do Sufi practice with such scarcity of pea cactus and water. The body needs fuel to twirl."

"My mother did so every day," Ataturka said, moving closer to Gran, studying the old woman's face.

"Then it is your job to take her place," Gran said, her frail voice trembling. "Madam President, you put us here. You shut off our water and drained the Euphrates. Allah is angry with you. Look behind me. Many of us will be driven into the sea when the de-salinization plant breaks down. Please, Madam President, go to the temple and twirl with the dervishes since we cannot. Ask Allah to solve the riddle, so you can share the Water Thread with the whole world."

"How can you say this, Gran?" Ruqia cried. "If Ataturka finds the Thread, we are all dead."

Gran leaned close, the wrinkles around her eyes like spider webs wilting in the sun. "This Ataturka is not what she seems. She knows she is bad, but she wants to be good. Otherwise, she would have watched Sara drown in the execution bowl."

A pulse throbbed through the hologram: *Time's Up. Time's Up.*

Sara reached for her beloveds. In an instant, she was gone, Gran was gone. Gonul was left holding Ruqia in his arms in the empty Hidden University. They held each other for a long time.

43 - Kethuda

Two figures in black escaped into the anonymity of the city. One tall, the rough cloth of her brown burka rustling as she walked, one arm inside her robe, as if holding a treasure. Her eyes were covered with light brown lace so that she saw the people rushing by through a pattern of budding flowers.

The figure beside her was short. A twin in apparel, but she had no hidden tool beneath her robe. No lace covering her eyes. On her wrist, an invisible tether, made of digital air, anchored to the waist of the other woman. Any attempt to escape would be met with a disabling shock. And yet she pulled the tether out as far as it could go, as if inviting a show-down.

"My Gai is commanding the *belekevi* who fight the Turks that search for the Water Thread, so I can't consult her on this matter," Kethuda said. "And her brother commands the Resistance, here in the city. He must stay one step ahead of the bronze soldiers of my father, or Hamza will throw me in prison, and you will be executed. How strange that you're the only person left to help me figure out the riddle."

"The answer lies outside the walls of power," Sara said.

"How do you know?"

"The Scientists for Humanity hate power. Some of their grandparents lost their souls at Los Alamos," Sara said as she slid into a dark alleyway. "If I find the meaning of the riddle, I may not tell you."

Kethuda laughed, her voice aggressive, amused, "Then at least I will know it can be solved."

Sara glanced back, equally amused.

Kethuda followed, on a quest not only to solve the riddle, but to learn from this girl. She couldn't stop thinking of the holograph with Sara's two virtual lovers, touching Sara so tenderly even though she was made of air. And the way she reached out for them... *I only know about this passion of love from movies and the memory of my mother's arms. I want to live it like Sara.*

"When are you going to stop calling me 'queen'?" Kethuda asked.

"When you take responsibility for the genocide of your ancestors."

Kethuda pulled the digital rope tight, reining Sara in. And yet, there was nothing to say. No way to counter what she knew in her heart to be true.

The coral sky turned purple as night descended. They came to a street lined with the towers of low-income housing. Torches lighted the sight of children in a central courtyard, swinging and sliding, their squeals and giggles a welcome balm.

"I remember when we had electric street lights in Rojava," Sara said. "Before quota. Did your parents take you to the playground at night?"

"I don't remember," Kethuda said, staring at the children with unexpected curiosity.

"In the summer, we always stayed out after dark. Papoo pushed me on the swing. I believed if I pumped hard enough, I could swing all the way to the stars. In those days the sand in our playground was so moist we could shape it into funny sculptures of towers and castles and horses and goats."

Kethuda looked down at the playground soil, tapping it with her foot: hard as rock.

Sara knelt and tried to pry out some dirt with her strong little hands. "Can't move it. This Earth certainly doesn't flow like water."

Kethuda glanced at Sara, her mind churning. "The sand in the desert is different."

"Not as hard, but so dry, you could never make a sand castle out of it."

"The desert does not flow like water."

"No. There is no Earth made of two parts hydrogen, one part oxygen. In arid countries, we don't even have mud, much less 'flowing' Earth."

Kethuda breathed heavily. "I remember mud. In the ancient city of Catalhoyuk, where my mother brought me as a child, they wouldn't let us make mud cakes inside the ruins, but Ayse always found a spot outside, where we could dig in the wet Earth and make glorious mud cakes, with layers of fresh wildflowers for "frosting.""

Sara smiled.

Kethuda looked away. They moved on.

In the Water Square they discovered one electric street lamp shining down on the line of people that stretched as far as they could see.

A man in line with his little boy stepped back, offering them his place. They shook their heads and backed away. Even speech could betray their identity, so they stood in the shadows, watching as the boy put his lips to the Kiss-Off station, his father holding the bucket until the ration shut off.

Kethuda and Sara studied the water, the people. Most were in a family group or young people on the arms of their sweethearts. Division of labor was well-practiced: one person holding the bucket, the other kissing the station until the water stopped. There was a lightness among the people, a sense of making the best of the inevitable. Children showed up in their nightclothes and took a moment to stick their hands in the water, to giggle, to play.

Sara and Kethuda walked the streets for hours, listening to the chatter of families, the music inside the houses, the yowling of a cat, the night cry of a T-Rex wren, bringing Sara great joy.

On the way home, two men came upon them. Kethuda whipped out her e-arrow rifle but faltered. Sara seized it, flipped it to *sleep*, and made quick work of the assailants. Kethuda stared at the unconscious men breathing at her feet.

"They will wake before sunrise," Sara spoke in a quiet tone. "My Flying Warrior showed me this feature, seldom activated, because it delivers no mortal blow. My teacher uses it, I'm sure, because he loathes the idea of taking a life."

"Your teacher. The man who put his holographic hand on your face?"

Sara looked off into the distance at a sliver of moonlight peering out from behind Ankara's tallest building.

"You have two lovers," Kethuda said, unable to mask the envy in her voice.

"Allah disapproves?"

"Do you care?"

Sara smiled. "Earth Divine lives in the water. That is my Allah."

Kethuda laughed. "You are a wild child." As she stared down at the unconscious men, her eyes grew so large, they shimmered like stars. "Your divine water, Sara, could that be a clue to the prophesy? I learned from my mother that the divine loves all people, all life forms. A 'flow' of the Earth could mean a change in how we are with each other—"

"Not set in our ways, like the dry, hard soil, but fluid, like soil flushed with water—"

"New tributaries opening, in ourselves, in others—"

"Owning the sins of the past." Sara's dark almond eyes caught a sliver of moonlight.

Kethuda sighed so deeply, the surrounding air fluttered. "This is what you want from me—the public confession."

Sara did not move.

Kethuda's lowered her eyes, as if looking down into the well of her own heart. "This breaking up of our 'solid' way of doing things, it would mean stripping away all we've done, all we've been."

"Do we have the guts to do it?"

"We?"

"The Kurds are not blameless. We have murdered. We know the corruption of the will to power."

Kethuda laughed in surprise, "I thought you were Ms. Fearless."

Sara looked skyward, "It's a well-kept secret."

"We are cowards."

"Thirsty ones," Sara said.

"We must use our brains to solve this riddle, our fear be damned."

They walked on, their minds encircling one another, thought building on thought. They talked of radical schemes, illogical consequences, and the heresy of breaking rules, as the moon peered through a break in the buildings, showering them with light.

44 – Gai

SHE dreamed of Africa, her little feet running through the bush, her brother behind her. Zebras up ahead, chewing on fresh grass shoots. She saw a baby, just born, wobbling to suck his mother's breast. "Lion!" cried Eng as a lioness leapt out of nowhere and charged straight toward his little sister.

She woke, gasping, sweating. She looked around. *Where am I? Where is my yeyo?* The warriors slumbering in the pea cactus tent slept in their green and white hijabs, in case they were called to arms. Devoted women, brave women, but strangers. *Not the women of home: my playmates, my aunties, Mama showing me how to shoot the bow, Papa taking my hand as we rounded up cattle on the red Earth road.*

Gai drank precious water, her longing for home so great, she could barely swallow. "Why this dream now?" she whispered to Engai, whose face she had never seen, only a presence in her dreams, a full-bodied, nongendered figure, made of Earth, more alive than anything in waking life. Sometimes Engai answered her questions in words or in pictures that floated through her mind like a solitary, sailing leaf. There was no answer this morning, only the peppery call of the T-Rex wren, *cha cha cha.* An irritating call. She longed for the soothing *korr-orr-orr* of the secretary bird echoing across the savannah.

Gai's thoughts went to her brother. *Have I robbed him of a wife's love?* Jealous ladies in their village said the twins acted like "more lovers than twins," for though Gai had one boyfriend briefly in school, it did not last. Nor did Eng pursue lasting connection with any women. He had once got mad at an old Aunty in the village who whispered nasty things. "You are jealous of this love I have with my sister," he said. "There is nothing carnal in it, only a meeting of mind and soul no other woman can match." He had been right. Gai knew this, and after they had fled North, survival was their only mission. Finding a mate, having children, would come later. Now this "later" was upon them. Partner-less, childless, she was grateful that she would meet Hamza's army today, having known one great love with all the passion of her soul.

She moved silently out of the tent. No ferry-cycle close by. Where could she go to get reception for her secret In-Phone pathway? "I will dance on rocks," she whispered to herself, scaling an outcrop that provided protection, or the illusion of it, for her bivouacked *belekevi* army.

She found a flat rock at the top and swayed, touching her right nipple, hoping her fancy footwork gave the implant in her breast the illusion of weightlessness.

"Hey, there, Sugar!" came the voice of the woman no longer in New Orleans. "You calling us from the heat of battle?"

Other faces appeared, all of them, from all over the world, peering at Gai with worry and love.

"I'm on a rock," Gai said. "From up here, pea cactus fields stretch out as far as I can see."

"Same here, in Itasca State Park. They Showboat-Sun-Shuttled us all the way up to Minnesota," said the woman, and she blew her trumpet.

"Why is your tune so happy?" asked Gai.

"I'm trumpeting you to victory, darling."

"We're all here, knowing you will beat those Turks back to the stone age," said a young illegal South African refugee from her new home on the banks of a woman-made river in Kansas.

"How's your new home?" Gai asked.

"Oh, it's so flat, the pea cactus a crispy gold. The people are nice, though. They call me the 'Black Dorothy,' because the style of pea cactus dress here looks like Judy Garland in her blue pinafore."

Thousands of faces burst into laughter. Gai drank it in like fresh water to her weary heart.

"I love you all," Gai said, her voice quivering.

"Long Live the Resistance," shouted thousands of women.

The transplant to Minnesota played her trumpet; the elderly woman on the porch in Paris raised her arms and directed them all in song:

> I have my women,
>
> I have my love.
>
> I am not alone in this world—

A *belekevi* ran toward Gai, waving her down from the rock. There was no time for goodbye. Gai pinched her right nipple and scrambled down the rock face.

"Turks coming over the mountain—" the *belekevi* said, breathless.

"Call to arms," Gai said, pulling her red Maasai scarf from her pocket and tying it around her neck, a talisman that, for a moment, anchored Gai in her African home.

Hamza's bronze soldiers swarmed down the dry mountain into the barren valley. Gai and her troops could find little cover in the arid patches of Earth. She led them into combat, shooting Turks to her right, to her left, killing one straight in front of her, a girl with bronze ribbons in her hair, her chest exploding with blood.

The *belekevi* had never been so fierce, streaming ahead of Gai, protecting her on all sides, some getting so close to the Turks they struck them in the head before delivering the fatal e-arrow.

No matter how many the Resistance killed, the Turks kept coming.

Gai noticed that some bronzies were falling from missiles outside the ranks of her army. A sniper? Two, maybe more, shooting from a distant pea cactus grove? Some of the Turks turned toward the snipers, suspecting another flank of *belekevi*.

Gai engaged the scope on her eyebrows, spotting the top of a head with spiky hair moving among the pea cactus; the flash of another person's dark hair. YPJ scouts? Whoever they were, it was a great opportunity. She called to her troops in code, imitating the secretary bird, *korr-orr-orr*.

Her *belekevi* shifted their position and closed in behind the Turks who were headed into the grove. The hidden snipers made quick work of the advancing bronzies, while the *belekevi* engaged the back rows.

Gai moved into the center column, shooting to the right, to the left, mowing down three young boys straight ahead of her. The blood of the closest boy flew out of his chest, and a droplet lodged in Gai's left eye. She lost focus for a split second, and an e-arrow missile sang its way into her heart. *Burned at the stake from within.*

The *belekevi* shrieked with alarm, their voices drowned in the growls of triumph from the Turkish boys. The smell of blood and spit filled the air.

The world of ordinary time and space dissolved, and a non-gendered figure appeared beside Gai whom she recognized at once, "Engai, you are here."

"I see you."

"I have killed," she said.

Engai smiled. "You think I cannot see wise Gai, sad Gai, loving Gai, foolish Gai, unwitting warrior Gai. You fulfilled your destiny. Let me fulfill mine."

Gai felt no sorrow, no fear, only love for the Earth, the water, the sky, and all living things. She saw her *yeyo*, her papa, the red Earth of the Maasai Mara, the *korr-orr-orr* of the secretary bird, calling her home.

45 – Ruqia

GONUL and Ruqia peered out of the pea cactus grove. The fighting halted. The Turks signaled that they found no Water Thread in the cave, and called for their soldiers to abandon the field. Through the unforgiving dust, Ruqia and Gonul could see Turkish soldiers dragging their fallen comrades away. "They put the stunned ones into the same pile?" she asked.

"Of course," he said with a chuckle, "how surprised they will be when those soldiers wake up."

"This is not warfare," she said, with a download of guilt.

"You're not a warrior any longer."

She smacked him with her cane, her heart knowing no humor. "It's very hard to give up who I was, to become a weak thing that cannot *win*."

Ruqia and Gonul heard the sound of wailing and made their way out of the grove to the women soldiers encircling the body of an African, her black braids resting on her breast. A soldier breathed into the mouth of the fallen one, pressing on her heart, "Gai, do not leave us—"

Ruqia knelt, touching the wrist of the victim, "She is gone."

"You are the famous Flying Warrior. You trained me in Rojava." Many young faces turned to Ruqia.

"You are the famous *belekevi*," she said with a bow of her head. "Shouldn't someone close the eyes of your Gai?"

"The person who closes her eyes will be our next General."

A heaviness consumed Ruqia's body, and with it, a silent song of destiny as if she were being pulled out of herself with such force it seemed impossible that her body was still in one piece.

She bowed deeply, as if praying to Allah, hearing the song of destiny grow stronger, even as the other part within her pulled toward a deeper destiny she could not see.

The *belekevi* joined her in prayer, chanting to Allah, wailing the name of General Gai, the noble one.

Ruqia joined in, scouring her brain for chants and songs she had overheard from Gran. The *belekevi* seemed warmed by such devotion. For Ruqia, it was all show, and yet, why was she doing this? They could all see the cast on her leg. She could never fly in battle, and yet, the pull within her to return to glory was stoked by the adoration on their young faces. Another voice within her said, "You can't do this. You are done with killing." It was her greatest battle, not of blood and singing arrows, but of the depth of her soul.

Who am I? There is no god dictating my destiny. It is all up to me.

The *belekevi* formed a circle around her, praying to Allah to grant them the gift of the great Flying Warrior, who could still fly as a genius of strategy in battle.

The sound of their sweet voices, the low notes and high notes, entered Ruqia's body until the buzzing thoughts in her brain calmed.

The women touched Ruqia's shoulders. "Shoulders so strong. You are a Kurd, like us. Carry the Resistance to victory. Protect us from harm. Free Sara Roxan, our hero."

The last words landed squarely in Ruqia's heart. She looked away from Gonul and addressed the *belekevi*. "I will be your General."

The women bowed with relief and offered song and praise.

Gonul gently took Ruqia's hand. "You must do this?"

She moved her finger across the back of his hand: the veins, the rough sunburned patches. She said to her soldiers, "This is my brother, Gonul. He will bear the body of your General Gai back to Ankara."

The *belekevi* murmured gratitude. One of them removed the red Maasai scarf from Gai's neck and tied it around Ruqia's. Too tightly. She loosened the knot and nodded in acceptance.

Many bodies of the fallen comrades were placed on the ground beside General Gai. Many tears of mourning flowed. Ruqia and Gonul held hands as they walked into the battlefield to retrieve the dead. Ruqia was nauseated. *This comes from the part of me that loathes war.* She knew Gonul sensed it. They said nothing.

The sun set as the stench of blood became the sorrowful smell of death. When the stars come out, a massive Sun War Car appeared, its panels flapping like a giant dragonfly with the last bit of stored syn-photosynthesis. It came to a stop beside the bodies of Gai and the other soldiers, and its back end opened with a great yawn to receive all the bodies.

"I don't want war for you, sister," Gonul said.

She looked at him, as if seeing him at the end of a long tunnel. "You are going to Ankara. Give Sara my love."

He hugged her fiercely. "You will join us, soon?"

The *belekevi* chanted the Sufi prayer for the dead as Ruqia closed Gai's starlit eyes. She lifted her body into the War Car beside the other victims. *Murder in battle is so wrong, and yet, here I am, bound once more for glory at all costs.*

Gonul boarded the front of the vehicle, and it took off like a hornet from its nest. Ruqia breathed slowly, gaining her balance. She was the General now. She had to be the one to protect and lead these young women.

She glanced down at the tiny flat button on her e-arrow rifle that would alter the setting from *sleep* to *kill.* The mantle of Gonul's love caressed her shoulders like a giant golden shawl. The memory of Sara weeping over the body of the ISIS Comrade, the little girl in the Temple of Return, dying with her baby bird…. Ruqia could not move her fingers. Could not alter the setting.

"Son of a bitch," she muttered, turning to face her troops.

46 – Sara

ENG intercepted Sara and Kethuda and pulled them into an alleyway. "What in the name of Engai are you doing out here?" He gestured at the streets around them.

"We didn't want to bother you," Kethuda said.

"We wanted to go on our own, without a babysitter," Sara said, hands on her hips in defiance.

"I will send a message to Gai," he said, escorting them quickly through the streets. "She will have short words for you both."

"We were looking for the answer to the riddle," the women said in unison.

Eng stopped, his face graced with moonlight: no judgment, only curiosity.

"If your sister were here, she would tickle you," Kethuda said.

"Are you asking for the job?"

Kethuda quickly turned away. Sara laughed to cover the tender feelings of the queen. *How odd, I'm protecting the queen like a—friend....*

Eng laughed nervously, aware of his impropriety. He hurried them through the streets and up the long stairs to Sara's prison cell.

Kethuda dismantled Sara's invisible tether with irritation. *She doesn't like putting me in bondage.* "Are you afraid of the disapproval of the women of the world?"

"How would you know about such things?"

"YPJ is admired by Nina Navalny in solidarity with her own Resistance. Women all over Europe, India, Afghanistan, America envy our courage and success. These women are mad at you, yes?"

"I am not running a popularity contest," Kethuda said, allowing Eng to pull out her chair and help her into it.

A *belekevi* brought water, coffee, and pea cactus angel food cake.

"We don't have a solution," Sara said to Eng as she gulped the water. "But we have a plan. It was the President's idea: the 'Earth' in the riddle is *us*, humans, hardened in our nature, inflexible in our hatred for each other." She bit into the cake and moaned with pleasure at the soft texture in her mouth. "To solve the riddle, we must break up this hatred in our hearts and 'flow' in reconciliation with each other."

Eng poured a cup of coffee for Kethuda, his hand trembling with excitement. "You women have great brilliance," he said. "To 'flow' as a human being is to be like water when it is not dammed or evaporated—"

"Generous to all people," Kethuda said, her eyes on his trembling hands.

"Generous to all living things," Sara said.

Kethuda chuckled, "Sara loves her birds and dinosaurs more than people."

"I agree with her," he said. "Engai lives in everything."

"My job is people first," Kethuda said. "If humanity is what needs to 'run like water,' this must involve a public moral reckoning."

Eng's eyes brightened. "There is a model for this in the history of South Africa. The Truth and Reconciliation trials that ultimately, however imperfectly, dismantled Apartheid."

Sara gasped, "My teacher told us about that." She placed her palm on Kethuda's forehead, the other on Eng's. The placement of a human palm on a human forehead, activated a projected image from the In-Phone onto the cold stone wall: twentieth century white oppressors listening to the testimony of Black South African women who were raped and tortured. One woman, called Selema, expressed her rage and hatred. Her oppressors knelt before her in shame, confessing their guilt. The images moved in montage through three days, until, miraculously, Selema forgave them.

"Enough," Kethuda said when they had watched for some time. She gently lowered Sara's hand. "Can we really do it here, with the Turks and the Kurds?"

A darkness took over Sara's body, as if she were stepping out on a mountain ledge with no way to turn back. She looked at the cake on her plate, no longer hungry for it.

Kethuda kicked off her golden sandals and paced on the wretched stone floor in bare feet.

Eng said, "If we are to emulate South Africa, the sins of both nations must have a full hearing, or it will seem a political ploy, not the answer to 'Earth flowing like water.'"

Kethuda flounced into her chair and drank down her cup of water. "If I do this, my father will literally kill me as soon as he gets the chance. If I don't do this, my people will dehydrate." Her body trembled, speaking the word.

Sara spoke in a clear voice, "If I do this, Madam President, will you grant me immunity from execution?"

"Lies stop here," the queen said, her eyes finding Sara's. "I saved you once. I hope I don't have to save you again. In truth, if we fail and power shifts, no promise of immunity can save you."

Sara's heart skipped as she reached out a sweaty palm. The queen encircled it, her palm sweaty as well.

47 - Kethuda

ENG escorted the President back to her apartment. "I will be on guard," he said, closing the door.

"You think someone will come after me?" she said through the door.

"I think you were foolish to go into the streets without me."

"No one talks to me like that, except Gai."

They chuckled. The aroma of Ankara at night penetrated the room: pea cactus peppers roasting on a crackling fire, the tink tink of ferry-cycle bells, lovers whispering. The longing in Kethuda's heart was like a soft animal coming out of its burrow, yearning to touch and be touched.

She gulped water and curled onto the floor beside the door. "Eng, are you there?"

"I am here."

Her body trembled. "Do you need water?"

"I am good. My ear lobe is quite sore from trying to message Gai about your misbehavior. I cannot get through. Someone must have disabled her In-Phone."

"Hamza?"

His breath shortened. She regretted her words, "I'm sorry. I didn't mean to worry you."

"My sister is my certainty mountain. Not to worry."

Kethuda placed her palm on the pea-wooden surface of the door. "Have you ever loved a woman, besides her?"

He did not answer at once. "Before I answer, can you tell me, Madam President, what you mean by 'love'?"

She leaned her cheek against the door, as if it were his chest.

His voice betrayed a deep curiosity. "What is it that you look for, Madam President, in the nature of the heart, beyond physical desire?"

She wanted to grab the hand of a woman for courage. With Gai at the front, the only woman she could think of was the Kurd. How absurd. She cleared her throat. "Love? I have known the love of my mother, though I did not respect her. She had no spine against my father. Beyond that, it is legendary that my father has kept me locked away from romantic love with a man, or a woman, or nongender, for that matter. In a way, I am like a monk, or a princess looking down from her tower."

"A lonely princess," he said.

"I know my fantasies," she said, eyes closed, as if talking in a dream. "A man who is everything my father is not. A man who delights in simple joys and cares for me, as I care for him. A better man than I: not torn between my love of power and my desire to love justice, to live as a simple woman, kind and free"

She heard subtle movement, but he said nothing.

"What is love to you, Eng? You who have only felt a deep abiding sister-love for your twin?"

His fingers tapped the door, a light, contemplative rhythm. "I am not as fine in character as my sister. I have known women. I have stolen. I have killed."

"To survive."

"Not so pure as that. I understand what it is to be of two minds. I say I am a lover of peace, and yet, when my sister and I were fleeing to the North, I killed for a liter of water. You have a weakness: the thrill you get from being Ataturka the powerful. Both of us long to be better human beings."

She felt a wash of relief, even joy. "Eng, will you open the door?"

He chuckled, "Is that an order?"

She giggled like a schoolgirl, "Absolutely."

He opened the door. His face was soft with sweat.

Her body grew warm, her lips parting.

He touched his ear, "Incoming message—must be Gai." As he listened, his face grew tight, as if he suddenly stood in a strong wind. "Oh my God, Kethuda, Gai is dead."

"No." She reached for him, her body cold with shock, her heart dissolving into his.

48 – Eng

HE could not talk her out of it. Kethuda came with him as violence erupted in the streets of Ankara, Hamza's soldiers flooding into the city, shooting *belekevi*, or worse, ripping off their hijabs and raping them before killing them.

Kethuda stayed close to Eng, never turning away as they came upon violated young women left for dead in alleyways. He helped her bind their wounds as she talked to them in soothing tones.

He watched her with admiration. Where did the President learn to show empathy so well? *Love thine enemy?* Surely it was not in the original meaning of the phrase that he should find himself falling in love with the Turkish President against his will. *Does the heart know politics, or is it an organ unto itself?*

The streets emptied with the dawn. Nothing left but the stench of blood and spent e-arrow missiles. Hamza's soldiers had gone off to find women and drink themselves to sleep. They would not sleep for long. Daylight would bring them out again, like baby burrowing lizards who crave the sun. An uneasy stillness settled on the dusty streets.

Eng put his arm around Kethuda. She rested her head on his shoulder. It warmed him to feel the strength and softness of her body, the scent of dust and perfume in her hair. They were standing in front of the Presidential apartment, waiting.

A Sun Car approached. *Belekevi* followed it through the streets to receive the bodies of their loved one. A Kurdish man in YPJ fatigues emerged from the Sun Car, carrying the body of Gai wrapped in a thin white cloth. Eng fell to his knees, wailing with rage and grief beyond the Earth and sky.

Kethuda grabbed his hand, weeping as she knelt beside him.

The Kurd asked, "Where shall I place the body of General Gai?"

Kethuda peered at him through her tears. "You are the man who touched Sara's face in the hologram—"

"I am Gonul. Sara is my beloved."

Eng rose unsteadily, looking into the eyes of this man. Soulful eyes, intelligent and wise. "I would carry my sister, but I haven't the strength. Not today."

Gonul carried Gai's body up the stairs and placed her on the bed. He took out a bottle of oil.

"I will do it," Eng said, pouring the rose-scented liquid into his hands, smoothing it onto Gai's face, still so beautiful, even in death. "I am now one half of myself," he said. "I long to join her."

Kethuda spoke through tears. "Please, Eng, I beg you not to leave this world, and me alone in it. I'm a selfish monster, but I cannot bear to lose you both. I love your sister so much. This apartment was our sacred women's space. How often we gazed at the sun coming through the white curtains and greeted the day with coffee and dance."

Eng reached for Kethuda and guided her fingers to touch Gai's face.

"How cold she is," Kethuda said.

"I feel the warmth of her soul," he said. "She loved you. So often Gai would say, 'Brother, this woman President wants good things. Perhaps she will learn the wisdom of the invisible heart, even as the zebra faces into the wind to catch the lion's scent.'"

"I will leave you in private," Gonul said, closing the door behind him.

Kethuda touched Gai's hair. "Eng, your sister spoke of you all the time."

Eng reached out to touch the President's small hand, pulsing with life next to the quiet darkness of his lifeless twin.

Kethuda trembled at his touch, her fingers brushing Gai's eyelids. "Your sister told me, 'My brother, he came out of the womb first, bigger, longer.' She said, 'Even as a little boy, he could bring down a cape buffalo with one shot.'"

His feet seemed to straddle two worlds, the one where Gai showed him how to shoot a Maasai spear and this one, where she lay dead. He touched his sister's nose. "She always made me feel worthy, whether I deserved it or not."

"You used to lift her up onto your shoulders, keeping her safe, as you went into the bush."

"She told you that?"

"I know you so well, Eng, the other half of your god." Kethuda pulled his face close and kissed his lips. His body opened to hers, grief and desire becoming one.

49 – Gonul

HE ran through the streets, his heart in a panic. Gai's death was a great distraction for Ataturka, an opportunity he must seize before it was too late.

He scurried past the Kiss-Off station, the street vendors crying, "pea cactus popsicles in new flavors: rosemary, garlic, octopus!"

He found the underground headquarters of the *belekevi*. Although Gai was neither Sufi, nor Muslim, the *belekevi* were predominantly Sufi, so they twirled slowly and prayed to Allah to protect Gai's ascending soul. Gonul joined them in prayer.

The young women begged him to tell them more about the new General, "R," who had taken Gai's place. He told them she was the greatest fighter in all Rojava. Even wounded she would lead the *belekevi* to victory. They were pleased and grateful.

What if Ruqia can't go back to killing? Then I'm lying to these devoted women.

He excused himself, saying he had to attend to important business of the Kurdish Resistance. One of the *belekevi* touched his forehead, downloading directions to a safe house onto his In-Phone. "Be very careful," she said. "The bronze soldiers of Hamza are everywhere."

Back on the street, he sensed that the bronzies were following him. He dodged into a narrow alleyway, slipping into a merchant stall beside an old man in a Kurdish turban. The sign over his shop announced *Pea Cactus Straws—Get The Most From Kiss-Off!*

"No law against sucking out the last bit with a straw," the old man said. Gonul borrowed a turban with face covering and helped the old man unload boxes, as the bronze soldiers passed by.

"Stay until nightfall," the old man said. "I could use the help, and you can get to wherever you're going in the dark, while the soldiers get drunk and chase women."

As the sunset blended the crimson sky into gray, Gonul thanked the old man, slipped into the streets, and came upon the back of the prison, guarded by the *belekevi*.

They ushered him quickly up to Sara's cell, where he found her with one finger on her In-Phone, the other writing words in the air.

He stood, breathing slowly, taking in the sight of her: the lines of her small body moving gracefully, her dark almond eyes searching for vertical patterns in the horizontal text.

He stepped closer, his boots scraping the floor.

She turned, startled, and swept the words away. "Mr. Askay— Are you virtual or a dream?"

"Neither. I am real."

"Real? How is that possible?"

He touched his ankle, and the cell door opened.

"What magic is this?" she said, barely breathing.

"I peeked into Ataturka's room. The African was making love to her. He didn't notice that I touched his ankle and copied the code."

"Making love to her?" she said with excitement.

"You care about this?"

"She has loved him for so long—"

"Not as long as I have loved you." He pulled her into his arms. She wept with joy, kissing him again and again, their hands moving across each other.

She pulled him toward a lumpy mattress on the stone floor.

"No, my darling, we don't have time. The safe house is far away, but we can make it, if we leave right now."

"Safe house?"

He combed her long dark hair with his fingers. "Sara, my Sara, I have come to set you free."

Her forehead creased, and she and looked at him with large eyes. He didn't understand. She should be weeping with joy and pulling him out the door. Instead, her eyes turned inward, as if looking for something in an unfamiliar landscape. "Safe house," she murmured. "Safe from what?"

"Hamza discovered that his troops were drinking and sleeping with prostitutes through the night. He shot a few of them to set an example and stationed soldiers on every street corner all night long. I've brought a burka to hide you."

"Hide?"

"Yes, for the duration of the Resistance. They want you dead, Sara."

Her breath became imperceptible; her body, which had moved in spirals of joy only a moment ago, grew quite still.

"Don't be afraid, my darling. I will protect you. Come. Now." He pulled the burka out of his pack.

"Hide? Is that what you think of me?"

"I think you want to live."

Tears moved down her face. "I do want to live. I do. I love you so, and I love R. Where is she?"

He cradled Sara's moist face on his chest. "She's in the mountains, assuming General Gai's command."

Sara looked in his eyes, her own blurred with tears. "Ruqia is leading women into battle, and you want me to hide in a burka?"

"You would stay *here*, Ataturka's pawn?"

"I see who she is, but I have a part to play in this. We all need to find the Water Thread. I can help Kethuda—that's her real name. I can help her find the answer to the riddle."

"What if it's a hoax?" he said, gathering the folds of the burka to slide over her head.

She stepped back. "No. You lie to me, to yourself. You know this in your own heart. The riddle was written in the handwriting of your friend, Joseph. It is a philosophy, a social policy, offered to the whole world."

Blood seemed to drain out of his body. "My God, Sara—you turn me away in favor of blind idealism?"

"This is not idealism, Gonul, my love. It is a truth that great mystics and scientists have known for centuries. The true nature of existence: it does not have to be hard, like our thirsty Earth, it can be fluid, in our connection to all living things, to the air, the stars, to each other. I lecture you as you used to lecture me, but the time for teaching is over. We are poised, like the dinostrich and the t-rex wren, to evolve or perish."

A great loneliness settled into his very being, "And you—and the Turkish President are going to lead this grand evolutionary shift? She's your pal now? What did you call her?"

"Kethuda. Her real name."

"She has blinded you."

Sara laughed warmly, "I see all sides of her. How can you presume to know what I have lived and seen with the eyes of my own mind and heart?"

He stepped closer. "Sara, Ataturka has no heart. I felt it, just now, when I carried Gai's body into her apartment. Being in her presence, I shivered, like a child standing in snow."

"Snow…" she said, recalling a bygone wonder.

"Come with me, now, quickly." He lifted the burka to pull it over her head.

Sara seized the rough cloth and threw it to the ground. "No, Gonul. You think you can force me to go against myself? I see the part of Kethuda that is obsessed with power, but she is more than that. She has a woman's heart, and that part of her desires to wed her power to the *good*."

"The good…?"

"If I leave, and hide out with you, making love and writing revolutionary pamphlets, I know which part of her will win."

The hot tears of awareness flooded his eyes. "You are her conscience."

Sara sighed, "Ruqia is in great danger. If Kethuda and I can solve the riddle, we can prevent an escalation of this war."

"Ha, now you're the one tossing bullshit. You don't want Ruqia to die, but you are dazzled by your *own* power. It outshines your love for both of us."

Sara breathed slowly, receiving the truth of it. "I don't deny it. The last thing I expected. I do feel a sense of my own power, but it is not a power to dominate people, or strum my own *oud*. It's a power deep within me to claim my own destiny."

He was quiet as the grave, feeling the loss of her.

She sensed it. "I love you so much, but something happened between me and Kethuda, this person I used to call 'the queen.' Not love, certainly plenty of hatred, but something else. A possible co-creating of a new world."

His body could not move. Even his bones didn't believe what he was hearing.

"And, you, my dearest Mr. Askay. What of *your* power? You don't need to save me." She reached out to him. They held each other, but he could feel her body stiffen, where it had once been the softest thing he had ever touched.

As dawn light filtered in from the high barred window, Gonul scooped the burka off the floor and left without a word, knowing that her eyes followed him, that her eyes would always follow him.

PART FOUR
WATER

50 - Kethuda

THE procession stretched for miles through the pea cactus fields, Kethuda deeply moved that so many people knew and loved Gai. Not just the fighters of the Resistance, but children, street vendors, the African water refugee community in Ankara. And dancers, so many dancers wearing brilliant colors to honor the woman who had been their teacher, their mentor, their friend.

The event was carried on the World Board at the request of the Sisterhood of African Mothers and Daughters. Their songs and trumpets were broadcast on everyone's In-Phone around the world, heralding Gai to her rest.

The body, carried on high by the *belekevi,* was wrapped in a translucent pea cactus Burial Cloth. Since the coming of the perma-drought, human and animal bodies had been placed vertically into a grave at the edge of a pea cactus grove. The Burial Cloth would dissolve into the soil, and Gai's naked body would join the legions of those whose bodies fertilized the field.

The procession came to a square hole of Earth marked by a cloth of white silk on a pole, waving like a flag in the breeze.

"Are you sure?" Eng said, leaning close to Kethuda. She was grateful for his warmth, the scent of his body, the low sweet growl of his voice.

She touched the white cloth. "My mother is in the next silo. Please, do us the honor to place your sister beside her." She took the white scarf and wrapped it around her shoulders. How soft it still was, after blowing in the drying air all these years.

Eng held the body of his sister, rocking her, singing cradle songs of the Maasai, *grow up, my child, Grow up like the mountain.* When his voice fell silent, Kethuda helped him lower Gai into the Earth.

The long line of mourners passed, bowing, praying.

When all had taken their time to honor Gai, the *belekevi* covered the body with Earth.

Kethuda and Eng placed a pea cactus blossom on the silent grave and followed the mourners to an empty field where dancers jumped straight up in the air like Maasai warriors. Mourners encircled them, weaving together, singing in the languages of the African ancestors.

Kethuda and Eng joined the circle, their bodies moving close, moving apart, shouting in grief and joy and love for Gai, who would live in their hearts forever.

Late that night, Kethuda woke in her canopy bed beside Eng's naked body. Moonlight penetrated the sheer white curtains. Their love-making was not gentle, an unmistakable act of aggression waged by both of them, fed by an appetite that grew more insatiable with each encounter. They did not speak of love but only "Does this hurt?" or "Do you like this?" or "Are you thirsty?" To speak of love implied they might lose one another. That was unbearable.

When they thought of Gai, they wept. When they released their tears, they pressed their bodies together, grateful for the explosion of pleasure that increased with time.

How did I live without this for so long? Always in control, always my image to consider, afraid if I surrendered to desire, it would destroy my power. Lies fed to me by my father. In truth, I feel more powerful now that I can throw this man down on my bed and dictate my pleasure, even as I satisfy his.

She was happy to see Eng sleeping. He had not slept since Gai's death, nor had she. They seemed to find respite only in love-making. She slid from the bed, adoring the feeling of her skin against the silk sheets. Never had she loved her body so much. *His hands touch every inch of me, his eyes see all of me, and I am changed because of it. I am a woman of desire, not too old to have a child. Something I never dared hope for, but must have craved and did not know it.*

She danced, quietly, naked, thinking of Gai: the first night, when they had danced before all those men. She needed to carry that confidence with her now, as she dressed, picked up Gai's e-arrow rifle, and slipped silently from the room.

She hurried down the back stairs, and a dark figure appeared, blocking the bottom step. A beast? A man? She moved into the moonlight. He had aged, the folds of flesh on his neck more iguana than man.

"Ayse?" Hamza said, peering up into the darkness.

"No, Papa." Her hand tightened on the rifle under her cloak.

His spine strained to straighten, his lips a bell curve.

She looked around. No bronzies, and in her haste to get to Sara, she had neglected to call *belekevi*. Father and daughter were alone. "I saw Mama's grave today. We buried General Gai beside her."

"The naked dancer, next to my wife. Allah will never forgive you."

"Both were great women, Papa."

"Shut up."

The old rage simmered in her. "I put a flower on Mama's grave, but the ground is so hard, so dry, it blew away."

His eyes lifted. "It's not my fault the water went away."

"Isn't it?"

"Oh, please. The fossil fuel lament. What the hell was my grandfather supposed to do, and his father before him? We needed fuel. We dug up oil. By the time they figured out it was burning up the planet, it was too late."

"Shame on you. Shame on your fathers."

His voice softened, "I flew in fossil fuel airplanes when I was a boy. Quite something. Tourists used to fly to Turkiye, especially Istanbul, to marvel at our ancient mosques, our modern cuisine."

"I hope to fly someday, when they perfect the Sun Sky Shuttle."

His eyes searched her face. "So, my army shot down your darling African Queen. Too bad. I remember her at the banquet. What a body. I was royally pissed off that you horned in. I had my bed all ready for her that night."

"I'll bet you did."

"I'm a man, and your mother is gone."

"You had many women when she was alive."

His eyes narrowed, "What do you want, Kethuda?"

"Oh, it's back to that. What happened to Ataturka?"

"You tell me."

"Ataturka is alive and well."

He smiled, "You play politics on both sides. You lie to me. You lie to the Resistance. You keep both sides guessing where you really stand."

She said nothing, her mind swirling: damn him for being so mean, so right.

He cackled like an old crow. "You don't stand for anything, do you? Hah! Poor baby, you have the insides of a jellyfish."

She cursed herself in silence: he had gotten to her again, stripping her down to *nothing*. Out of the chaos of her mind, she said, "How did you know you loved Ayse?"

His eyes found hers in the darkness. "I'll be damned. No longer the Virgin Queen. Who is it, your African lackey? I'm jealous. Where's *my* whore?"

"I think I love him. A man of great integrity and honor. You can't possibly understand."

"That's a load of crap. I know what it is to love what you cannot *be*. Your mother was the love of my life. All gentleness and honor. So much so, it was hard to find the woman in her. I didn't want to twirl and pray; I wanted to make love to her!"

He had never confessed this before. An unwanted warmth entered her heart. "I can understand why that was hard for you, Papa."

"I gather you don't have any problem getting it on with—what's his name?"

"Eng, the other half of 'god' in Maasai."

He smirked. "Just keep it quiet, if you value your neck, not to mention your Presidency."

She choked down her fury, the silence between them like two vultures on the plains with nothing to eat.

He climbed a step toward her, his breath like burnt pine needles. "How much longer must we keep up this charade, my dear?"

"Until my soldiers find the Water Thread. Then we will see what happens to the Resistance."

"Do it now," he said. "Take your civil army, the ones without those infernal Kurd hijabs, join my bronzies. We will find your damned Water Thread. If it exists."

In the silence, she felt the jellyfish inside of her transform into a different species: an elegant amphibian, rainbow colored, swimming through man-made coral reefs. She knew what she wanted: Eng, and she wanted the Resistance to win. Earth Goddess be praised, she wanted to be *good*.

"Consolidate the armies of father and child. Our true allies will love us—the Russians, the Chinese. We don't need RAT. All those countries are going under anyway. We will find your Water Thread and save it for our new alliance."

She stared down at the man, his leathery skin darker in the shadow of the moon.

"I don't know if you've ever tasted fine Russian caviar, my darling. The finest sensual orgasm on the planet."

I could shoot him right here and be done with it. The bronzies would fall apart, the belekevi take over the city. I would bury him in a field far away from Mama.

He coughed, bending over, as if choking on her thoughts.

She pulled the weapon from her cloak, flipped the setting to *kill*.

A scent came to her on the wind, her Papa's scent, no words for it, just *him,* and with it, sounds of his steps in bare feet, her mama's laughter, her papa's steady hands as he lifted her out of her high chair.

She shut off the rifle and ran upstairs. Eng still slept. As much as she wanted to curl next to him, she needed something else at this moment. She poured a glass of water and slipped into the adjoining room that had belonged to Gai. There was only one high window, its rough brown pea cactus curtain bobbing slightly in the night breeze. *What an entitled bitch I was, to make Gai stay in this tiny servant room.*

She crawled onto the scratchy covers of the single bed, pressing her In-Phone with little hope. She was surprised when the sleepy face of Nina Navalny appeared. "I'm sorry. Did I wake you?" Kethuda said in a rush. "Please, I want to talk to you."

Nina peered closer. "Ataturka?"

"No, call me Kethuda if you can manage it. My given name. Is Nina yours?"

"Nina Pavlova Navalny. Always just Nina. You sound different, Kethuda. What's happening?"

"The riddle."

Nina rubbed her eyes. "Your hoax? We've been making jokes about it."

Kethuda breathed slowly. *Of course no one believes it, any more than they believe the Water Thread is real.* "Never mind, tell me what is happening in Russia, or wherever you are."

"My rebels, we are in hiding. I won't tell you where. There is plenty of water here, but in my country, it is very bad. Even in Siberia they have imposed stiffer rations."

"I want to know—I am doing an experiment, based on South Africa, Truth and Reconciliation. In Russia, did your grandfather's grandfather ever find a way to make your terrible dictators apologize for the genocide of Stalin, the war in Ukraine, the closing of the country to water refugees?"

Nina lowered her eyes as if suddenly very tired. "You sound like a child to ask these things. The Russian people have never been free; we still have apartheid of the soul."

Kethuda reached for a comb on Gai's nightstand, smelled it, taking in the scent of Gai's hair. "It has never happened in my country either. We are going to attempt it, the Kurd and I. I wanted to know if you had any advice for me?"

Nina was quiet, resting her chin on her hands. "I have an advantage over you, Kethuda. My rebels and I, we have nothing to lose, because we have nothing. I am not a President. I am a gambler. I am betting that the water will go so low, the coasts be so flooded that our dictator will have no solution. All the people will rise up and join me. They will set aside their fear. I don't care if I live or I die. I don't care who hates. If you can get to this place, Kethuda, where you don't cling to your power, or even your life, you can lay bare the sins of your dictators, and the people will see your truth and follow you."

Tears streamed down the President's face. "I want to be that person. I want to be as brave as you. I try, but I am weak. I could have killed my father just now, and claimed my country for the Resistance. I couldn't do it."

Nina pierced the energy veil of the In-Phone with her finger, wiping off Kethuda's tears.

"Thank God you didn't kill him," Nina said, "Not that he doesn't deserve to die, but it must not be by your hand. I will put your tears in a bottle, Madam President. When humans have left this Earth, visitors from another galaxy will come here. They will find this bottle and say, 'What treasure! The tears of a woman who found the courage of her heart.'"

51 - Ruqia

SHE pulled herself up the face of the cliff, her bad leg hanging off the end of her body like a T-rex wren with a broken wing. This image gave her strength as she remembered Sara calling for Rexie after they had made love in the desert. The answer had come, *cha cha cha cha,* and Sara had run barefoot across the sand, her body like an angel ready to take flight. The bird had landed on her shoulder, cried out, and flew away. Later, as they curled together under the stars, Sara wondered if the bird was trying to tell them to flee. But they were warriors in the YPJ, guarding the Water Thread. Flight would be treason, and they were so in love, they didn't want their time in the desert to end.

Ruqia's exhaustion was more than physical. In every skirmish between the *belekevi* and Turks, she had used her disability to stay behind in combat, fearing that the *belekevi* would discover the dark secret that she had set her e-arrow rifle on *sleep.* This deception chewed away at her heart as she watched the *belekevi* kill and be killed.

This is my job, said her head.

Not any longer, said her body, sending her crushing headaches that blinded her with pulsing, purple light.

Using what was left of her strength, she reached the top of the mountain. *Belekevi* swarmed up the cliff beside her. They could see a distant cave where, it was rumored, Joseph and his team had built a secret chamber for the Water Thread.

If we find it, all this blood and horror will be worth it.

She pressed her forehead to no avail. The In-Phone was out of range. Her scouts had not returned. Not a good sign, but the cave was so close, just across the plains. "Advance!" she shouted, ignoring pain in her leg as she led the charge, her brave young soldiers swarming ahead of her toward the cave.

The *belekevi* shrieked in alarm as a flank of bronze soldiers poured onto the field, e-arrows singing through the air. Ruqia could not stay behind when her soldiers were being ambushed. She shot down Turks, to the right, to the left, to center.

A *belekevi* noticed that a bronzie felled by Ruqia's rifle spilled no blood. "What are you doing?" she said. "They slaughter us and you put them to sleep?" An e-arrow sank into the girl's heart, and blood covered the ground. In horror, Ruqia looked out across the field: bronze figures advancing, as far as she could see. "Retreat!" she shouted, lifting the fallen *belekevi*, but the woman who had spoken truth to Ruqia's power was dead.

The other *belekevi* closed in, protecting their General, many falling as their column retreated to the hilltop, descending the side they had just climbed, firing, pursued by the Turks. As Ruqia stumbled down the hillside, bronzies pushed *belekevi* off the cliff. One by one, the young women's bodies were crushed on the white rocks below.

The Turks retreated in triumph. What was left of Ruqia's army found shelter in a pea cactus grove down valley from the mountain. Many were wounded. Many more had died. They wept and sucked raw pea cactus stems.

A nongendered soldier wiped blood and sweat off their face. They stared at Ruqia.

Humiliation flowed warm and ugly through Ruqia's body. She dropped her eyes.

"You led us into a trap."

"I didn't know. I heard rumors about the cave. We all did. All I thought about was finding the Water Thread."

"The bronzies heard the rumors too," they said. "It was satisfying to hear them squawk when they found an empty cave. Small joy in the face of so much blood." They seized Ruqia's rifle, their face draining of color when they read the setting. "*Sleep.* It is true then."

Shame clustered in Ruqia's throat. The ungendered held out their hand. Ruqia surrendered Gai's red Maasai scarf. They tied it around their own neck, brandishing their weapon, set on *kill.*

The *belekevi* did not look at Ruqia.

As the sun set, they followed their new General out of the grove.

Ruqia sat alone, her e-arrow rifle on her lap. *How many of my women died today? Fifty? A hundred? Two hundred? Why did they let me live?*

The answer came as she stared down at her rifle. *Of course, men would shoot me and be done with it. Women assume I will be my own executioner. Why stain their hands with my blood?*

She managed a soft smile. Gonul would call her out on gender bias. He always insisted that compassionate men behave just like women. Well, maybe.

She cradled the weapon in her arms and ran her fingers over all its nicks and scratches. A tired weapon, but capable of performing one last violent act. She changed the setting to *kill* and lifted it to her temple.

52 – Sara

CHA cha cha cha!

"Rexie II! It has been so *long*."

cha cha cha cha!

She climbed up the jagged bricks of her cell wall, a cup of water in one hand, a morsel of a *saltie* between her teeth. "My darling, today of all days, you are *here*."

The dawning sun warmed the eager bird as she passed the cup through the bars and watched his long tongue extend into the water. She reached out to touch his feathers. He quivered, but let her pet him, one shimmering black eye mirroring hers.

"Thank you, babe," she said. "Your feathers are the softest thing I've ever touched, except, maybe, Ruqia's eyelids, or the underside of Gonul's wrist... When your species becomes a full-fledged dinosaur, please keep your feathers. No scaly lizard skin. Always stay as silken as you are."

Some things of beauty need to remain in a world of constant change. Even as this thought came to her, Rexie II flew away into the sun.

A door slammed on the floor below. She climbed down and pressed a finger to her third eye, but Ruqia did not answer; must be out of range with her army. *Should I try Gonul? No. How could I call him after sending him away?*

Kethuda would be wearing her white gown and blue hijab. Sara mused that she, in contrast, would appear in sweaty fatigues, her hair in greasy ringlets, but what had any of this to do with it? And yet she knew perception was part of the theater of the day. She had not seen Kethuda for several days.

Their public event was planned, but not rehearsed. In truth neither of them knew what the other was going to say.

Kethuda arrived with Eng, their bodies moving in a subtle rhythm that betrayed their intimacy. Kethuda wore her mother's wedding gown, her mother's blue hijab. She glanced at Sara, her face a mask.

The sun seared Sara's eyes as they stepped outside the prison walls. *Belekevi* surrounded her but did not speak. They too had a role to play.

Eng ushered Sara onto the stage, the brilliant lights of the World Board reminding her of the bowl of water. The juices in her belly boiled.

Kethuda swept onto the platform, a hand raised to greet those who cheered and those who booed.

Sara's thoughts raced. *Was Gonul out there in the crowd? Was Ruqia fighting a great battle? Would I ever see them again? Had Gran already died in the water refugee camp?*

Eng guided Sara to a chair.

Kethuda's voice was modulated like a musical score, "Welcome, Turks, Kurds, water refugees, heads of state, and all citizens of our beleaguered planet. We gather today, the prisoner and I, to do our best to unravel the riddle: 'The Thread Will Bare When the Earth Flows Like Water.'"

She looked into the eye of the World Board: "Scientists for Humanity, you wrote this challenge. May our truth break open the hard Earth of human transgression, allowing it to flow like a river, with our confessions."

Sara lifted her eyes, blinking into the light.

"I will begin," Kethuda said, sitting down, her face still a mask, but her eyes holding the same quality as Sara's: a quiet hope.

"I, Ataturka, am guilty. But I am not alone. We, the nation of Turkiye, we are guilty. We have done violence, genocide, to the Armenians, to the Kurds."

Murmurs of shock rippled through the crowd.

Kethuda's voice rose. "Countless atrocities, in the name of the glory of the Ottoman Empire. Atrocities justified by those in power." She breathed out, her body trembling.

Sara widened her eyes as if to say, *stay with it, bitch!*

Kethuda cleared her throat. "It is time for Turkiye to take responsibility. For me to say, on behalf of my country: we did these horrific acts. Crimes against humanity. We are guilty."

The crowd rumbled with shouts of anger, betrayal, gratitude, and awe.

Sara rose from her chair. "Ataturka, I have good cause to hate you. Turkish soldiers killed my mother as she attended Equal Voice Council in the Kurdish town of my birth."

Kethuda remained seated, calm: "I regret the killing of your mother. It was not of my command. My father ordered the slaughter of terrorists like your YPJ, not ordinary citizens."

"How are we 'terrorists'? We fight against your oppression. Every act of violence we committed was in reaction to your aggression against us."

"You lie. Do I need to cite every act of your PKK, your YPJ, and all the other alphabet Kurds who bombed our people?"

"Retaliation is not aggression." Sara scanned the crowd for *belekevi*, and for civilian Turkish Kurds in the Resistance. She saw many.

Kethuda turned away. "You force me to give an example. You call yourself 'Sara,' the code name for your Revolutionary hero, Sakine Cansiz."

"Yes, and I am proud to admire her legacy. She was tortured for ten years in your Diyarbakir prison."

"She was tortured for her *crimes*. She trained her women in suicide bombing for use not just against ISIS, but against *us*."

"Lies!' Sara cried, even as she knew this dark truth must be real. "We defended ourselves against your annihilation. That is our pride. Not a crime. You denied us our language, our faith, our culture, our basic human rights. Your father said, 'Kurds are worse animals than dogs.' We had to fight you or die!" She stood tall, breathing hard.

Shouts of rage came from the crowd. Someone threw a piece of bread onto the stage, shouting, "Eat it, doggie Kurd!" It landed on Sara's head and bounced off, hitting the floor in front of her. A large gray bird dived to retrieve it. An e-arrow sung over the crowd and into the bird's heart. It spat out the morsel and landed on the floor, thrashing, until the golden glow of the missile fizzled and the great gray wings lay still.

Sara stared at the bird, tears filling her eyes. Kethuda knelt and picked it up, studying its twisted body, its long brown tongue hanging loosely from its beak. Tears came to her eyes as well. She held out the body of the bird to Sara. "I'm so sorry, Sara Roxan. So sorry, that we were—that we *are*, so horrible to your people. I shut off the water to the Euphrates, sending your people into exile. We don't deserve your forgiveness, but I ask it." She turned to the eye of the World Board. "And, to you, down-streamers, refugees who line up each day for your pitiful ration of water. I am sorry."

The crowd was still, not from empathy, but from shock.

Sara took the bird from Kethuda's arms and stroked the gray feathers moist with blood. She spoke through tears, "Madam President, if I do not forgive you, we stay as we have been: encased in our hate, murdering each other, the love in our hearts as dead as this bird. And what is its crime? Wanting to live and be free, in dignity and sisterhood." She held the bird against her heart. "I forgive you, Ataturka."

Kethuda knelt to her, "Call me by my real name."

The blood of the bird soaked into Sara's chest. "Kethuda, daughter of Ayse, I forgive you. And I ask your forgiveness in turn. We Kurds killed the sons and daughters of so many Turkish mothers. For that, I am deeply sorry."

"Thank you, Sara, daughter of Gita Roxan." Kethuda addressed the World Board. "We come to you today not to please, or appease, but to do what is right. To make amends. To ask that you not leap to judgment but consider joining us in this confession and reconciliation in your own countries. So much killing has been done through the ages by men, and a few women... Yes, I speak that as a truth. It is time for you to confess, America—confess, Russia—confess Taliban—confess all champions of violence on our planet. Confess as they did in South Africa in the twentieth century, as we did today. Confess, and see your enemy with new eyes. We believe this is the solution to the riddle. It is what the water wants."

The silence of the crowd became an uproar: half of the people cheering with tears of joy, half jeering in fury. Sara extended a bloody hand to grasp Kethuda's as they faced the crowd.

53 – Ruqia

"END of the line," said a soothing recorded ungendered voice. Ruqia opened her eyes slowly, lids heavy, pupils dry. She pulled her body to standing: no thought, no feelings, only an uncertainty about how she had gotten here. Someone told her the desal plant outside Beirut had broken down, and the refugee camp had been relocated near the city that had been Damascus.

As Ruqia dragged herself out of the Sun Shuttle, she saw a familiar sight: people surrounding a desal plant on the shore of a sunken city, the spires of Damascus reaching up in the warm current of the sea.

How to find Gran in this deluge of humanity?

I'm not ready to find anyone.

She stabbed the sand with her cane, the weight of her e-arrow rifle heavy on her back, the sunlight oppressive. She walked away from the masses lining up for rations.

Her In-Phone: Gonul again. She pressed her finger hard against her forehead, hoping to disable the whole damn implant. He needs me, and I have nothing. I can't tell him I have been de-commissioned. I even failed to carry out my own suicide.

She walked until she found herself down beach from the camp, the sun on the water diamond white. She stared at it for a long time, light upon light.

Her body gave way, and she curled onto the sand at the shoreline, peeling off her boots, running a finger across the frayed laces. She remembered how proud Sara had been of her first pair of boots, the symbol of belonging and power for a YPJ warrior.

Ruqia's e-arrow rifle slid off her shoulder and landed in the tidewater. She had thought to toss it out to sea, but knew the current would only bring it back, and some doe-eyed girl would find it, see the initials, a great golden "R." This kid would gush, "This is the e-arrow rifle of the disgraced Ruqia, who lost so many lives in her final battle. I will reclaim it and kill many Turks in retaliation!"

Or so the fantasy played out in her mind.

I could take it apart and bury the pieces, but that will only pollute the beach.

Why are the tools of violence so hard to destroy? Violence was in me once. I could kill and never look back; feel pride that I had done my duty. Did I turn my back on my inherent female nature? Was I trying to "be a man?" Or does any of that gender crap mean a damn? The Women's Protection Unit trained me, telling me what I was doing was noble. I became a hero, avenging the death of my family.

She screamed in despair, cursing the heavens, the Earth, this life she could not live in, could not get out of. She slept at last, curled into a ball as the sea lapped gently against her.

Late that night, she was awakened by a hand on her shoulder.

"Praise Allah, I found you." Gran's voice.

"I didn't want to be found."

"You must have, dearie. You did something to your In-Phone. I got all this buzzing and directions to your possible whereabouts. You couldn't have been more specific."

"Leave me alone."

"Not happening." Gran held her tight, the stars so bright that dino-seagulls sang a song, thinking it was daylight.

54 – Sara

WHAT have I done? Sara pulled off her blood-soiled shirt, her breasts moist against her olive-green undershirt, "the pea-fabric that breathes with your body." When the fighting had started, she held onto the bleeding bird until a *belekevi* seized it and tossed it in a curbside compost that littered cities all over the world. The rest was a blur.

Sara peeled off her soiled pants, her heavy boots, until she stood in her undergarments, smelling her own sweat.

She reached for her tin cup. Only a sip left. It cooled her dry throat. *We had such hope*, and yet, both Sara and Kethuda had known there would be strong reactions on both sides. The *belekevi* praised Kethuda for confessing her crimes, but they hated Sara for those two little words on behalf of the Kurds' violence against the Turks: "I'm sorry."

"How dare she speak for all Kurds?" they had shouted. "We have nothing to apologize for." "Fatima Roxan is no 'Sara.'" "She is a traitor to the Kurds."

And Kethuda? She had been swept away by bronze soldiers arriving from the field. They had given up their search for the Water Thread, answering Hamza's call to return to Ankara and restore order. Kethuda's apology for the sins of the past was met with shouts of "Treason!" The bronzies had murdered the *belekevi* guards at the prison and thrown Sara into her cell with no provisions.

She licked the last drops of water from her cup, thinking of the one bright moment: as she spoke her truth, she saw Gonul in the crowd, his face looking up at her with love and pride and fear. How could one human face express so many emotions at once? Only her Mr. Askay. "What does it mean to be free," he had asked often, in class.

"I don't know," she said in her cell, as if he sat beside her. "I stood before the whole world, exposed to the hatred of the Turks, and, as it turns out, the hatred of my own people. I am now the slime on the bottom of the shoes of everyone. And yet, Gonul, my love, you taught me that even in the greatest darkness, there is the freedom of the soul."

Where is my soul? I can no longer be the Sara who blindly worshiped Sakine Cansiz. My hero trained suicide bombers.

She pressed one finger to her forehead. Surprisingly, her In-Phone responded. In the chaos the bronzies had forgotten to disable it. Knowing she must use it wisely, Sara brought up a much-viewed photo of Mamoo and Papoo. "I rage at you. You must have known of the darkness in Sara Sakine, and yet, you let me use her name. Who am I now? Nothing but a traitor to my own people and a confirmed terrorist to the Turks."

A chill ran through her body. She stepped onto the sunlit circle of the stone floor with bare feet. It did not warm her.

The In-Phone vibrated, activating the Holographic Locator. Sara's digital self suddenly stood in a makeshift hospital. Gonul was helping with the wounded. Surprised that Sara was able to answer his call, he left a *belekevi* patient with a nurse and hurried onto a small balcony above the chaos of the city. There, he held Sara close, stroking her hair made of air.

She caressed his gossamer shoulders. "When we made our Truth and Reconciliation, we thought your Joseph would be so proud that we had solved the riddle, and he would send the Water Thread to the whole world. It only sparked violence. What did we do wrong?"

"Nothing. You were magnificent, strong, and true. So was the queen. Maybe regression is part of transformation?"

"Who said that?"

"Me."

They laughed, their translucent bodies moving inside each other.

"Where are your clothes?" he said.

"I can't wear a uniform anymore, those heavy boots. I'm no warrior, no hero."

He traced her leaf-shaped eyes with his fingertips. "You are a new animal, like the dinostrich or the T-rex wren."

"I'm devolving?

"No, my darling. Even though you're made of air, I can feel it, the new dimension of you: the truth of your own darkness, and the darkness of your namesake. You are not pure, my beloved, but you and your Kethuda have brought the world to its knees with two words."

"I'm sorry?"

"Yes. General Eng has coined a new slogan for the Resistance: 'For the Blood of the Bird.'"

"They don't hate me?"

"Not everyone, dearest. Many could see the evolutionary leap: you and Kethuda, holding bloody hands, both of you good, both of you evil: two humans, joined as one."

"I love you."

"Be patient," he said, as the In-Phone flashed red. He faded away, and she was back in her cell, alone.

But the walls looked different: the gray stone, the jagged bricks, the iron bars were luminous, the world wide open, blistering with promise.

55 – Kethuda

SHE reclined on a divan in her apartment, surrounded by men. Her father sat in an Ottoman armchair, smoking a cigar, his forehead creased, but this was no "triumph" cigar: his mouth sucked it like a baby on a tit.

Kethuda's "uncles," the ministers of finance, war, and peace, were studying streams of data in the air, muttering anxiously.

The scientists of engineering, hydrology, and climate, clustered at the other end of Kethuda's apartment, studying vast virtual charts. Their bodies moved, not like men, but like broken sticks trying to glue each other back together.

She sat among them, trying not to think or feel, but thoughts and feelings intruded. The shame of defeat: Ataturka, guilty of "female arrogance," her own people calling her "Heretic," "Traitor." She and Sara believed that their Truth and Reconciliation would "bare" the Water Thread and save the world. Instead, only a deafening silence from the Thread's inventors.

Damn them—what more do they want?

And my own people? I thought that they would take the stage and tell their own stories of violence against the Kurds, begging forgiveness. Instead, they hate me, call me "wicked witch" and cry "hoax" on the riddle. They turned to my father, who promised water at all costs. I lost my power. I lost my Eng to full-scale Civil War.

The members of RAT and other leaders around the world responded in turn. Shogofa in Afghanistan took it as inspiration to stage her own version of Truth and Reconciliation, calling the Taliban before a tribunal of women. At first there was great resistance, but the mothers of the Taliban shrewdly insisted that their sons would gain new esteem in the eyes of the Afghani people if they cooperated. Shogofa began each hearing by showing In-Phone archive movies of Archbishop Desmond Tutu in the twentieth century as the he broke down in tears when a Black woman forgave white South Africans for murdering her son. These hearings opened great controversy and agony in Afghanistan, but Shogofa and her women held strong, sending a thought-message to Kethuda, expressing gratitude.

Nina Navalny came out of hiding, demanding public confession for the crimes of the centuries, beginning with the attack on Ukraine in the early twenty-first century. As disorder came to the Kremlin, the revolutionaries took their cue, calling out elderly patriarchs to confess genocide to the families of their victims. The result was mixed. Young Russian soldiers gunned down some of the participants at Truth and Justice Forums. But many young people supported the forums that went on, unchallenged, all over the country.

Nina sent a bouquet of Moscow lilies to Kethuda, their soft pink blossoms filling the President's apartment with the scent of political spring. The card read, "To Madam President, my sister."

Kethuda wiped away tears at the thought of Nina's kind regard.

America, predictably, responded with silence, Boatwright reportedly too busy dealing with uprisings among Blacks and Hispanics to think about the genocide of Native Americans, oh, and that war in Viet Nam, and Iraq, oh and Closing the country to water refugees who then died in Temples of Return on the Southern border....

Elena Maria Juarez wrote in *The New Yorker*, from her new office in Northern Canada, "This is the woman we hoped Kethuda would become. Not the war mongering imprint of her father, but a woman of vulnerability and principal."

Kethuda sent a thought-message back, thanking Ms. Juarez, and congratulating her on her move to Canada. Elena messaged back, "Oh, how I miss the Big Apple. You will find that Water Thread, won't you, so we can all go home?"

And, most unexpectedly, an African woman called Kethuda from the headwaters of the Mississippi River in Minnesota, bringing with her the Sisterhood of African Mothers and Daughters. She played her trumpet and the women sang, "When the Saints Go Marching In." The African water refugees in the United States teamed up with African Americans to start Truth and Justice Forums all over the country to address the history of slavery and oppression of Black people shamefully still going strong in the twenty-second century. "If we can't have good water," said the trumpet player, "we can have truth!"

Kethuda thought of Gai and Eng. The Thread could pull water out of the sea, extract the salt, and pour it into the heart of the African continent. Eng could go home, though she didn't want him to. She dreamed every night that he was beside her. Dawn was a cruel monster, exposing his absence. She couldn't even send a message on her In-Phone; it would be intercepted by Hamza's men and put Eng in danger.

Hamza approached her with preening arrogance, his cigar smoke wafting into her face. She waved the smoke away but caught something in his eyes beyond the delight of holding her hostage: a contained agony. He turned away quickly, joining the scientists.

No one looked at her.

I am invisible, but still useful as a mouthpiece. When they've arrived at their strategy, they will have me waddle out onto the World Board and claim what? That Sara is a witch who put me under a "confession spell?"

A great exhaustion came over her, as if a beloved had died after a long illness. She reclined deeper into the lavender scented divan, noticing a strange blob on her desk across the room. She stared at it, numbly: the Seated Woman of Catalhoyuk, her belly heavy with child, her breasts distended from nursing, her feet on human skulls. Nausea seeped into Kethuda's belly: what an ugly thing, this slab of clay. *I will replace her with a replica of naked Aphrodite from ancient Greece: youthful breasts and rump, no head, no arms, no delusion of identity, no pretense of power. That is the way men see women. What an idiot I was to think I could create a feminine form of power that would transform the world.*

Her In-Phone shivered with red light: A Hologram Request, from Sara.

Kethuda's body tensed, the nausea swelling. *Sara, calling with her wide-eyed energy. Doesn't she know it is over? We inspired the rest of the world, but here, we lost. What if I ignore it? Not step up to meet her, just this once...*

Another throb of the red light. The tightness in Kethuda's body persisted, urging surrender to a desire she had never been able to resist: her own curiosity. She darted into the bathroom, shut the lid on the Gai-inspired Sucking Toilet, and pressed a finger to forehead until Sara appeared beside her. The child looked pale, dark circles under her eyes, a few dark, greasy ringlets curling onto her shoulders.

"Why're you looking at me like that?" Sara said. "Like you don't know me."

Kethuda's eyes went from Sara's sheer pea cactus undergarments, to her dusty bare feet. "Where's your uniform, your boots?"

"It's too hot to wear them."

"It's hot here as well," Kethuda said in a forced-casual voice.

Sara's eyes grew large at the sound of male laughter in the apartment. "You've joined your father?"

"I'm his lackey. It's my own fault. He gave me power, and I miscalculated. The people don't want Truth, much less Reconciliation."

"No. We did well."

Kethuda scoffed.

"It was a good beginning. Joseph and the Scientists for Humanity want more. I'm not sure what. The Earth doesn't flow with only one proclamation, no matter how bold."

"How lofty you sound, poor muffin."

Sara laughed, warm as spring rain on a dry creek bed. "Not lofty, but I keep remembering the moment when I took your hand, the blood of the bird smeared between us. It changed me somehow. It changed *us*. Gonul said it changed a lot of our people."

Kethuda turned away, unable to tolerate Sara's infernally innocent face. "Did it? Maybe for the Kurds."

"What did your dad do, drug you?"

Kethuda laughed bitterly. "Only with ultimatums. The room buzzes with scientists and flashing data."

"It doesn't take a scientist to see that the mountains are as dry as the soil in the desert."

Kethuda looked deeply into Sara's eyes.

Sara's ghostly image gazed back, her head moving slightly to the side, like a dinostrich listening for underground streams. "We don't have time for this, K."

"K?"

"Whatever," Sara said. "I was a puddle of misery at first, like you, hating myself, blah blah blah. I couldn't reach Ruqia, my beloved. I don't know if she's dead or alive. But then I heard from my teacher, Mr. Askay—"

"Poor little girl, running to your teacher, begging the older man to tell you what to think, since you can't think for yourself."

Sara's voice deepened. "Gonul is my lover, my friend. It doesn't matter what shape his genitals are. We all need friends to lead us back to our best selves when we are lost."

Kethuda lowered her eyes, an unusual sensation spreading across her heart: *shame.* "I'm sorry. That was a horrible thing to say. I have no such friend."

"Why didn't you follow Eng? Renounce your power?"

"I am my father's prisoner," Kethuda said, not looking at Sara.

"What a load of crap. You're only a prisoner of yourself."

Kethuda heard this as a home truth from a true friend: the Kurd, her enemy. "What are we to do now, Sara?"

"Don't call me that. Cansiz was a suicide trainer. I am Fatima, the Kurdish Cinderella."

Kethuda smiled gently. "As you wish, but your Sakine was a revolutionary hero. She taught her women the combat tactics of the day. Nothing is pure, 'Sara.'"

The girl's eyes opened so wide, their leafen shape became round. "We are changed, Kethuda. I gave you grief, like a friend, and you flipped it back to me. Maybe Truth and Reconciliation was about *us*, no one else, and we needed the bond of the blood of the bird, to finally be able to trust each other."

Kethuda knew the truth of it. She extended her hand. Sara smiled and took it. Their air hands become one.

A battering knock rattled the bathroom door. "My poor Aysetta," Hamza said. "Hiding out in your shame. And why not? The Kurd lured you into a blood bath."

Sara's face hardened with hatred.

The red warning light *beeped* on the In-Phone.

Hamza raised his voice, "Come, dear. My servants will give you a dry scrub, soothe your irredeemable guilt."

"I have no water," Sara said, her image flickering. "No food. They mean to kill me slowly—"

Kethuda gasped, as Sara disappeared.

56 – Ruqia

SHE sat on the beach beside the desal plant of the city that had been Damascus, towers of brine littering the thirsty Earth.

She stared at her e-arrow rifle, moving a finger across the flat buttons.

If I sell it or give it away, or drop it down coast, someone will find it. They will kill with my weapon.

Gran came with a bowl of hot liquid.

Ruqia sipped the thick green pea cactus soup, tasting vaguely of artichoke. "Where on Earth did you get it?"

"Aid boat. Made it through the hurricane."

"Did you have some?"

"Eat it," Gran barked, edging herself onto the sand with cracking knees and hands. But there was grace in her movements as the soft lemon-yellow silk of Sara's hijab settled on her shoulders, "Let me mother you just a little, R."

"The way it used to be," Ruqia said, "before Little Mama came on the scene."

Gran smiled, patting Ruqia's knee. They were quiet. Ruqia drank the soup. When it was gone, she asked, "May I see it again, please?"

Gran's voice was weary, "I've used up my quota."

"Please. I will pay you back. Somehow."

"Why won't you let me enable your In-Phone? You are way under quota, and I have almost no energy units left."

Ruqia stared into the empty bowl. "I can't talk to Askay or to Sara. I just want to watch her standing there with Ataturka, holding that dead bird, getting all bloody, that look on her face: like she sees something no one else can see."

Gran took the bowl. "Always your shame, your failure, hating yourself because you don't have it in you to kill anymore. What about the people who love you?"

Ruqia studied the bent body of her old friend. "My splintered heart caused the death of a legion of *belekevi*. Sara has to hate me for that."

"Your head's gone sideways. What did Sara do when she accidentally murdered the ISIS woman?"

"She wailed like an animal."

"What did you do when you were attacked in the grove by those young boys?"

"The Turks?" Ruqia said, in a flat voice.

"Yeah. So? What did you do?"

"Changed the setting of my rifle to *sleep*." Ruqia sat in silence, her mind numb, her eyes burning. The air was so hot, the sea so warm. Gran fanned them both with a sand dollar as big as a dinner plate.

Ruqia said, "I think of our beloveds in Ankara in the thick of the Civil War, and here I sit, unable to kill the enemy, unable to kill myself."

"Sometimes, it is given to us to wait."

Ruqia studied the deep crevices of her friend's face. The ocean smelled of rancid seaweed. "What would you do, Gran, if you were with them, in Ankara?"

She looked at Ruqia, with cloud-grey eyes, "The endless life of a refugee has rubbed my nose in a hard truth I've avoided for so long: I'm *old*. The e-arrow rifle is too heavy for me to lift without pain. My only gift is building an Equal Voice Council. We're making progress, believe it or not, though Fidan and Nazan hate the ISIS women—but here's the good news: they all hate me more."

"Allah must be so proud." They laughed until tears came, and they hugged each other and laughed some more. Gran passed a canteen, and they each took a sip of water, giggling with the sheer joy of loving each other.

After a while, Gran said, with philosophical lightness, "Murder is easy. Democracy is hard. We're attempting to re-habilitate Fidan and Nazan and the ISIS women by allowing them to carry rations to other people. Trying to teach service, emphasizing it is the will of Allah. Then we found out Fidan and Nazan were making deals on the side to sell the young ISIS women to the guards for sex. I would love to kill them, but Allah came to me in a dream and said, 'No. Find another way to include and transform the nasty biddies.'"

"Allah said that?"

"Word for word."

Ruqia felt a great tide rise in her body. Blindly, with the empty soup bowl, she dug a deep hole, flinging sand right and left, jamming the metal butt of the rifle into the unyielding Earth, shrieking like a madwoman. "There's no way to get rid of it! The tide will eat away at the sand and expose it. If I bury it inland, the wind will expose it. Whatever I do, it will come back, for Fidan or Nazan, or any other wicked person to dis-cover." She faltered, gasping, as her mind saw a deeper truth. "And what about this thing in *us* that made this gun? How do I destroy the killer in *myself*? She is still very much alive, in spite of all my whining that I can never kill again. I dream of leaping in the air, shooting soldiers, and seeing their blood soak into the soil. How do I kill *that*?"

Gran looked out at the warm, lapping sea. "What if there's no getting rid of the 'killer' in *us*, General R?"

Ruqia looked deeply into her friend's weathered face. Something about Gran was like Sara standing on the podium with the bleeding bird: a seeing far beyond.

"What if we accept this indestructible darkness in all of us, don't fuss at it or try to send it away, but invite it to sit at the table, like a badly behaved child that we don't want to send to foster care for fear he, or she, or ungendered, will become a tyrant and take down the whole world."

"Treat the killer in ourselves like an unloved child?" Ruqia asked.

"Yes. I'll bet little Hamza was sent to his room, or shipped off to live with abusive aunties instead of being invited to the table to eat his pea cactus gruel with everyone else."

"I think you are a dreamer, Gran."

"I am. I admit it. Not a bad theory, though."

"Askay would be proud," Ruqia said, wondering if such an idea could be true, wishing she could call Sara, fearing what would happen if she did.

A new wind came from the ocean, cooling their faces.

Late in the night, Ruqia woke from a deep, dreamless sleep. A softer wind and full moon beckoned. She picked up her cane and walked along the shore, the moonlight following her like a bioluminescent fish in a dark sea.

And then, there was no "then," no time, no thought, no life, no death. She was suspended in an undiscovered country, alone, no "other," no Ruqia, no Flying Warrior, no crippled leg, no failure, no glory.

A voice within her said, "Why think of suicide? If I am not 'I,' I cannot die. Nor was I ever born." She walked for hours in stillness, nothingness, and peace.

57 – Kethuda

SHE ran down a narrow side street, followed by a bronzie, only a boy, who had smuggled her out of her apartment building in a gray burka, claiming she was his grandmother. He had done well, and she was still puzzled about why he had done it. Why risk so much in spite of her generous payment of a Presidential ration of water?

She clutched the bag of food and water inside her burka, terrified she would drop it, or that her burka would be blown open by the wind whipping through the canyons of the buildings.

The air. Something was wrong with the air. It was so bereft of moisture, her throat was as dry as the soldier's bloodshot eyes.

Fighting broke out at the end of the street, an exchange of e-arrows between the *belekevi* and the bronzies. As bodies fell, the boy guided her into an alley.

"We have to wait," he said.

"We cannot wait. Sara has no food or water."

"We have to wait." Moonlight covered half of his face. She trembled. She had seen him before, but the memory remained in darkness.

The fighting at the end of the street died down. She heard the scurrying of feet from survivors, the smell of death from the others.

"Come on," the boy said. "You're my gray granny. Wail like one."

They came upon the slaughter of young ungendered. Kethuda stared at them, some from Hamza's army; some from her own.

The soldier hurried her on. As they approached the Water Square, they heard the cries of women, children, and men; a cry of such alarm, Kethuda thought it must be from a slaughter of opposing forces, but, no, a new death opened before her.

The Kiss-Off station was dry.

Children thrust their mouths onto the spouts, licking the last drops. Old and young walked the streets, some in nightshirts, some in fine robes, crying, "Hamza, Ataturka, where is our water?"

"It is the end," the young soldier said.

"I don't care. We have to get to Sara. Hurry."

"What can you possibly offer me as a reward now?" he asked.

"One last shot at living on this planet," she said, looking into his red eyes.

He spat on the ground, a pitiful effort since his mouth was so dry, but he took her arm and hurried her through Water Square to the outer wall of the prison.

"Death row visit for a grandmother," he said to the bronzie guarding the door.

The guard laughed bitterly, "We're all on death row." He let them pass, unquestioned.

As they ascended the stairs, Kethuda thought, absurdly, of the night before, when she lay in bed, a minion under house arrest. Her father had entered without knocking, pulling up a chair beside her bed.

"What is it, Papa? Why are you here?"

His voice was strangely calm. "You shamed our nation on that platform with the Kurd, but it took great courage. I am proud of you." His eyes found a memory, "The day you were born, your mother and I cried and laughed and kissed you again and again. I had not known it possible to love so much." He looked at her as he would have looked upon a ghost. "I am so sorry, my daughter, my soul."

"He *knew*—" she said, climbing the stairs to Sara's cell. "He knew the Kiss-Off station was shutting down. He, Hamza the Great, could do nothing but watch himself die with his beloved daughter."

She heard voices on the top floor. Sara was the only prisoner, and yet two women conversed. "Wait for me," she said to the soldier as she opened the door and saw Sara sitting on her sagging cot, holding the face of a woman made of air who said, "Sara, darling, I had to come and tell you. It wasn't a religious deal; it was like, I was dead, but not dead, totally alone, no Flying Warrior, no 'I,' but somehow it didn't matter."

Kethuda hurried into the cell and thrust a canister of water into Sara's hands.

"My enemy brings me life!"

"Sip it slowly," said Kethuda.

"This is Ruqia," Sara said between gulps.

"I am so pleased to know you," Kethuda said, stepping toward them. *I am no longer nothing. I belong with these women. In choosing to belong to them, I claim the best angel in my corrupted soul.*

Sara rested her eyes on Kethuda, as if she could read the President's mind.

"There is a quality of magic between you two, "Ruqia said. "Some union of mind and spirit I don't understand, but I can see it is very real. I came to tell Sara I am no longer the Flying Warrior. I am nothing, and that is good. It doesn't mean I'm worth nothing, quite the opposite—but I still don't know how to destroy my weapon." She held up her holographic e-arrow rifle. "It looks so harmless, when it's made of air. It is not harmless in its material form. It's indestructible, from molten metals deep in the Earth. We crafty humans pulled out what was liquid and made it hard. Made it death."

Silence.

The three women stared at the gossamer gun.

Kethuda placed her hand through the hologram, stirring the molecules of air until the image of the gun blurred into a fluid swirl.

"Ruqia, you are a genius," Kethuda said, lifting the image into an ascending spiral. "The original properties of this weapon, from the veins of the Earth, are longing to be set free."

58 – Sara

IN Water Square the peach light of dawn shone upon two women approaching. One wore bloody pea cactus undergarments; the other had thrown off her gray burka, revealing a sleeveless, paper-thin nightgown. Their abundant black hair moved gently across their shoulders in the first winds of dawn. They were followed by Hamza's bronze soldiers, e-arrow weapons raised. One young soldier led the rest, his face gloating with satisfaction.

This morning, the only sounds were the moaning of the thirsty. No singing of e-arrow missiles in a city without water.

At first no one recognized the women. Kethuda was hard to identify without her white flowing robes and blue silk hijab. In her silvery sheer night gown, she seemed naked, like a madwoman roaming the streets.

Sara stepped to the center of the Square, the bird blood dried to a rusty brown on her undershirt, the leaf-shape of her eyes bringing recognition. "It is the betrayers!" shouted a woman in the crowd, "Ataturka and her Kurd!"

Soldiers from both sides aimed e-arrow rifles at their heads.

"We did not shut off your water," Kethuda said. "Our mountains are barren, our reservoirs empty."

A grumbling quiet settled among the people. Even the children grew still, staring at the women in the center of the Square.

Sara touched her forehead, using the last of her energy quota to summon the internal World Board buried inside the In-Phone that could reach all users across the globe. "You, inventors of the Water Thread, are you listening?"

The World Board trembled within all of those assembled, and all of those listening around the world.

Kethuda placed her finger on Sara's forehead and spoke in a voice as calm as the stones under her bare feet. "Turks, Kurds, water refugees, people of the world, we need you to surrender your weapons. We will make a great furnace and melt them down, returning them to the molten state in the Earth from which they came." Her eyes closed. "Inventors, Scientists for Humanity, we pray this is the meaning of your riddle. By making the tools of our violence liquid, we hope to gain your trust, your respect, and that you will release your Water Thread to the whole world."

No sound in response, the wind deserting the dry air.

A *belekevi* rushed into the Square, her rifle pointed at Sara's head. "I will kill you first," she said. "The Turks killed my mother too. And you, our 'hero,' are friends with this murderer!"

Sara breathed slowly, her eyes resting on the girl. "I have killed as well. An ISIS commander who had kidnapped me. It did not justify taking her life. And you, *belekevi*, you have killed. There is no justice in killing."

The hands of the girl trembled "You think you are so noble. You are no better than me."

"I am not," Sara said.

The smug bronzie lifted his rifle. "I am the one who shot down the bird. The Kurds burned my village."

"And yet you helped me escape and give sustenance to Sara?" Kethuda said.

"I thought you meant to feed her and then execute her."

Kethuda let out heavy breath, "As you executed the bird."

"Now it is your turn, Ataturka," he said, pointing his rifle at her head. "I will kill you for making friends with this filthy Kurd—"

Sara knocked the weapon from his hands and grabbed it. He cowered, but she did not harm him. Instead, she placed the rifle at Kethuda's bare feet, addressing the crowd. "We have come to the end of ourselves. There is no other way. I beg you to follow the command of your President and surrender your weapon to the fire."

The stillness in the crowd churned. The *belekevi* girl kept her e-arrow rifle pointed at Sara.

Kethuda grabbed Sara's undershirt. "If it is to be. We die together."

There was no movement but the rustle of the wind.

Slowly, as if walking in a dream, a bronzie licked his dry lips and lowered his e-arrow rifle. Breathing haltingly, as if this could be his last, he carried his gun to the center of the Square and placed it at Kethuda's feet.

A long, slow exhale came from the crowd, like the tide going out to sea.

The young *belekevi* lowered her weapon from Sara's face, screaming with frustration, then, her dry lips set to the future, she kissed her e-arrow rifle and placed it at Sara's feet.

The movement of the people unfolded like the dance of a million sleepwalkers, the sound of metal clacking against metal deafening as soldiers from both sides tossed their weapons onto the pile, some with anger, some with resentment, some with relief, some with gratitude.

Hamza and his bronzies found their way through the crowd, holding their weapons tightly to their chests. "You think you are powerful," he said to his daughter. "You have no power. This will not work. You would destroy the last tool man has forged to save himself from annihilation."

A calm settled on Kethuda's face. "I honor my beloved Gai to say this: I am *humble*, of the humus of the Earth. That is the greatest power there is."

A collective sigh radiated from the crowd. They pressed in on Hamza and his men, leaving them no way out. *Belekevi* put their strong hands on the backs of each man, pushing as they chanted in the name of Allah, "Surrender to God."

One of Hamza's bronzies, then the other, dropped their e-arrow rifles at Kethuda's feet.

Hamza would not budge. Sara gave the order. *Belekevi* swarmed down on him and pried the weapon from his grip. He screamed and tried to bite them. The women laughed, tossing his e-arrow rifle at Kethuda's feet.

Hamza stared down at his weapon, resting on the stone pavement beside his daughter's bare feet. He seemed to age in the moment, the skin on his face going slack, his eyes clouding over. He looked into the face of his daughter, as a boy lost in the wilderness. He reached for her breast. She slapped his hand away.

"No, Papa. Never come to me again in the night."

He shivered with what could have been true loss, but his face was a martyr's mask.

"Go, Hamza," Sara said. "You have no place here any longer."

He squinted, as if unable to see Sara in the light, and turned to his daughter, but there was no empathy in Kethuda's eyes. Hamza the Great sighed, as if it were his last, and walked away, ignored by the crowd.

"Follow him," Sara said to a score of *belekevi*. "He's not done with his rage, only paused it."

Eng appeared in the Square.

Kethuda's face exploded with joy. He placed his weapon in Kethuda's arms. "You have found your goodness, Madam President."

"I love you," she said.

He answered with a passionate kiss.

Gonul found his way through the crowd, dropping his e-arrow rifle at Sara's feet, his eyes swollen with inexplicable wonder.

She grabbed his hand. "Your rifle has only been on *sleep*." He folded into her arms, brushing back her stringy hair. She laughed, touching his face, his eyebrows, his bushy beard.

Nourished by his love, she said, "Inventors of the Water Thread, are you watching? We are not heroes. We are not noble. We can burn our weapons, but not the sickness in our hearts. We ask your forgiveness. We will try to do better, try to hate less, kill less, if you give us the chance, for our country, for Turkiye, for Rojava, for every country of our Mother Earth."

Sara reached for Kethuda. They wrapped their arms around each other, as twin trees entwine.

Eng and Gonul gestured to the crowd to come forth. More weapons clattered onto the pile. With each sound, the hearts of the people opened, until there were no words, only the clanking of the weapons and the lark heralding the dawn.

59 – Ruqia

SHE pressed her face to the window of the Sun Shuttle, one arm hugging a parcel marked with a red "X": her e-arrow rifle, on its way to the Square in Ankara, where she would place it at Sara's feet. Thoughts of ecstasy filled her mind. *Sara, to touch her, to be touched by her. And Gonul. How good it will be to see him.*

Gran sat beside her, studying a map of the Turkish town where she and Ruqia would set up an Equal Voice Council, a pilot project of the new Arms-Free Turkiye. "There will be a Fidan and Nazan in every village," Gran muttered.

Across the world, people were giving up their arms, burning them in great fire pits. All countries were also required to destroy their nuclear weapons in exchange for the Water Thread, especially meaningful to the Thread's creators descended from the men at Los Alamos who made the atomic bomb.

"In-coming images," Ruqia said.

She and Gran touched their foreheads: a World Board set up on the outskirts of Ankara: Kethuda, no longer calling herself "Ataturka," sat with Sara downwind of a massive furnace melting the weapons. Beside her in hologram was Nina Navalny, stoking a bonfire of weapons in Red Square. The old men of the Kremlin had aged out of power, paving the way for Nina's Democratic Russia to take hold.

Shogofa was there, with her educated women, in front of a massive furnace, thirsty Taliban tossing their weapons into the flames.

A montage showed fires all across America. Elena Maria Juarez posted a message in *The New Yorker*, "It took the end of civilization for America to destroy her guns. Pathetic, but today we say, 'Hallelujah.'"

Gran chuckled.

Ruqia smiled. It was all very gratifying, but she could not take her eyes from Sara's luminous face, looking out with such love.

Their In-Phones flashed off as the Sun Shuttle turned, aligning with the Euphrates.

Ruqia leaned out the window, her heart beating like a wild drum. People ran alongside the Shuttle, shouting as it came into view: the Water Thread filling the Euphrates. Flocks of dinostriches and hundreds of people waded into the river, drinking, splashing, laughing.

Ruqia wiped away tears in time to see a Water Thread Rainbow arching over the river. She shielded her eyes from its brilliance: so much yet to conquer, such a long road ahead, but the wind on her face was *moist*.

Notes for the reader:

What is Real:

The ancient history of Catalhoyuk and the statue of its Earth Goddess, the Seated Woman.

The Women's Protection Unit of Kurdistan (YPJ) the fighting force of Rojava in Northern Syria. Sakine Cansiz, revolutionary hero.

Engai is the Maasai manifestation of the divine, neither male nor female; inclusive of both.

Other historical figures: Cyrus the Great, Golda Mier, Benezar Butto, Joan of Arc, Jean August Dominque Ingres, Alexi Navalny, and Nurbanu Sultan.

The projections of the impact of climate change, including water shortage in the Middle East and sea level rise from the Mediterranean, are based on current scientific data.

What is fiction:

All characters, imagined technological inventions, and evolution of species is entirely fictional. Any similarities to those living or dead, or actual inventions created outside my awareness is coincidental.

Acknowledgments and deep gratitude to Timmi Duchamp and Kath Wilham for transformative guidance, and eagle-eye editing, and for their feedback and support throughout: Megan Seaholm, Susan Scott, Beverly Olevin, Marc Olevin, Ginny Rohan. Donna Lee, Kevin Filocamo, Peggy Farah, Tim Nelson, Ann Blake, Tori Allen, Karlie Markendorf, Lucy Ostrander and Megan Chance. Worlds of gratitude to you all.

About the Author

Elizabeth grew up writing stories and plays, which ultimately led to a career as a television screenwriter. Her produced credits include the critically acclaimed *All I Could See from Where I Stood* (PBS), *Having Babies II* (ABC), and *Help Wanted* (CBS), the latter nominated for an Emmy. She is particularly proud of an independent documentary, Home from the Eastern Sea, which she wrote and co-produced with an all-female creative team. Originally aired on PBS, now distributed through Kanopy, the film was honored with a NAFTA American Scene Award, and a Cine Golden Eagle. In tandem with screenwriting, she worked on novels, drawn to the duel reality of inner and outer life. This eventually led to a new calling as a psychotherapist. She worked with the most vulnerable populations, seeing first-hand the tragic impact of class, race, gender, and mental health inequality. She studied the depth psychology of Carl Jung, and opened a practice offering the healing modalities of sand play and dreams. This work brought her writing to a whole new level, a world of symbols and archetypal forces not limited to the conventions of time and space. She was presented with an Achievement in the Arts Award from the Seattle Psychoanalytic Community for producing and publishing four plays and *Soul Stories*, a collection of two novellas. Elizabeth's dearest treasure is her loving and laughing family. The image for her Aqueduct debut novel came to her in a dream.

www.elizabethclarkstern.com